A PORTRAIT OF ANDREW

Also by J. P. Bowie

A Portrait of Phillip

&

A Portrait of Emily

A Portrait of Andrew

A Novel by J. P. Bowie

iUniverse, Inc.
New York Lincoln Shanghai

A Portrait of Andrew

iUniverse, Inc.

For information address:
iUniverse, Inc.
2021 Pine Lake Road, Suite 100
Lincoln, NE 68512
www.iuniverse.com

ISBN: 0-595-30223-8

Printed in the United States of America

For my partner Phil—and for my good friend Mavis, who gave me the idea for the New York setting of this story—and for Michael, Tony, Bryan and all of you who have allowed me to have so much fun writing these books.

My grateful thanks to Dee Warrick, of the San Diego Police Force, who graciously answered questions about police procedure—of which I knew very little!

Some months earlier…

The driver of the Jeep Cherokee took the sharp bend in the road just a little too quickly and, for a moment, the vehicle's tail end swung violently near the soft shoulder. With a quick intake of breath, she straightened the vehicle out and gripped the steering wheel harder, trying to take more control.

She glanced at the man in her passenger seat. He had not stirred, but slept on in his drunken stupor. She looked at him again, her face twisted with dislike.

'Why the hell am I the one driving the son-of-a-bitch back to the house?' she thought bitterly. 'I should have let him try to drive himself. Serve him right if he'd gone off the road and killed himself!' That would be the answer to everything—he'd be dead, and no longer a threat to her happiness.

The road in front of her was dark and winding, lined on both sides by tall trees that obscured what little light the moon could provide. She had driven this road countless times before on previous visits, but tonight it appeared alien and hostile, and she was unable to make out any of the familiar landmarks that told her she would soon be at the narrow turn off, that led to the house. Had she already passed it? Had her scattered thinking made her miss the unmarked road? Muttering a curse under her breath, she slowed slightly and peered ahead looking for something she could recognize. She jumped as blinding headlights rounded the corner and seemed to come straight at her.

"Jesus!" she screamed, wrenching the steering wheel hard to the right. The Jeep skidded on the soft ground as it left the pavement, causing her to lose control of the vehicle. It spun into the trees and bushes and plunged over the side of the embankment, stopping only when it crashed into a pile of logs at the bottom of the incline.

The blow she felt to her chest, she realized, was the air bag wedging her between the seat and the steering wheel. She struggled free of her seatbelt and pushed the door open, crying out as an agonizing pain shot through her left arm right up to her shoulder. She fell out of the vehicle moaning, then staggered to her feet and looked back at her passenger. He was still asleep, or had been knocked unconscious. Gritting her teeth against the pain, she went round to open his door, then jumped back as a burst of flame shot out from under the Jeep.

"Oh my God!" Her shriek finally awoke the man in the passenger seat. Dazedly he looked around him, at first not comprehending the danger he was in. Then, he saw the flames rise around him, and realizing he could not move, he called to her for help. His face contorted with terror as smoke filled the vehicle, and the heat from the flames engulfed his body.

She stepped back from the vehicle, her mind spinning crazily out of orbit. Here was the answer! The problem solved…He stared at her in horror, as he saw the expression on her face change to a cold mask.

"Help me!" he screamed, but she turned and ran, scrambling madly up the steep incline that led to the road. The force of the blast from the explosion behind her pushed her into the soft damp earth, and she lay there for a long time listening to the roar of the flames—and somewhere above that, she could swear she still heard his screams…

CHAPTER 1

Peter Brandon groaned softly as he reached across to switch off the alarm by his bedside. "Time to get up," he muttered to himself, none too convincingly. He hated getting up when it was still dark outside, but today, he and his partner, Jeff Stevens, had an early morning plane to catch.

"C'mon, sleepy head." Jeff appeared in the bedroom doorway with two mugs of coffee. He set them down on Peter's nightstand, and kissed him lightly on the cheek. "Up and at 'em, or we'll miss that plane."

"You showered already," Peter said, still half asleep. "You smell all clean and nice…come back to bed." He lay back on his pillow and wrapped his arms round Jeff's neck. He gazed into the warm gray eyes he loved so much, and ruffled Jeff's thick chestnut colored hair.

"No chance," Jeff chuckled. "The cab's going to be here in forty-five minutes—so move it!"

Peter groaned again, but sat up and sipped some of his coffee. "Okay, can't win this one I guess."

Jeff grinned at him. "Andrew just called to remind us to bring overcoats—he said the temperature in New York is going to be barely above freezing for the next few days."

"Lord, what we do for our friends," Peter complained. "It's going to be in the seventies here today, and we're voluntarily flying to the frozen wastes to spend Christmas—up to our asses in snow."

"This was your idea, remember? You and Andrew have talked about nothing else for the past month. 'Oh, it'll be so neat to have a real white Christmas this year—and spend it with you guys—we can't wait!'"

"Yeah, yeah, yeah. Go on, rub it in." Peter slipped out of bed, stretched mightily, then padded to the bathroom and turned on the shower, while Jeff busied himself making the bed and tidying the room.

Jeff had to admit that he too was looking forward to the trip. It would be good to get away for a couple of weeks, and to see their friends Andrew and David again. It had been over a year since David had accepted a promotion at work, that involved he and Andrew moving to New York.

He knew Peter missed his buddy, Andrew. They had become close friends from the time Peter had awakened from his coma. For three years Peter had languished in a hospital bed after a murderous attack had left his lover Phillip dead, and Peter in a deep coma. Andrew had been hired by Peter's mother to carry out the program of passive physical therapy recommended by the doctors. He had been at Peter's bedside when he awoke, and had been a key figure in ensuring his total recovery. He had become Peter's personal trainer, and inseparable friend.

Jeff had entered Peter's life when he was hired to investigate the crime that had put Peter in hospital. The strong physical attraction they had both felt for each other almost immediately, had deepened into a loving tender relationship that had helped ease the despair and loneliness both men had experienced in their separate lives.

Now, two years later, they were more in love than ever, and enjoyed each other's company and conversation despite their disparate views on many issues. Jeff's work, as a private investigator, sometimes got in the way of Peter's social plans for them. Peter was a talented artist, creating portraits and landscapes that were much in demand, but he could freely organize his time off without much restriction. Jeff, on the other hand, was sometimes forced to reschedule his time at a client's whim, much to his partner's chagrin.

Sometimes, Peter would suffer in silence, but occasionally he would get vocal about his disappointment, and that could lead to a row, as Jeff would refuse to give in to Peter's petulance. They would never stay mad at each other for very long, for Jeff refused to let the sun go down on any difference of opinion they might have, and the making up process was always thrilling. Besides, one look into Peter's startlingly cobalt blue eyes, and Jeff's strong resolve would turn to putty.

Not that he would ever admit to the effect they had on him…He smiled gently now as he heard Peter warbling "New York, New York." in the shower. The last couple of years had been a heady experience for Jeff. His business had thrived, due mostly to the notoriety he and Peter had gleaned from their involvement in one or two high profile cases. Despite the stress and sometime danger of the situations, the up side of it all had been that they had made new friends along the way, and their relationship with each other had been strengthened.

Sometimes he tried to remember what his life had been before Peter, and it was becoming increasingly more difficult to imagine he had ever been happier in his entire life. His reverie was interrupted by Peter bouncing back into the bedroom.

"Did you already pack my deodorant?" he demanded, hands on hips.

"And if I did?" Jeff smiled salaciously, taking in Peter's slim, lightly tanned body still glistening and damp from the shower.

"You will have to be punished, I think." Peter advanced on him, eyes flashing, a smile tugging at the corner of his mouth as Jeff caught him in his arms and held him in a bear hug. Peter giggled and wound both his legs round Jeff's waist. Just then they heard the doorbell chime, and Peter yelped as Jeff dropped him unceremoniously on the bed.

"The taxi's here. Get dressed!"

"He's *early*." Peter dived back into the bathroom. "I'll just have to go stinky."

"There's a spare deodorant in the cabinet..." Jeff laughed, as he ran down the stairs to answer the door. He informed the driver they'd be a few more minutes, and helped him load the suitcases into the cab. Peter appeared in the doorway, pulling a sweater over his head.

"Got the tickets and everything?"

"Everything—don't worry. Just grab your coat and let's go!"

"Right...New York here we come..."

Jeff smiled wryly. "I just hope New York's ready for *you*."

Andrew Connor frowned as he looked at his appointment book for the day. "Damn," he muttered, noticing the time of his last appointment was for 4pm.—a sports massage for Roy Harmon. He had meant to reschedule that one. Peter and Jeff's plane was arriving around five, and he and David were planning on being there to meet them at the airport. It would take them a good couple of hours to get there with the rush hour traffic. He'd have to call and cancel this last appointment. He ran his hand through his fair curly hair in exasperation. He hated having to do this, as he always tried to avoid letting his clients down, but he had no choice today. He'd see if Mr. Harmon could make it early tomorrow morning. That would free him up around 2.30pm today. Just time to meet David at his office, and get to the airport in time.

He was so looking forward to seeing Peter again. Jeff too, but Peter was his best buddy and he had missed him more than he could have imagined. A lot of it, of course, was the fact he had made few friends in the city. David's job involved long hours, and many nights he arrived home, tired and depleted from the stress of his new position, and in no mood to go out or socialize. Andrew recalled the happier days in Laguna, when he and David, Peter and Jeff, and their close friends, Rob and Maggie would get together frequently for a lively evening of dinner and laughs, or a trip to the theatre.

They'd all had their busy lives, but always had found time for each other. Things were different now, and though Andrew did not want to burden David with his complaints, he had to admit to himself—he loathed New York. He hated the impersonal and unfriendly attitudes he encountered almost on a daily basis. The fact that no one cared what happened to those around them concerned Andrew, and made him wonder just how much longer he could put up with it. David's promotion was an important step in his life, and Andrew knew that he would be loath to walk away from it and return to California just because Andrew was unhappy living in New York. He had tried to hide it from David as much as he could, but every now and then his exasperation would surface, and lead to an awkward silence when David questioned him about it. He just didn't want David to worry about it, and he kept thinking to himself that eventually, he might be able to settle down in the city and make the best of it.

Rod and 'A', the two Englishmen whom they had met in Laguna through Peter, always made a point of calling when they passed through New York on their many trips to Europe. Sometimes they would get together for dinner or the theatre, and Andrew always loved to get the news of his friends who seemed so far away. It had been 'A' who had let it slip that Peter and Jeff were planning this Christmas trip. Andrew smiled as he remembered the look of consternation on 'A's face as Rod had reprimanded him for giving away the 'secret'.

"You and that bloody big mouth of yours. Nobody can tell you anything without you blabbing it all out at the drop of a hat!"

"Oooh!" 'A' had giggled like an errant child. "Pretend you didn't hear, my darlings—it's not like me to let the cat out of the bag."

"Hah!" Rod had snorted. "You couldn't keep a secret if your life depended on it."

Andrew had called Peter that night to have him confirm the good news, and his friend had laughed when Andrew told him how he'd found out.

"I told Jeff the one sure way you'd know is if we let 'A' in on our plans. Yes, it's true—we want to come see you at Christmas. But, only if you want us to, of course."

"Are you kidding?" Andrew had positively yelled. "There's nothing I'd want more."

The one friend he had made, Morgan Kennedy, was the only person in New York he felt he could confide in. He had met her a few months previously when she made an appointment for some physical therapy following an accident she'd been involved in. Her doctor had failed to recommend a therapist so she had called Andrew on her own, after seeing his ad in the paper. Andrew had warmed to her immediately, and over the weeks of her treatment, they had frequently gone for lunch, indulging in long conversations and sharing their frustrations about New York living.

Morgan and her husband Jeremy lived only two blocks from Andrew and David's apartment, but it had taken some time before their mutual partners joined them socially.

"Jeremy doesn't want to hear me bitching about living here," Morgan had confessed to Andrew at one of their lunch dates. "And he wouldn't appreciate the two of us agreeing with each other."

Andrew knew they did not have a good marriage. Morgan had told him so on many occasions with an almost resigned complacence that he found unacceptable, and had told her so.

"You shouldn't be so easily accepting of a bad marriage, Morgan. You deserve better than that."

"Andrew, you haven't known me long enough to know what I deserve," she had admonished him. "It hasn't been an easy street for Jeremy either—I can be quite the shrew when I want to be."

"Have you thought of seeing a marriage counselor?"

"My dear young Andrew, you are quite the naif, aren't you?"

"Am I?" Andrew had retorted, stung and flushed with annoyance.

"Sorry, I don't mean to be patronizing. Jeremy and I have been married for twelve years. It was wonderful to begin with, but as time goes by, people change, and you don't always like the things you used to, in the beginning."

"Meaning what?"

Morgan swept a hand through her dark red hair and her green eyes glittered as she replied, "Meaning…I have a big mouth, and I'm speaking out of turn. I shouldn't be talking about this behind his back."

"About what?"

"Better you don't know, even though you would probably be simpatico."

"Morgan, you are being really obtuse! What the hell are you talking about?"

"Nothing, Andrew. Forget it, I'm just rambling, that's all."

That conversation had troubled Andrew for weeks afterwards, but if he ever tried to broach the subject again, Morgan would cut him short, and pick another topic. When he and David finally got to meet Jeremy Kennedy at an impromptu dinner Morgan gave for them, he decided he detested Morgan's husband.

The one thing he had never imagined happening was that the man would sit and openly flirt with David, for almost the entire evening. Even though David handled the situation with his usual grace and good manners, Andrew squirmed with embarrassment for Morgan, and was extremely relieved when David suggested they all get an early night, as he had an important meeting in the morning.

"Jeez, Andrew," he had half laughed as they walked back to their apartment. "Did you know Jeremy was gay?"

"Morgan has never mentioned it, David! I can't believe she wouldn't tell me that little snippet of information."

"Maybe she doesn't know."

"How can she not know? The man's a *flamer*."

"It *is* a little hard to miss," David had chuckled.

The next time Andrew met Morgan for lunch, she apologized profusely for her husband's behavior. "I guess I should have warned you—Jeremy can be a real tease at times. He really doesn't mean anything by it. It's just his silly sense of humor,"

"What do you mean?"

"Well, he was just pretending to be gay, Andrew. He's really not, and it's not done to embarrass anyone or put you down. He just gets a kick out of it."

Andrew looked at Morgan incredulously. "You mean, you think that's all an act?"

"Of course it is. He does it all the time—even in front of our straight friends. They get quite a charge out of it."

I bet they do, Andrew had thought, grimly.

Sighing at this disquieting memory, Andrew dialed Mr. Harmon's number and left a message saying he hoped he was not inconveniencing him, but he would have to change the 4pm appointment for today, to sometime tomorrow. Putting the phone down, he began to wonder if he'd made a mistake by inviting Morgan and Jeremy to the party he and David were throwing to welcome Peter and Jeff to New York. What if Jeremy behaved as atrociously in front of them? God, Peter would have a *fit*—and probably bop Jeremy on the nose if he got too close to Jeff.

For a moment, Andrew grinned happily at the thought.

Oh, boy.

He'd just have to be on his toes to make sure there were no altercations. He was probably being paranoid, he thought. In a larger crowd, Jeremy might behave himself impeccably—hopefully.

Oh well, he'd just have to deal with it when, and if, it happened.

Morgan Kennedy sat in front of her dressing table mirror, and gazed grimly at her reflection.

God, I'm looking old, she thought, grimacing at the dark smudges under her eyes and the creases on either side of her mouth. Her skillful application of make up would take care of this, but it depressed her that her once smooth and supple skin was giving in to the march of time that suddenly seemed to be speeding up with every day that passed. Another year almost over, and her forty-sixth birthday on the horizon!

She shuddered at the thought as she picked up a sponge and began applying a smooth coat of foundation, then glared through her mirror as she saw her husband enter the room behind her.

"Finally pulled yourself away?" she asked between clenched teeth.

"Am I late?" Jeremy Kennedy ambled over to where his wife sat and kissed her shoulder. Despite herself, she shivered with pleasure at his touch. After all the years, and the knowledge of his infidelities, she still could not resist him, physically. She gazed at him now, taking in his smooth good looks, the tanned skin stretched over his chiseled bone structure, the smoldering dark brown eyes, and the curly black hair that bespoke his Greek heritage.

She wanted him, while she hated him.

"You know we're having dinner with Bruce and Jennifer at eight o'clock," she reminded him, as she tugged her fingers through his hair, forcing him to keep his lips on her bare skin.

"Boring."

Jeremy sighed, straightening up and stepping away toward the bathroom. Morgan stopped herself from asking him why he was so late; he would only lie anyway, and what difference did it make? He had come home—to her. With all his faults, she still felt lucky to have him. Any woman would. He was amazingly handsome, and attentive to her every need. At thirty-five, ten years her junior, he still exuded enough sex appeal to turn every head in a room, man and woman alike.

Jeremy stood in front of the bathroom mirror and stripped off his shirt and tie, throwing them carelessly on the ground. He stepped out of his pants and briefs, then turned on the shower. Languorously, he soaped the hard muscles of his chest and arms, his mind slipping back to an hour before, when he had been engaged in one of the most overwhelming sexual experiences of his life. He closed his eyes at the thought, and massaged his growing erection as his fantasy took control. Now, in his imagining, he could feel the silky smooth skin beneath his fingers, the full soft lips pressed against his own…

"Are you nearly ready?"

He winced as Morgan's voice cut through his fantasy and brought him down to earth in a hurry. Grabbing a towel, he hastily started to dry himself.

"Be right there, sugar!" he called, then muttered to himself, "Oh, I'll be right there—*bitch*."

He splashed on some cologne and pulled on a pair of clean briefs. Morgan stood in the bathroom doorway watching him. He smiled at her. "Pick me out a shirt sweetheart, please?"

Smiling benignly, she walked to the closet and pulled out an ice blue silk shirt by Armani, she had recently bought for him.

"Good choice." He kissed her lightly on the cheek.

"Now hurry!" Morgan cajoled. "We are way late."

"Oh, don't fuss. They'll forgive us. You know they live for a night out with us."

"With you, maybe. They think you're such a *riot*."

Jeremy looked admiringly at his reflection in the mirror, then smirked. "That's because they have no life. All that money and not a clue how to enjoy themselves, unless someone else is showing them how." He knotted his tie expertly, and pulled on a dark blue silk blazer. "What's on the agenda for tomorrow night?"

"Andrew's throwing a party for his friends from California. One of them is an artist, and the other a private investigator."

Jeremy raised an eyebrow. "Quite a combo. Well, at least it should be more interesting than tonight."

CHAPTER 2

Andrew hopped from one foot to the other impatiently as he and David waited for the passengers to disembark from the plane. They had arrived early, only to find the flight delayed and an extra hour's wait ahead of them.

"Calm down honey," David whispered, then louder, "Look, there they are!"

With a whoop of glee, Andrew charged forward and grabbed Peter in his arms, hugging him mercilessly.

"Help!" Peter laughed, hugging him back. "Don't crack a rib, please."

"God, I've missed you!" Andrew felt tears springing to his eyes as he grinned happily at his friend. Jeff and David meanwhile, had exchanged a slightly less emotional greeting, and were busily engaged in catch up conversation.

"Are you OK?" Peter looked at his friend with concern as Andrew rubbed his eyes. He still exuded the fresh and open-faced appeal Peter remembered, but there was an air of dejection that he was quick to pick up on.

Andrew forced a smile. "Yeah, yeah I'm fine. I've just been looking forward to this so much."

"Well, now we're here." Peter squeezed his arm. "And you've got to put up with us for two whole weeks."

"It'll be the best two weeks of the year, believe me."

Peter dropped his voice so David could not hear. "Do you hate it here that much?"

"Later. I don't want David to get upset with my belly aching."

"Right." Peter smiled across at David and opened his arms. "Come here, you handsome devil!"

David grinned at him. "Glad you guys are here. Andrew's in seventh heaven, seeing you again. Let's go find a cab. We're having dinner at the apartment tonight—just the four of us."

"Sounds great," Jeff said, shouldering their carry-on luggage. "Lead the way!"

The apartment, conveniently located in mid Manhattan, had been a great find for David and Andrew. David's bosses at his office had pulled some strings in getting it for them, so anxious were they that David come work for them. It was a large two bedroom on the twelfth floor, and had been professionally decorated and furnished by the owner. As they unpacked in the guest bedroom, Peter admired some of the artwork on the walls.

"This guy has a fortune tied up in some of these," he remarked to Jeff, as he hung clothes in the closet.

Jeff gave the painting over the bed a mock critical look of appraisal. "I like your work better."

"That's because you're biased, as of course, you should be."

"I just can't figure out what the heck it's supposed to be."

Andrew tapped on the door and peeked in. "Ready for a cocktail?"

"You bet." Peter beckoned him in. "We can do the rest of this later."

"How do you like the room?" Andrew asked.

"Very nice. I was just saying, the owner has spent a fortune on this artwork."

"Yeah," Andrew said, looking around. "David's boss said the guy is a real art fanatic. Buys from all over the world."

"Where is he now?" Jeff asked.

"Who knows? He's leased the place for two years to David's company. Which means we'll be living here for another year, I guess."

"Andrew, you seem really down." Peter looked at his friend with concern. "Can you tell us what's wrong?"

"Look…" Andrew closed the door behind him. "Let's not get into this right now. I'll explain later. Tonight, I just want us to have fun and not talk about things I can't change. Believe me, it's not that bad." He smiled at them, and opened the door again. "Come on; let's have that drink."

They walked out together into the living room. The glow from the fireplace and the twinkling lights on the Christmas tree gave the large room an inviting atmosphere as the four friends toasted each other, then settled down on the comfortable sectional couch to talk. Jeff looked appreciatively at the portrait of Andrew that hung over the fireplace. Peter had painted it and presented it to

David and Andrew as a Christmas gift. He had captured an image of Andrew after a strenuous workout, his bare chest and shoulders gleaming with perspiration; his head tilted back slightly, his eyes half closed with the euphoria that a good work-out could often bring. The overall effect was both strong and sensual.

"That is just so *good* Peter," Jeff murmured, leaning back into the couch's soft cushions.

"Yeah." David looked up at the portrait with admiration. "That dreamy look in his eyes still turns me on."

"This could be more information than they need." Andrew slipped an arm round Peter's shoulders. "You have no idea how many people have admired your work. If you lived here you could make a fortune painting portraits."

"Thanks, but I make a nice living in Laguna. Sorry, but I'd find it hard to trade places at this point in my life."

"Well, there's certainly enough crime here to keep Jeff busy," David remarked.

"He's busy enough. I hardly see him as it is, these days."

"He's full of it," Jeff protested. "I'm home every night by six. Sometimes I have to cut my clients off in mid sentence, just to get home in time and escape the Wrath of Brandon!"

"Somehow, we don't see you as the henpecked husband Jeff," David said, as he and Andrew laughed at the expression of feigned indignation on Peter's face.

"You bet he's not," Peter chuckled. "Anything but."

"How's Eve doing?"

"Mom's just great," Peter replied. "She and Fred will be with friends in San Diego for Christmas. They're taking Martha Harley. Don Harley's wife—or I should say, widow."

David grimaced. "How could we forget the Harley saga? Martha's lucky to have such a good friend in your mother."

Peter nodded. "It's been rough for her. I never could quite understand the bond between Martha and my mother. Martha's always seemed a little…*vapid*, if you know what I mean. But they've been friends since they were little girls, and now, since Don's death, Martha's really dependent on my mother and Fred."

"Do you think Eve will ever marry Fred?" Andrew asked.

"I wish she would. I'd love for her to be as happy as I am—finding the man of my dreams, I mean."

"Hey you." Jeff smiled at him. "You're getting me all hot under the collar."

"We had a card from Rob and Maggie," David said. "Hard to believe little Robbie is going to be a year old."

"Yeah," Jeff agreed. "Too bad we're all at opposite ends of the country right now. It would have been great to see them for Christmas."

Andrew stood up suddenly. "I'm going to get dinner started."

Peter watched him as he disappeared into the kitchen; then, he too got to his feet. "I'll just go see if he needs any help."

"Okay…" David called after him. "You guys can catch up on the gossip. I want to show Jeff the designs I'm doing for the company's new project."

Peter joined Andrew in the kitchen. The two friends smiled knowingly at each other. "Come on," Peter said, quietly. "Put me to work, and tell me what's ailing you."

"Is it really that obvious?"

"Andrew, you're my best friend. The guy I almost owe my life to. Don't forget where I was when I came out of that coma. Without you and my mother, I could very well have done myself in. I think I'm right when I say we are closer than many friends ever get a chance to be. So, if I happen to notice that you're unhappy, it's because you've let me be privy to your moods in the past—and I've got to say, you are not being your usual sunny self." He put his arms round his friend and hugged him gently. "Come on, 'fess up. What's the problem?"

Andrew sighed. "Just about everything. I hate this city, I hate this apartment, and I hate the fact I'm three thousand miles from my best friends…and I hate myself for feeling this way. This is so important to David—this promotion, I mean, and he's doing so well. How the hell can I tell him, 'I'm unhappy—and please can we go home?'"

"You've never mentioned this to him, at all?"

"I can't, Peter. I just can't. I don't want to put him in the position of choosing. I'm afraid if I do, I'll lose."

"You don't know that!"

"You're right, I don't know that. I just don't want to take the chance. And it sounds so damned melodramatic anyway. 'David, you have to choose between your career and me…' I can't *do* that to him."

"I understand, believe me," Peter said. "Jeff wouldn't stand for that either, not for a minute. But I think you have to let David at least know how you feel. Maybe he's not so in love with his new position as you think."

"Well, of course it's hard work for him. The hours are brutal sometimes, and he comes home exhausted most of the time. Our…uh…special times are almost non existent, lately."

"That's not good!"

"Tell me." Andrew sighed again. "Maybe I'll hang my portrait over the bed—he did just say it still turns him on." He looked at Peter with a lopsided grin. "Oh, I just don't know what the answer is. Please don't bring this up in front of him, though."

"Of course not. This is something you have to work out between the two of you. I just wish there was something I *could* do."

Andrew touched Peter's arm gently. "Hey, having you and Jeff here for two weeks is the best thing I could have hoped for. David's actually managed to get a few days off, so we'll have a wonderful time—and, just being able to talk to you about it all has helped."

"Good, now we better get cracking on that dinner, or the guys will be coming in here to rape and pillage."

"I wish!" Andrew gave a rueful laugh. "Okay. Why don't you throw the salad together while I get the pasta going?"

"So tomorrow night," David said as they relaxed after a satisfying dinner, "We've asked a few friends over to meet you guys and have a little early Christmas cheer."

"I'm glad you've made friends here," Peter remarked, looking at Andrew.

"Well, they're mostly from David's office. His boss, and his wife. What's her name again, David?"

"Jennifer. Graham and Jennifer Mitchell. You'll like them—they're very easy to get along with." David poured them all another glass of wine as he continued, "Then there are a couple of other guys and their wives, and Bob and his partner Michael. They're a hoot. It's too bad Rod and 'A' aren't in town. They said they might be, but at the last minute Rod's sister insisted they go visit her in London." He paused, then chuckled. "But we mustn't forget Morgan and Jeremy. They'll probably make it a memorable evening."

"Yeah," Andrew said, quietly. "I don't know if that was such a good idea of mine."

"Now, this sounds intriguing." Jeff looked at Andrew with interest. "Who are Morgan and Jeremy?"

"Morgan was a client of mine for a while. She was recovering from a car accident. We hit it off and became lunch buddies. Then we met her husband,

Jeremy. Frankly, I can't stand the guy. The first time we met him, he spent practically the whole evening trying to make David."

"What?" Peter looked at him in surprise. "Did she tell you he was gay?"

"Well, she says he's not. He just likes to pretend he is—sort of a party piece to entertain everyone with."

"Oh, what a crock," Peter laughed. "What kind of heterosexual male wants people to think he's gay—even in jest?"

"I think he has to be bisexual, at least," David commented. "Morgan probably just turns a blind eye to it."

"But isn't she embarrassed by his act?" Jeff asked.

Andrew shook his head. "Doesn't seem to be. She just laughs it off. Actually, she's had quite a difficult time for the last few months, since the accident."

"How come?"

"Well, she told me how it happened, and it's all a bit devastating."

"Go on," Jeff urged with interest.

"She and Jeremy went to some wild party in New Hampshire with another friend who got really drunk, so she insisted on driving him back to the bungalow before he made an ass of himself. Jeremy didn't want to go with them—would've spoiled his fun, I guess, so she said she'd come back and get him. Anyway, some jerk ran her off the road—her car went down an incline and hit a tree. She managed to get out, but the guy with her was such a dead weight, she couldn't budge him, so she decided to get back up on the road to get help. Here's the really bad part…the car caught fire and exploded with their friend still in it. There was no way she could help him. By the time help arrived, he was burned to a crisp. Morgan was hysterical of course. Well, you can imagine; she didn't even know she had a broken arm till the paramedics examined her."

Peter and Jeff stared at Andrew in silence as he finished his story.

"Oh my God," Peter said, finally. "That's just awful!"

"Did they ever find the guy who ran her off the road?" Jeff asked.

"No. She couldn't describe the car. Said the headlights were blinding, and of course, he didn't come back to help. It took her a long time to get over it—especially as Jeremy blamed her for the whole thing."

"Oh, he sounds like a total charmer," Peter gasped.

"Tell me. I don't know why she sticks with him. He's such an asshole."

"A very good-looking asshole," David interjected. "And younger than her."

Andrew frowned. "David, that's so shallow."

"Yes it is—but we all know you can never tell why a person puts up with a rocky relationship. A lot of times it just comes down to familiarity—or good sex. After all, they have been married for over twelve years. There must be something there to keep it together."

"But, if he's gay or bisexual," Peter wondered, "Surely she must have a problem when he goes off with some guy."

David shook his head. "That part of the story we don't know. She's never admitted to Andrew that it even exists. Only thing she's ever mentioned is that they have screaming rows, now and then."

"Right," Andrew agreed. "And she only mentions that when she's really depressed."

"Has she said whether he still blames her for the accident?" Jeff asked him.

"That doesn't get talked about anymore, apparently. No, I think their problem stems from the amount of time he spends away from her during the day. It's not like he's got a job or anything. He used to be a male model. Did the runway stuff in Rome and Milan from all accounts, but now he doesn't work. She's loaded, so he doesn't have to."

"Aha!" Peter cried. "There's the answer. He's only staying with her for the money."

David laughed. "Yes, Sherlock—we already came to that conclusion."

"She makes no bones about that aspect," Andrew said. "She knows her money is a huge attraction. Let's face it—I hate the guy, but I have to agree with David—he *is* very good looking, and Morgan is…well, past her prime to be polite. She's still an attractive woman; but—and I hate to say this, he does look more like her son than her husband."

"Ouch," Jeff murmured.

"Well," Peter said. "I think we now know more than we really need to about Morgan and Jeremy. Gee, what'll we find to talk to them about tomorrow night? The accident, their turbulent marriage or whether Jeremy likes men or women?"

Andrew moaned. "I *knew* I shouldn't have invited them."

"Get out!" Peter laughed. "If what you've told us is only half the story, they promise to be the most interesting couple here."

"I hope you're still saying that after Jeremy puts the make on one of you—or maybe both of you."

Jeff and Peter looked at each other speculatively.

"I know I can handle that with dignity," Peter said, airily.

"Well..." Jeff grinned. I'm not sure I can. If he comes on to you, I may just have to play the injured lover, and sock him one."

Andrew grinned at them both. "I'd pay good money to see that!"

"Would you really put someone's lights out if they came on to me?" Peter asked later as he and Jeff lay in bed, nestled in each other's arms.

"Probably not," Jeff yawned. "I'd ask for money, instead."

"You!" Peter buried his face in Jeff's armpit.

"Argh," Jeff growled. "Stop, or I'll have to have my way with you."

"You'll have to make me stop..."

Jeff pulled Peter on top of him and kissed him hard on the mouth. Peter returned the kiss passionately, thrilling to the feel of Jeff's strong body beneath him. He smiled wickedly as he felt the hardness of Jeff's erection against his thigh.

"Now I've got you," he murmured sensually. He lowered his head and nibbled gently on Jeff's left nipple, enjoying the writhing reaction it caused.

"You know just how to drive me mad..."

Peter continued to drive him mad as his lips and tongue traced an erotic pattern over his chest and abdomen.

"I love you so much," Peter murmured as Jeff rolled him onto his back and lay over him, smiling into his eyes. He encircled Jeff's slim waist with his legs, and his heart raced with anticipation as he felt Jeff's rock hard penis slip between his legs. This was the complete fulfillment he longed for; this feeling of total belonging to the man he loved. He gazed up into Jeff's eyes, now half closed with sensual pleasure as he moved rhythmically above him. Jeff's breathing became more labored, and Peter's own climax became too strong for him to control. They clung together as one, Jeff's face buried against Peter's neck, a gasping shout escaping his lips as they came together. They lay spent, in their deep embrace for some time, without moving.

"God, this gets better every time," Peter sighed happily.

"Practice makes perfect."

"Wanna go again?"

"Are you crazy? Haven't you ever heard of jet lag? You've worn me out, young man, and now I need rest!"

"Me too," Peter smiled sleepily. Within minutes, still curled together, they were fast asleep.

CHAPTER 3

Peter woke next morning, feeling totally refreshed. Ambling into the kitchen he found Andrew sitting at the table sipping coffee.

"Hey, Peter." Andrew got up and gave him a good morning hug. "Coffee?"

"Love some."

"Jeff still asleep?"

"Still in the land of Nod. I think I wore him out last night."

"Lucky you! David was asleep the minute he hit the pillow."

"He does look tired, Andrew."

"He's *always* tired." Andrew frowned, then looked up at Peter. "Sorry, I'm being a bitch."

"Andrew, are you sure you want a bunch of people over here tonight? You don't have to entertain us, you know. We're happy just being here with you guys."

"Oh, it's all arranged. David's having it catered, would you believe, so there won't be anything to do except keep everyone's glass full."

"Are you working today?"

"Just this morning, then I'm meeting Morgan for lunch. I thought you could join us if you'd like. We'll be at Alfredo's. It's just a couple of blocks from here…say around twelve-thirty?"

"Sounds good. So we get to meet the famous Morgan without the infamous Jeremy?"

"Yeah, I'd like you to meet her first. You'll like her, and she's dying to meet both of you. I've told her all about your adventures."

"Adventures?" Peter laughed. "That's one way to describe all the weird things that have happened in the couple of years.

"What weird things?" Jeff asked, appearing in the doorway, yawning mightily.

Andrew smiled at him. "Good morning, Jeff. Looks like you need a coffee fix."

"You bet I do. This guy kept me up all night."

"Sounds like a personal problem to me," Andrew said—then added, "and not one I'd know anything about lately."

"Oh oh," Jeff sighed. "A bit early for true confessions isn't it?" He slumped down on a chair and looked blearily at Peter who shook his head slightly. "Sorry, I'm a little grumpy this morning. Must be the jet lag."

"We're having lunch with Andrew and Morgan later," Peter told him.

"Uh huh." Jeff took a sip from the mug of coffee Andrew had put in front of him. "Is there a gym near here, Andrew? I could use a workout to clear the cobwebs."

"Just round the corner. You can use my membership card for a free pass."

"Thanks. Want to join me, Peter?"

"You bet. I'm not having you on the loose in New York surrounded by naked sweaty men, without me there to protect you."

"Like he needs protection." Andrew stood up. "Okay you guys, I've gotta go. I'll see you later…at Alfredo's."

"We'll be there."

"Make sure you bundle up for the gym, guys. It's colder that a witch's thingy out there, and you don't want to catch your deaths coming out after sweating up a storm."

"Yes, Mother!" Peter grinned at him.

"See you later guys. Have fun."

"Later!"

Andrew was right. It was freezing cold on the street, but the gym was well heated and well equipped. After they had warmed up on the treadmills, Peter perched himself on a leg-raise machine while Jeff did some bicep curls with free weights. Peter glanced around at the men and women all seriously working out around him. He couldn't fail to notice that some surreptitious glances were being cast in Jeff's direction, as he cut a fine pose seated on a bench, concentrating on the steady rhythm of his exercise.

Peter smiled to himself, as he too admired Jeff's muscles rippling under smooth tanned skin. Not for the first time, he found himself reflecting on the strange circumstances that had brought them together. Peter was convinced that it was not just by chance, but rather by design.

Phillip's design.

He would never be able to prove his theory, of course, but he had talked it over with Andrew, and with Jeff himself. As improbable as it seemed, both of them had been prepared to go along with Peter's belief that his dead lover, Phillip, had orchestrated the events that had led to Peter's first stormy meeting with Jeff, and the subsequent developments that had ended in justice being meted out to Phillip's murderers.

Peter counted himself lucky in having Jeff in his life. Not just because of the fact that he was so easy on the eye, but that he was such a caring and thoughtful person—a good guy, Peter reflected, and a lot more patient and understanding than himself.

Jeff caught his eye and smiled back at him, seemingly oblivious to the attention he was getting from the men and women exercising near him. Peter's smile turned to a slight frown as a tall man, wearing a body hugging black unitard, moved in front of him blocking his view of Jeff, and obviously engaging him in conversation.

He could hear Jeff's pleasant laugh sounding just a little uncomfortable as the man continued to monopolize his attention. He noted the man's stance was touched with an air of arrogance and self-assurance, as though he was used to the admiring looks of lesser mortals. His back was a perfectly sculpted V-shape, from his wide shoulders to his slim waist and hips. He stood with his hands resting lightly on his hips, and Peter noticed with some amusement that he flexed his buttock and thigh muscles as he stood there, obviously for the benefit of the crowd he seemed to know, without a shadow of a doubt, was watching him confer with Jeff.

Peter's eyebrows arched as he saw the man sit down next to Jeff on his bench and lean in closely, in an almost intimate fashion. He was about to hop off his machine and make his way over to them, when he saw the man flick his eyes in his direction. Jeff had obviously told him of Peter's presence, for he stood up, shrugged his shoulders slightly and sauntered off, turning just once to look at Peter again. Jeff walked over, shaking his head.

"Who the heck was that?" Peter asked.

"Didn't introduce himself," Jeff chuckled. "Just fed me a line about how great I looked, and he'd been watching me, and maybe we could work out together. Just baloney, really."

"The nerve! Trying to pick you up right in front of me."

"Well, to be fair, he thought I was on my own."

Peter smiled at him sweetly. "He was right about one thing—you do look great."

"Thanks. Wanna spot me for a little while?"

"Sure."

"Good. That way I can look up your shorts without anyone noticing."

Laughing, their arms around each other's shoulders, they made their way to the workout bench, unaware of the envious eyes that followed them.

Morgan Kennedy's day was proving to be a difficult one. First, her father had called from Connecticut demanding to know why she had canceled her plans to visit them over the Holidays.

"Your mother is really upset, Morgan!" he had ranted in her ear. "Tell that selfish bastard of a husband that I'm going to give him a piece of my mind when I talk to him."

"Jeremy is as sorry as I am we're not going to see you this Christmas," she had replied. It was a lie of course, but she felt she had better try to sweeten the old man as much as she could. "He didn't know his brother and his family were going to land on us until just last week." She had repeated the lie Jeremy had told her to use as an excuse.

"Damned irresponsible, if you ask me," her father had fumed. "Expecting people to give up their plans at the last minute."

Then, the headache that had started the night before to which she had attributed too much wine with dinner, had returned with a vengeance, leaving her feeling nauseated and irritable. Jeremy hadn't helped, of course. His cavalier attitude to her problems had led them to a row, causing him to flounce out of the apartment.

"For God's sake, put on a new attitude along with your face, this morning!" he'd yelled before slamming the door behind him.

Last evening had been awful.

Jeremy was right—Bruce and Jennifer were boring people, with very little conversation. She had worked overtime to try and keep the talk flowing, while Jeremy had sat very silent, unlike him, seeming to mock her attempts at keeping the party alive. Usually he was the life and soul, being screamingly funny with his take off of gay men, but last night he had hardly said a word. His moroseness had continued on the way home, and he had gone to bed almost immediately, without a word. He'd been fast asleep—or was pretending to be—when she eventually joined him.

She sighed as she opened a bottle of painkillers and swallowed three of them with her coffee. Surely, she would feel better before her lunch date with Andrew and his friends.

After she showered, she sat in front of her mirror, gazing at her reflection, as she seemed to do with increasing frequency, these days. Cosmetic surgery was probably the answer, now, she thought. She could no longer disguise the bags and crows feet around her eyes, or the sagging of her skin under her chin. She dreaded the thought of being cut for the sake of vanity. She'd read so many horror stories of botched surgeries. Yes, she could afford the best, but even then, sometimes the results were not always pleasing or natural looking. She shuddered at the thought of living the rest of her life scarred, or with one eye lower than the other. She'd seen one woman interviewed on TV a few nights ago, suffering from just those results of an unsuccessful operation

"God, I'm being ridiculous," she said aloud.

Of course, that would not happen to her. Several of her friends had already had facelifts, and kept encouraging her to do the same. Perhaps then, Jeremy would show more interest in her again. That was the real reason she wanted to go through with the surgery—Jeremy's dwindling interest in any sexual relations between them. No matter how hard she tried to get him in the mood, he now rarely ever responded.

Damn him! she thought. He might save just a little for me.

She knew he was finding his sexual release elsewhere. Had been, for a long time. At first, she hadn't minded too much. He was being safe, and he always had enough reserve to keep her satisfied. But gradually, over the years, his passion waned, and when they did have sex, it was just that. It felt like he went through the motions, and she knew his mind was a million miles away.

Of course, she could have thrown him out, divorced him, found someone else to replace him. She was still attractive—and she was rich. She could have any one of a hundred good looking men she encountered at parties and social gatherings every year, but—and this was the part she found the hardest to understand—despite all his infidelities, his arrogance, his uncaring attitude, his *thanklessness*—she still desired him.

Even when she found out what he was really up to.

Her eyes strayed to the photograph on her husband's nightstand, and her mouth tightened as she looked at the faces smiling back at her. There she was in the middle, Jeremy on one side, his arm around her waist—and Kevin on the other, his arm across her shoulders, his hand resting on the back of Jeremy's neck.

How could she have been so blind to not see what they were doing—what they had been doing for years behind her back? Of course, when it was all out in the open, after she had walked in on them, and caught them in that most compromising of positions—then she remembered the furtive glances, the stolen smiles, the odd innuendo that had, theretofore, gone completely over her head.

What a fool I was, she thought, still gazing at the photograph. And all the time I thought we were the best of friends.

She had felt especially foolish, because it was not the first time it had happened. There had been others before Kevin. Bright shiny young men who came into their lives and stayed until Morgan paid them to go away. She had not suspected Jeremy was gay when she first met him. He was so virile, so eager to bed her and make love to her every night. He was a beautiful man, he made her laugh—and he was there to carry out her every wish. She knew her money was the main attraction, but she loved having him by her side, loved the way other women looked on in envy, loved the attention he gave her…loved *him*. How easily she had fallen—how easily he had made it happen.

They had been married for two years before she became aware of his true sexual nature. She couldn't remember the boy's name now—just someone he had picked up while she was out of town, visiting her parents. She discovered them in bed on her unannounced return. She had been horrified and hysterical at first, but had believed him when he said it had never happened before—and it never would again. When she found out he had lied, she had tried to console herself with the fact that, at least, it was not another woman.

Surely he would get over these useless infatuations, as he grew older. When she suggested he go to therapy to see if he could be cured, he had flown into a rage and threatened to leave her. Over the years, she endured the company of these young men who flitted in and out of their lives, some for a few days, others a few weeks until Jeremy became bored with them and cut them loose. Two or three of them stayed far too long, and Morgan was forced to come up with large sums of money to get rid of them.

Then, there was Kevin.

She had never suspected he and Jeremy were having an affair, after all Kevin was married to her best friend Sylvia and he seemed so…*masculine.* For years, the four of them went everywhere together. She and Sylvia were glad the men got along so well, spending hours talking, keeping each other company while the women went shopping.

Silly Morgan, she had chastised herself later. You thought that Kevin's influence would make a man of Jeremy!

Feeling totally betrayed by her discovery, she had told Sylvia everything. Kevin and Sylvia were divorced within a few months, and Sylvia had never spoken to Morgan again. But Morgan could not bring herself to end her marriage to Jeremy. Even when she found out he and Kevin were still seeing each other, still feverishly arranging times and dates when they could meet—even then, she could not let him go. They became the "Three Musketeers" as Kevin dubbed them, and although she knew certain friends were laughing behind her back, she would not end it.

Secretly, and without ever discussing it with Jeremy, she had offered Kevin a lot of money to give up his relationship with her husband, but he had smilingly refused.

"How could you begrudge me just a little of his time, Morgan?" he had asked her. "He lives with you. He'll never leave you!"

She had prayed that Jeremy would tire of the relationship, as he had done so many times in the past, but he did not. If anything, it seemed to grow stronger. She lived in fear that Jeremy would indeed leave her to be with Kevin. That she could not tolerate, and then, Kevin was dead—killed, in that awful crash that Jeremy still blamed her for.

She blinked back tears as she looked around the bedroom with it's pale rose colored walls, and remembered the night in this very room when Jeremy had screamed at her for what had seemed hours, calling her every vile name he could think of, while she stood trembling with fear and humiliation.

"I will never forgive you for this!" he had ranted at her. "You have destroyed my life. You couldn't bear to see me happy, not for a second. Your jealousy killed him."

"But it was an *accident*," she had whimpered, pleadingly. "I could have been killed too."

"You should have been!" he had screamed at her. "I would give everything to have him standing here, instead of you—you useless bitch!"

He had flung himself out of the apartment and disappeared for days. She'd had to endure the questions of the police and investigative officers alone. What was left of Kevin was further cremated and his ashes flown to his parents in Seattle. With one or two exceptions, most of her friends shunned her socially. It was a tragedy they could not seem to handle.

Then she met Andrew, and his natural warmth and caring disposition endeared him to her almost immediately. Under his therapeutic touch, she had relaxed and opened up to him like she had done with no other. She had been disappointed when he'd told her he was a gay man, living in a loving relationship with David, but she knew it would have been delusional of her to think he could be interested in her in any way, other than friendship. He was so much younger than she was—almost fifteen years. Nevertheless, at times she'd wished she could simply curl up in his arms and that he would protect her from the miseries of her life. The comforting hugs he would sometimes give her, made her crave more. She loved the feel of his strong athletic body against hers.

In the meantime, of course, Jeremy had returned, and a truce of sorts was forged between them. It was a far cry from the way she had hoped her life would be, as she grew older, but at least he was there by her side again. Almost as if because of this, things seemed to return to normal. Her so called friends appeared to have forgotten the events of the past months, and called to invite them to their various functions. Even if she never felt completely at ease with any of them again, at least it could be assumed that all was well with her and Jeremy.

Her make up complete, Morgan dressed quickly, topping off her outfit with a thick wool coat and fur hat. She hated the winter weather. She never felt glamorous in all these layers. It was just a short walk to Alfredo's, but she decided she'd call for the car. She was looking forward to her lunch date with Andrew and his friends. Her headache felt better, and as she stepped off the elevator, she straightened her shoulders and flashed the security guard a cheery smile.

It was a new day, and with new people to meet.

CHAPTER 4

Alfredo's was a popular restaurant and Andrew had been wise to make reservations. He waved, smiling, as Peter and Jeff entered and looked around at the sea of tables and people.

"We're lucky," he said, as they sat at his table by the window. "They were over-booked, but they had a couple of cancellations, so we don't have to wait."

"Welcome to New York," Jeff said, wryly.

"Is it always like this?" Peter asked.

"Always." Andrew picked up his menu. "Especially at lunchtime."

"Where's your friend, Morganna?"

"*Morgan*," Andrew laughed. "She's on her way. She just called saying she was waiting for her car."

"It's certainly a different life here," Jeff remarked. "How are you coping?"

"Some days are better than others. I think you know I'd rather be back in California—but please don't mention it to David. I don't want him to think I'm whining to you."

"Don't worry Andrew…" Peter touched his hand. "Like we said, it's up to you and David to work this out."

"Thanks guys. Oh look, here's Morgan." He stood up and waved as Peter and Jeff turned to see an elegant, chicly dressed red haired woman coming toward their table. They also stood as Andrew made the introductions.

Morgan gave them both a large smile. "I'm so happy to meet you both. Andrew has told me so much about you—I feel I already know you." She sat down next to Andrew, who helped her remove her coat. "Jeremy couldn't make it, but he's looking forward to the party tonight."

"Oh…right," Andrew's smile faded for a moment. "You'll meet Morgan's husband at the party."

"Can't wait," Peter said mischievously, ignoring the pressure of Jeff's foot on his.

"So, how are you enjoying the City?" Morgan asked them.

"Well, Andrew and David have made us very welcome." Jeff turned his killer smile on Morgan, and she let herself drown in the depths of his smoky gray eyes. "They made us a wonderful dinner last night. Then today, Peter and I had a great work out…and now, here we are."

Morgan felt herself coloring slightly as she realized she had been momentarily mesmerized by Jeff's physical presence. She cleared her throat and sat back in her chair. "Well, we're looking forward to Andrew's party tonight, and we must have you both over for dinner as soon as we can arrange it."

"That would be great." Peter started to smile, but a sudden sick feeling slid over him like a clammy blanket.

"Morgan's an excellent cook," Andrew enthused, putting his arm round her shoulders and giving her an affectionate squeeze.

As Peter stared at the two of them, trying to throw off the feeling of nausea, he felt an ominous presence hover over them. He became light headed and his stomach knotted in a painful spasm. He could feel sweat break out on his forehead and in his armpits.

Jesus, what is this? he thought, gripping the edge of the table tightly, fearing for a moment he might topple from his chair.

Andrew, who was sitting opposite him, took his arm. "Are you all right, Peter? You've gone white as a sheet!"

"I…I feel a bit nauseous, actually."

"Here, take a sip of this water" Jeff handed him his glass and massaged the back of his neck. "You going to be OK?"

"Yeah. I'll be fine. I must have overdone the treadmill on an empty stomach, I guess." He tried to smile as he put down the glass of water. "Phew! That was nasty, but it's passing off now. I think I just need something in my stomach."

"Perhaps an omelet or something light like that," Morgan suggested.

Jeff agreed. "Good idea. An egg white omelet and a salad—that shouldn't upset your system."

Peter smiled at him and nodded, but deep inside him he knew that what he had just experienced had nothing to do with his digestive processes. Fortunately, he began to feel better, and he pushed aside the ominous presentiments he'd had earlier. He'd wait to discuss this with Jeff, when they were alone.

The rest of the time was spent in pleasant enough conversation and Morgan showed a great deal of interest in Peter's artwork.

"I've only seen the portrait of Andrew, of course," she remarked. "But I could tell it had been done by someone who really understands his craft. I would love to see more of your work."

"You might just be able to," Peter told her. "While we're here, I'm supposed to be talking to some dealers about an exhibition—here in New York, for next year."

"How marvelous." Morgan's eyes grew wide as if a thought had just occurred to her. "If you wouldn't mind, I'd like to host a cocktail party for you on your opening night."

Andrew gave her a hug. "That'd be terrific…wouldn't it Peter?"

"Why, yes." Peter tried hard not to show his surprise at this generous offer. After all, he thought, we've just met. Isn't this a bit much, even for a wealthy woman like Morgan? And there again, was that strange insidious feeling that stole over him as he looked across the table at her expectant expression. "That's…that's very generous of you, Morgan."

"It will be my pleasure," she assured him with a smile as the waiter finally descended upon them to take their orders.

As they left the restaurant, Andrew threw his arms around Peter and Jeff's shoulders. "Okay, you two. Try and stay out of trouble till I get home. I only have two more appointments today, then we can kick back together till the guests arrive."

"Sounds good." Jeff turned to Morgan. "Good meeting you, Morgan. We'll see you later at the party?"

"Yes. Till then." She smiled at them both, then walked quickly up the avenue, pulling her coat around her against the cold. Peter watched her retreating figure for a moment, his mind going to a place from which he had to almost physically wrench it back. He shook his head quickly to dispel the strange thoughts that had invaded his brain.

Jeff gave him a worried look. "You're still not feeling right, are you?"

Peter tried to shrug it off. "It's not anything you can't take care of," he replied, giving Jeff a sly look.

"Oh boy!" Andrew laughed. "I'm out of here…I'll see you guys later."

"Right…" Jeff said, as he unlocked the door to Andrew and David's apartment. "Now will you tell me what really happened to you in the restaurant?"

"Can't fool you, can I?"

"No, you can't—and don't ever try to, either." Jeff pulled Peter close and kissed him roughly. They clung together for a moment then Jeff began to unbutton Peter's heavy overcoat. "C'mon, tell me what it was," he coaxed.

"I really don't know what the heck it was, Jeff. One of those creepy feelings I get now and then." He watched as Jeff hung their coats in the hall closet. "It happened when Andrew put his arm around Morgan. He was showing her pure affection, and I suddenly got this strange sensation of…oh, how can I describe this? I want to say a menacing presence, directed toward Andrew."

"From Morgan?" Jeff asked, raising his eyebrows in surprise.

"Yes, from her. Like she was a real danger to him."

"My God," Jeff said, quietly.

Over the time he had known Peter and lived with him, he had come to respect these intuitive feelings that his lover was prey to, now and then. Ever since he had awakened from his coma there had been some form of psychic link that had, on more than one occasion, been helpful to Jeff and other people faced with danger.

At Jeff's insistence, they had consulted a couple of reputable psychics who had shown a deal of interest in Peter's 'feelings' as he referred to them. One of them, Adele Cummings, was candid enough in her approach to suggest that Phillip's death, Peter's coma and the 'feelings' were all linked.

"It seems, from what you've told me, that when you awoke from your coma, the psychic bond between you and Phillip was established—and has not diminished." She had looked seriously at them both as she continued. "In fact, if anything, the link has been strengthened, perhaps by the dangers you have faced and his realization that you still need his help."

"You mean, you think Phillip's still looking out for us?" Peter had looked at her in amazement. He had always been convinced that Phillip had indeed set in motion a chain of events that had eventually led to his murderers' destruction, but he had never considered the notion that Phillip might somehow still be watching over him.

"Try to think of him as a guardian angel," Adele had smiled at him. "He's not here to interfere, or to spy on you—only to help if he's needed."

Afterwards, he and Jeff had talked it over, and although Peter found it hard to believe that what Adele had told them was in any way plausible, he had never come up with an alternate reason for the sensations he sometimes felt.

"If what she said is true," he'd said to Jeff later. "How do you feel about it?"

Jeff, knowing that Peter was a little upset about this whole revelation, chose to try and lighten the situation with humor. "Well, I've never really been into three-ways myself—but for *you*…"

He'd had to dodge a well aimed punch at that moment, but fortunately Peter had taken the joke well, and Jeff had told him, in a more serious tone, that he thought it was just fine—if indeed it was Phillip, still looking out for them.

"Nice to know I still have the seal of approval," he'd said with a smile, and this time, Peter was not sure if he was joking or not.

Now, as they discussed this latest event, Peter frowned as he asked, "But what could it be, Jeff? On the face of it, Morgan seems like a really nice person, and Andrew is obviously very fond of her. How could she be a danger to him?"

"You don't think this menace you felt could have been coming from someone else in the restaurant?"

Peter frowned as he thought. "No, I really don't think so. It was so *close*—and besides, who else in the restaurant knew Andrew?"

"Good question. If I didn't know better, I'd say you had to be imagining this, but…" he added with a wry smile, "I do know better. We'd better be on the look out for any sign from her tonight, that she's not the lady Andrew thinks her to be."

David and Andrew got home within minutes of each other, David having left work early to get the arrangements for the party under way. "The caterer will be here around seven," he explained. "It's a buffet, so people can just help themselves all night. He'll be back in the morning to clean up."

"What's the dress code?" Peter asked.

"I told everyone to come casual. Everyone wants to get out of their business suits—I know I do," he laughed, stripping off his tie and unbuttoning his shirt collar.

"You guys get ready," Andrew said. "Then we can have a drink before everyone arrives."

Jeff nodded. "Okay. We need to shower, but we'll be quick."

"There's a first time for everything, I suppose," Peter chuckled, pulling Jeff toward their bedroom.

"God, you have a one track mind."

"And you love it!"

Andrew watched them go, a smile playing around his lips. "They're so good together. I'm so happy for them."

David put his arms round him and held him close. "I'm happy too, Andrew. Happy for us."

Andrew leaned his head on David's shoulder. "I've missed this a lot lately."

"I know…I'm sorry I've been neglecting you. I love you very much. You do know that, don't you?"

"It's wonderful to hear you say it, David."

"Come on. We've got an hour before the caterer gets here, and I don't think Peter and Jeff will be hurrying through their shower. Let me make up for some lost time here, with you."

"I like that idea." Andrew smiled at him and they walked hand in hand into their bedroom. David closed the door gently behind them, then pulled Andrew into his arms. He unbuttoned Andrew's woolen shirt at an almost feverish pace. Beside themselves with desire now, they tore at each other's clothing, then fell on the floor in a tangled heap.

Andrew looked up into his lover's eyes. "I think abstinence brings out the animal in you."

"Let me show you the ways," David growled into Andrew's ear, sending delicious thrills coursing through him. Any further conversation was stilled by their lips meeting in an all consuming kiss.

When the four friends gathered in the living room again, Peter did not fail to notice the smile of satisfaction on Andrew's face. While Jeff and David talked on the couch, he cornered him in the kitchen.

"You're looking mighty smug," he chuckled, watching Andrew make their drinks.

Andrew turned and gave Peter a Cheshire cat grin. "I'd only tell *you* this, but we had the greatest sex I think we've ever had!"

"Is that what it was? I thought for sure we were back in California having an earthquake."

"Liar…I bet you and Jeff were far too busy to notice what we were doing."

"You're right—but I'm happy for you. It's certainly put you in a better mood."

Andrew smiled at his friend. "You know," he said quietly. "It wasn't just the sex. It was the fact that I felt *needed* again. These last few months, I've felt I was drifting somehow—out of place. Like I had no purpose. David has been so consumed with his business, and I can understand why. He's felt he had to do his best for the company—make a big impression. But, it left me at a loss, because I wasn't sure what my part in all of this was. I haven't wanted to complain because I knew how important it all was, *is*, for him. I know this makes me sound like the most co-dependent person in the world, but it's the way I feel."

"David's a lucky guy, having you in his life."

"Hey, we're all lucky." Andrew handed Peter his drink and they clinked glasses. "We've both got the best men in the world—and they haven't done so badly either!"

Out in the hall the doorbell chimed loudly.

"That'll be the caterer." Andrew made for the door.

Peter walked out into the living room and delivered Jeff's drink as Andrew ushered in two young men pushing food carts. While David and Andrew helped the men set up the buffet table, Peter and Jeff strolled over to one of the large windows and looked out over the city.

"Quite a view," Jeff remarked. "Look, it's starting to snow."

"Perfect," Peter murmured, leaning seductively against him. "A Christmas tree, a glowing fire, snow flakes outside the window. Now, if we were just alone…"

Jeff laughed gently and put his arm around Peter. "Will you ever stop being insatiable?"

"Not as long as *you're* around."

The doorbell rang again, and they turned to see David welcoming the first two guests.

Morgan sat fretting by the phone. Why the hell hasn't he called? she thought for the hundredth time, since she got home to an empty apartment. They were already late for Andrew's party.

Well, she wasn't going to wait another minute. She'd simply go over there on her own, leaving Jeremy a note telling him he could either come on later, or stay home. She would never have even contemplated leaving without him had they been going to any other of her friends, but she knew Andrew would understand. Pulling on her fur coat over an elegant black silk dress, she quickly scrawled a few lines and left the note on the dining table. She called her car service, and they told her they'd be right there.

Sighing, Morgan picked up her bag, and headed for the door. She jumped back quickly as the door suddenly burst open and Jeremy rushed in, out of breath.

"Where the hell have you been?" The stress had sharpened her tone.

"Sorry, sorry, sorry!" Jeremy sang as he ran past her. "I'll be changed in a second. Did you call the car?"

"Yes," she answered, slipping off her coat and following him into the bedroom. "Jeremy, where have you *been*?"

"Oh, just hanging out with some friends. No one you know."

"I have no doubt I don't know them." She did not bother to hide her sarcasm. "And how long have *you* known them? More than a few hours?"

"Now, now, Morgan dearest…no bitchiness, even if it *is* your style. If you must know, I've known them for years."

"You are such a liar." Morgan turned on her heel and left the room. She crossed to the bar and poured herself a neat Scotch. "Bastard," she muttered, tossing back the Scotch. She stood for a moment, feeling the strong amber liquid course through her blood. Jeremy came into the room and stood watching her, a mocking smile playing around his sensuous lips.

"Here." He offered her a tiny silver spoon laden with cocaine. "A little toot to put you in a better mood." He held the spoon to her nostril and she snorted the white powder it contained, reeling slightly from the effects.

"Better?" Jeremy smiled at her.

"You are so inconsiderate Jeremy," she groused, not willing to let him off the hook so easily. "You've kept me waiting for hours, we're late for the party, and…"

He silenced her by kissing her seductively, his full soft lips causing her to tremble with desire. She leaned against his chest, giving in to the lust she still felt for him.

"I don't think Andrew is going to be too upset because we're late," Jeremy chuckled. "He's probably hoping I won't show up at all."

"Why on earth do you say that?"

"Because he has the hots for me, and doesn't want David to know."

"*What*?" Morgan looked at her husband incredulously.

"You haven't noticed how agitated he gets around me? He keeps casting these soulful looks my way. Doesn't trust himself around me, I can tell."

"You're crazy," Morgan snapped, stepping back from his embrace. "If you must know, Andrew doesn't like you very much at all."

"Of course that's what he wants you to believe, my darling. It wouldn't do for him to let you in on his little secret, now would it? Might spoil that perfect friendship of yours."

"You're being really crass, Jeremy. Andrew was furious that you flirted with David that night."

"Of course he was. He wanted to be the one I was interested in—he was jealous that I was paying so much attention to his lover."

"Stop it!" Morgan cried. "I don't want to hear anymore of this. It isn't enough that you carry on behind my back with any man that'll give you a second look. Now you have to try and ruin my friendship with Andrew—one of the sweetest men I know." She peered at him suspiciously. "Are you jealous of our friendship? Is that what this is all about?"

"Now who's crazy?" Jeremy asked with a nasty laugh. "Anyone who wants to take you off my hands for a while is welcome to it."

Morgan reached out to slap him, but he caught her arm roughly in a strong grip. "I'll prove to you that I'm right, Morgan dearest. Tonight I'll show you just what 'the sweetest man you know' is capable of."

"No!" Morgan screamed at him. "You won't do this—I won't allow it! We're not going to their party. I'll call and say I'm not feeling well. I won't be lying—you've made me sick to my stomach."

"Fine," Jeremy smirked. "You stay home. I'll go by myself."

Morgan gave a low moan of despair. "Why must you do this? Why must you try to destroy me any chance you get?"

"Because of what you did to Kevin—but you know that already."

"That was an accident. An *accident*, for God's sake."

"Was it?" Jeremy sneered. "A fucking convenient accident, wasn't it?"

"What are you saying? You think I deliberately killed Kevin?"

"You wished him dead, and then he *was* dead. It's the same thing."

Morgan's head was swimming from the effects of the Scotch and the cocaine. "I…I don't feel well, Jeremy."

"So go to bed. I'll let you know what you missed later."

"No! You're not going over there without me."

"Then put on your coat and let's go…" Jeremy headed for the door, then looked back at her with a mocking smile. "I'm in a party mood."

Numbly, she obeyed, pulling her coat on as they left the apartment. The car was waiting for them and Morgan huddled herself deep inside her fur coat in the backseat, looking miserably out at the snow that had begun to fall more thickly on the city. This night, to which she had previously been looking forward, now loomed ahead of her, filling her with dread.

CHAPTER 5

"**How's** it going out there?" Andrew asked David anxiously as he pulled a tray of hot hors d'ouvres from the oven.

"Great! Everyone seems to be having a good time. Peter is regaling Graham and Jennifer with the story of Jeff's last murder case. You know, the father who molested his daughter?"

"Oh, right. I think her name was Emily. Peter says she's really happy now. Married to a really nice guy."

"And Bob and Michael are already in love with Jeff," David laughed.

"What a surprise." Andrew looked at David questioningly. "No sign of Morgan yet?"

"Nope. It is snowing pretty hard out there. Maybe they've decided not to come."

"She would have called by now, and besides, they have their own car. Here..." he handed the hot plate to David. "Take these out and I'll make us another drink."

"You got it," David said, pausing to kiss Andrew lightly on the lips. "By the way, thank you for earlier."

"You are entirely welcome. You have no idea how it brightened my life."

"You're the best," David murmured, "Oh oh, I think I heard the doorbell."

"That'll be Morgan and you know who—I'll go." Andrew walked off quickly to open the door. He swung it open, trying quickly to hide his alarm as he saw the haunted expression on Morgan's face.

She embraced him tightly. "Sorry we're so late—Jeremy got delayed."

"No problem. I'm just glad you could make it." Andrew hugged her to him.

"Wouldn't miss it for the world, buddy." Jeremy smiled at him as he eased Morgan out of Andrew's arms and began unbuttoning her coat. "Terrible night," he added, in a conversational tone. "We may have to stay over if it doesn't ease up."

"Well, we do have a sofa bed in the den," Andrew said, taking Morgan's coat from him and hanging it up.

"Mmm. Sounds like fun." Jeremy gave Andrew a hard stare. "Just as long as we can put you between us."

"Jeremy!" Morgan snapped. "Don't start that already." She walked ahead of them into the living room, and Andrew jumped, then gasped as he felt Jeremy's hand caress the curve of his buttock.

"What the…?"

"Oh, don't be offended Andrew," Jeremy sniggered. "Such a pretty ass. I couldn't resist."

Andrew glared at him for a moment, then decided it was best to not make a fuss. "What can I get you to drink?" he asked politely.

"Dry martini, shaken, not stirred—a la James Bond."

Good God, Andrew thought as he went to prepare the drink. He really is a sleaze!

Morgan had found Jeff and Peter and had greeted them as if they were old friends. It was obvious to them that she was extremely tense and on edge. Jeff could tell right away that she was on something.

Probably coke, he thought, watching Morgan introduce herself to David's boss.

"And you must be Jennifer," Morgan gushed, shaking hands with Graham's wife. "David just loves both of you."

Peter looked at Jeff apprehensively as Morgan babbled on.

"Excuse me one moment." Jeff spotted David and Andrew coming out of the kitchen, each carrying drinks for their guests. He touched David's arm and whispered. "You might want to get over there. Morgan is trying to do a PR job for you with your boss."

"Is she drunk?" David looked over at where Morgan stood, still apparently extolling his virtues.

"She's high, I would say. Coke, I think."

"Oh God!"

"I'll take care of it," Andrew said firmly, handing Jeff the martini glass he was holding. "Can you take this over to Morgan's husband? David will introduce you."

"Sure. Lead on Dave." Jeff's eyes widened slightly in surprise, as David led him over to where a tall man with black curly hair and aquiline features was standing surveying the crowd, with an amused air.

"Hey Jeremy," David greeted him. "This is Jeff, my old high school buddy."

Jeremy extended a languid hand for Jeff to shake.

"We've met before…" Jeff smiled coolly. "This morning, at the gym."

"Really?" Jeremy's expression showed not a trace of surprise. "I don't recall. I'm sure I would remember meeting someone as handsome as you."

Oh brother, David thought. Here we go.

"Well, I remember you Jeremy," Jeff laughed lightly. "You tried to pick me up and I pointed out my boyfriend to you who was with me at the time. Maybe you remember him? He's standing over there talking with your wife."

Jeremy looked over at Peter and shook his head. "Sorry, can't say I do. You must have me confused with someone else. Is that my drink you're holding?"

Jeff nodded and handed Jeremy his drink.

"Thank you. Now if you'll excuse me, I must join my wife."

Jeff and David watched as Jeremy made his way across the living room.

"Can you believe that guy?" Jeff muttered. "He just totally lied."

"I don't think for the first time either. His life has to be one big cover up story."

"I wonder why Morgan puts up with it?"

"Well, like we said earlier, she's in denial of the whole thing. At least we think she is, and as you can see, he *is* very attractive."

"In a slime-ball sort of way," Jeff chuckled. "Look, Peter's just recognized him too. I knew I wasn't hallucinating." The two friends laughed as Peter approached them with a comical—"Can you believe it?"—look on his face.

Jeff grinned at him. "I knew I was right—the guy from the gym?"

"The one and the same. What a trip—him showing up here."

"He does get around," David chuckled. "I bet he's not as cool about this as he appears to be."

Peter looked over his shoulder. "Well, he couldn't look me in the eye when Morgan introduced us. By the way, what's with her? She's acting like she's looped, or something."

David touched his arm. "Look out. Andrew's bringing her over here. Notice that hubby isn't joining us."

Andrew led Morgan over to them, and once again, as they approached him, Peter was uncomfortably aware of an unsettling feeling in the pit of his stomach.

What the hell…?

He couldn't put his finger on just what this feeling was. He'd had many of them in the past since awaking from his coma, but now he was filled with alarm as he felt his friend, Andrew, in danger. He took a deep gulp of his drink, hoping that would help. Maybe I'm coming down with the flu, or something, he tried to convince himself.

Jeff glanced at him. "You OK?"

"Yeah, I'm fine," Peter lied.

"Morgan's feeling a bit under the weather," Andrew was saying.

That makes two of us, Peter thought.

Morgan sighed, leaning on Andrew for support. "Too much Mr. Johnny Walker I'm afraid."

"Come on, you can lie down on our bed," Andrew told her. "You'll feel better in a little while." Morgan allowed herself to be led away by Andrew who returned a few moments later.

"Well, she's out." He looked gloomy. "Can't think what's got into her. She's never done this before."

"She's a very unhappy woman," Peter remarked quietly.

"Wouldn't you be if you were married to Jeremy?"

"If Peter were married to Jeremy, at least it would be the right mix!" David said, trying to lighten the atmosphere.

"Puh-leeze," Peter exclaimed, derisively. "Never in a million years. Can you imagine living with a man who doesn't know if he's Arthur or Martha?"

"I think he knows very well who he is," Jeff said, without a smile. "And if you ask me, he's a dangerous kind of guy to have too close to you."

"What do you mean, Jeff?" Andrew asked.

"Too much to go into right now. This is a party, remember? You have enough to keep you occupied tonight."

"Well okay, but I want you to tell me later."

Andrew and David moved away toward their guests and Peter looked quizzically at Jeff.

"What *did* you mean?"

"Don't know for sure, but I would hazard a guess, that any man, who is willing to live his life in a total charade, bears some watching. Let's face it, he's lying to his wife, to his friends and to some degree, to himself. It's amazing he's never been caught out. Here we are in New York only one day and we catch him in a lie right away."

"He strikes me as arrogant enough to feel he can get away with just about anything."

"Maybe…" Jeff watched as Jeremy excused himself from the couple he was talking to, and disappeared toward the bathroom. "I wouldn't be surprised if he's about to give himself a boost right about now."

"A boost?"

"He's cut a few lines tonight already by the looks of him."

"You mean he's doing drugs here? In Andrew and David's apartment?"

"You are naive sometimes," Jeff chuckled. "I don't think Jeremy cares where he does his drugs."

"Well, I think he's got a colossal nerve, bringing that crap in here!" Peter glared across the room as if to make his disapproval felt across the hall and through the bathroom door.

"Calm down. Let's not make him aware we know what he's doing. I want to keep an eye on him for a while. I have a feeling he's up to something."

They were interrupted at that moment by David's associate Bob, and his lover Michael. Both in their late thirties, they were the exact opposite of each other in looks. Bob was short, stocky and sandy haired with baby blue eyes that gave him a perpetually anxious look. Michael was well over six feet tall, broad shouldered, dark haired with a Native American cast to his attractive face.

"Andrew tells us you painted that incredible portrait of him over there." Bob looked up at Peter with admiration. "I'm sure you've been told a hundred times how talented you are, but we'd just like to add ourselves to your fan club."

"Thank you," Peter laughed. "If I had one, you'd certainly be welcome."

"Andrew also tells us you're to have an exhibition in town soon."

"Andrew's been busy…Actually, that's under discussion at the moment. I have no idea when it will be."

"Peter will be meeting with a couple of dealers while we're here," Jeff told them.

"Great!" Michael said. "Please make sure we get an invitation. We'd love to see more of your work."

"You bet. I'll make sure Andrew gets enough invitations, if and when it gets done."

"Did I hear my name taken in vain?" Andrew joined them, putting his arm round Peter's shoulders.

"We were just ingratiating ourselves into Peter's favor," Bob said. "So we can get an invitation to his exhibition."

"Yeah, you know the one you're promoting tonight." Peter grinned at his friend.

"Well? Can I help it if I'm all excited about you becoming the toast of New York?"

The group grew suddenly silent as Jeremy approached them.

"Oh oh," Bob whispered none too subtly, as he watched Jeremy walk purposely toward them. "Here comes the Queen of Denial!"

"Ssh!" Michael warned him.

"I've just come over to apologize to your Laguna guests, Andrew." Jeremy was all smiles. "I just remembered I did see you in the gym this morning. I'm sorry if you thought I was trying to pick you up…Jeff, is it?"

"No problem." Jeff grinned affably at him, ignoring the patronizing attitude Jeremy affected.

"It's just that I know so many people there," Jeremy continued. "It's such a social scene, as you probably know. I quite forget whom I talk to after a while."

"Yeah, right!" Bob snorted before he could help himself.

Jeremy fixed Bob with a disapproving look and was about to say something when his eyes flicked over to where Morgan stood in the hallway. "Morgan darling," he exclaimed, rushing to her side. "Do you feel better, sweetheart?"

"Like he cares," Andrew muttered, as Jeremy led his wife over to them. Morgan did look better. She had fixed her make up and combed her hair.

"Sorry Andrew…" She still looked slightly embarrassed. "I threw up in your bathroom, but I do feel better now."

Andrew took her hand. "Can I get you something?"

"Just some tonic water, I think. Better lay off the booze for the rest of the night."

"Good idea," Jeremy murmured smoothly. "Come and sit over by the window for a little while." As Andrew went into the kitchen for Morgan's water, Jeremy led her to the couch.

"What a snake he is," Bob hissed.

"Bob!" Michael remonstrated. "He'll hear you, for goodness sake."

"I take it you're not a fan," Peter said, grinning.

"Can't stand the guy." Bob lowered his voice to Michael's satisfaction. "He makes this big deal of pretending to be gay in front of his straight friends—for what purpose we have no idea—when, in reality he's a total closet case—with the door wide open. I bet he *was* trying to pick you up this morning in the gym, Jeff."

"No doubt about it. I know when I'm being hit on, believe me."

"We don't know why Morgan puts up with the pretence," Michael said. "She can't be that stupid not to know."

"How do you know them?" Jeff asked. "I thought Andrew and David were the only ones they knew here."

"We met them a couple of years ago at a party," Bob explained. "They were guests of friends of ours, and Jeremy asked Michael for our phone number. He seemed so nice and friendly—said he and Morgan would like to meet us for dinner, which we did. Once—never again! He spent the entire dinner trying to make Michael. I was pissed, I can tell you. But, I felt so sorry for *her*. We just can't work out the relationship, or why she stays with him."

"Andrew says Morgan told him Jeremy isn't gay at all," Peter said. "Just pretends to be, to amuse their friends. Do you believe that?"

Bob's eyes widened. "Not for a moment! We know for a fact he's been seen at the baths—and then there was that rumor he'd been having an affair with the guy that got killed earlier this year."

Jeff asked quickly, "What guy?"

"We didn't know him. Kevin somebody, I think," Michael replied. "From what we heard, Morgan was driving him home from a party. The car went off the road and the guy was killed—she was lucky to get out alive, apparently."

"That's the story Andrew told us last night," Peter said. "But he didn't mention anything about Jeremy being involved with the guy."

Jeff looked at him thoughtfully. "Maybe Andrew doesn't know that part of the story."

"Hey, you guys!" David appeared suddenly in their midst. "Quit standing here gossiping like a bunch of old ladies. Come and eat, before everything gets cold."

"Sorry David," Bob said contritely. "We didn't mean to hog the guests of honor." They walked over to the buffet table and Peter glanced at where Morgan still sat with Jeremy at her side. Jeremy caught his eye, and Peter could not fail to notice the speculative look the man was giving him.

What's going through that devious mind of yours? Peter thought with a shiver, then looked away as Andrew joined them at the table.

"I guess Morgan's feeling a lot better. She said they'd stay for a little while longer. I'm just going to get her something light to eat."

"You're very fond of her, aren't you Andrew?"

"I like her a lot. I just wish she'd get rid of that jerk. She'd be a lot happier without him."

"Maybe, maybe not," Peter remarked quietly.

As the evening progressed and the conversations drifted between politics, the weather and what everyone was planning for Christmas, the atmosphere became more mellow and the earlier altercation almost forgotten. Peter noticed that Morgan seemed relaxed and appeared to be enjoying herself, chatting to Graham and Jennifer and another couple whose names Peter had forgotten. Jeremy still sat attentively at her side. Neither one of them had drunk anything other than water, nor had Jeremy excused himself to go to the bathroom again. He did not join in the conversation very often, but appeared to be listening to his wife's chattering with faint amusement. Jeremy's performance, the one Andrew had led them to believe was inevitable, had yet to be realized. Peter was almost disappointed, but at the same time, relieved by Jeremy's failure to run true to form.

Perhaps there are too many real gay guys here for him to do his party piece, he thought, though from what he'd heard, he doubted if Jeremy would show much compunction about offending other people. He looked carefully at Morgan and tried to determine just what is was about her that troubled him so much. Twice now, he'd had these strange feelings in her presence—but why? Like he'd said to Jeff earlier, she seemed to care for Andrew a great deal. Why then did he have these unsettling moments when she was near his friend? What was it she was hiding—if anything? Was there a dark, hidden side to her psyche that he had somehow tapped into unwittingly? He shuddered slightly as that thought crossed his mind. Will the *real* Morgan Kennedy please stand up, he thought wryly. He felt slightly relieved when, around eleven, some of the guests began to make their apologies for having to tear themselves away.

"Great party," Graham, David's employer, enthused. "Seems a shame we all have to work tomorrow."

Jennifer, his wife, patted David's arm. "Only a couple of more days to Christmas Eve—then, you can all relax for a few days."

"I can't wait," Graham said. "Thank you David, for a very nice evening. Nice seeing you again, Andrew—and meeting your out-of-town guests."

Bob and Michael held back until most of the guests were gone. "We'd love to have you over to our place before you go back," Bob said.

"That'd be great," Jeff replied. "Shall we leave it to Andrew to arrange it with you?"

"Yes, we'll be in touch," Michael said. "We'll be out of town over the holidays, so maybe we can get together before then."

Morgan and Jeremy were the last to leave, Morgan again apologizing for her earlier behavior.

"Don't worry sweetheart," Jeremy said silkily. "Dave and Andrew have already forgiven you."

Andrew frowned. "There's nothing to forgive. I'm just glad you're feeling better."

"Thank you Andrew." Morgan kissed his cheek. For a moment she looked at him speculatively, as if she had just recalled something—then the look was gone and she smiled wanly at Peter and Jeff. "Nice seeing you again," she said as Jeremy shepherded her toward the door. He did not bother to shake hands with Peter or Jeff. Instead, he looked back at them from the doorway.

"Well, you boys have a wonderful Christmas," he said with pseudo-sincerity. "Sorry we didn't have time to get to know you better."

"Eeuw!" Peter exclaimed laughingly, after Andrew had closed the door. "What a total jerk!"

"I told you," Andrew said. "There isn't a bigger one anywhere."

"Oh come on," David laughed. "Surely there must be!"

"Well, not anywhere I know of."

"Why don't you guys go sit by the fire," David suggested. "I'll go make us all a nightcap."

When they were all comfortably seated, and David had brought out some glasses of eggnog laced with a little brandy, Jeff looked at Andrew sitting in the flickering firelight, beneath his portrait. "Andrew…Bob added a little side bar to the story you told us last night, about Morgan's accident."

"Oh yes?"

"Seems there's a rumor that Jeremy and the guy who was killed in the crash might have been having an affair."

"What? No, I never heard that. Morgan never even hinted at it."

"Well, she wouldn't, would she? She apparently doesn't acknowledge her husband's supposed sexual proclivities to any of her friends."

"That's true," David agreed. "It's all supposed to be an act."

"But, according to Bob and Michael, Jeremy's been seen at the baths."

"That doesn't surprise me," Andrew said. "Jeez! Why would Morgan put up with that?"

"She's got to be either totally oblivious—or just plain stupid," Peter suggested.

"Actually, I don't think she's either one." Jeff paused to sip his drink. "I think she knows exactly what's going on, probably always has done, but whatever arrangement they've worked out for themselves, she's happy to go along with it. Well, probably not happy, but certainly willing."

"Just so that she can keep him by her side?" Andrew looked unhappily at Jeff.

"Looks that way."

"How fucking sad," David muttered grimly.

CHAPTER 6

Jeremy awoke the next morning, pleased to know his wife would have already left the apartment for her weekly visit to the beauty parlor. He stretched luxuriously under the covers, rubbing his hands over his naked chest and stomach, enjoying the feel of his own hard body and smooth skin. His hand lingered on his growing erection as he remembered the sexual encounter of yesterday afternoon.

The beautiful Christopher—what an incredible face and body that young man has, he thought, slowly stroking his penis till it responded by hardening from his touch. He remembered how Christopher had held it and kissed it, all the while looking up at him with those beautiful green eyes. Fostering that image brought him to a shuddering orgasm.

Eventually, he rose, threw on a silk robe and padded into the kitchen where he poured himself a cup of coffee. What a different evening last night had turned out to be, he thought as he perched on a stool at the breakfast bar. Who would have thought those two guys from the gym would have been there? He laughed softly at the memory. Andrew probably hated him all the more now his friends had told him of that meeting.

Andrew…

"I'm going to have to do something about Andrew," he muttered aloud. He could see a certain amount of danger in his wife's friendship with that guy. They were getting way too chummy, and Andrew was getting too damned protective around Morgan. Jeremy didn't need anyone pushing into their lives that he did not have control over.

No. Andrew would have to go.

He had to go through with his plan to break up this friendship. He had already planted the seed last night. If Morgan suspected that Andrew and he were involved sexually, she'd feel sufficiently betrayed to ace Andrew out of her life for good. Of course, he'd have to put up with the repercussions also, but he knew how to handle her after all these years. She'd scream and cry and try to hit him, but he could control all of that. Some assurances and promises and of course, some sex, would take care of it.

His position in her life would once again, be secure. God knows, I'd love to leave the bitch, he thought bitterly. But then what? His income was totally reliant on Morgan's father's wealth and he knew the old bastard would gladly cut his son-in-law off at the merest whisper of a complaint from her. No, he'd have to stay, if he wanted this way of life he enjoyed so much to continue, and of course he did.

Who wouldn't?

He had an apartment and a wardrobe to die for. He had glittering functions to attend where he could preen and flirt with society's echelon. But, best of all, he had his pick of any young and beautiful man he wanted. And he wanted them all. He wanted that Jeff—Andrew's friend. He'd love to tangle with that wonderful physique. If it hadn't been for that blond guy Peter, being there, things might just have worked out. Then again, a three-way might have been fun.

Well, Jeff might be a little out of reach, he reflected sourly. That might just be a little too much involvement for even him to handle. But he smiled at the thought of just how destroyed Peter would have been, if he could have hooked up with his boyfriend. Jeremy chuckled nastily at the thought.

First things first, though. He picked up his address book, and found Andrew's cell phone number. A plan was forming in his mind. Not very complicated—simple really, but it could be very effective. His timing just had to be good. He glanced at his watch and noted that it would be another three hours or so before Morgan came home, around noon. He dialed Andrew's number, and was pleased to hear a background of traffic noise behind Andrew's voice when he answered. That meant he was already away from the company of his friends.

"Hi Andrew, it's Jeremy."

"Jeremy?" Andrew sounded very surprised.

"Where are you?" Jeremy asked.

"Just going into the clinic. What can I do for you?"

"Do you have a lot of appointments today?"

"No. Why?"

"Actually, I'm calling for Morgan. She still feels very bad about last night, and I wondered if you could come by the apartment this morning and talk to her. She'd feel so much better if you did."

"I told her last night there was nothing to worry about. Put her on. I'll tell her again if you think that'll help."

"Uh, actually she's asleep right now. I'd rather not wake her. But if you could come over around noon say, she's bound to be up and about by then."

"Well…okay," Andrew was still somewhat reluctant. "I guess I could swing by on my way home. I'm meeting Peter and Jeff there for lunch."

"Thanks Andrew," Jeremy said, with as much sincerity as he could muster. "Morgan will be pleased to see you." Smiling, he put the phone down, and walked into the bedroom preparing to shower. His eyes fell upon the photograph of himself, Morgan and Kevin. He noticed it had been moved from its usual position. That bitch must have been peering at it, he thought viciously.

His gaze took in Kevin's handsome looks and, for a moment, he felt suddenly alone and lost. If only Kevin was still alive. He could never have believed that he would miss another human being as much as he missed him. For the first time in his life, Jeremy had given his love and his trust to another man. Kevin was more than just a sex partner. He had loved Kevin, been *in* love with him—feeling emotions he could never have anticipated he ever would feel for another person—man or woman. He wanted to live with Kevin, run away with him, leave Morgan forever and never see her again.

All that would have been possible if Kevin had lived. They had talked of it on numerous occasions. Kevin had an excellent job in advertising and made a lot of money. Jeremy had even offered to get himself a job once they had found an apartment. They would have had a life together.

Sadly, he replaced the photograph on his nightstand and walked into the bathroom. As he showered, his thoughts went back to the last night he and Kevin had made love together. If only he had known it would never happen again he would have savored each moment even more. If only they hadn't gone to that party. If only they hadn't got so drunk, he would never have allowed Kevin to leave the party without him. Then, he would never have been in the car with Morgan—the bitch that killed him!

If only, if only…

* * *

Andrew sighed as he stood in the elevator that was taking him up to Morgan's apartment. He didn't mind seeing her, even though it was just a tad inconvenient today, but he could really do without having to see *hubby*, two days in a row.

A smiling Jeremy answered his knock at the door. "Come on in, Andrew. Thank you so much for coming over."

"Where's Morgan?"

"She just stepped out for a breath of fresh air." Jeremy said, still smiling at him, showing his perfectly capped white teeth. "Here let me take your coat." He began to unbutton Andrew's coat.

"I can do that!" Andrew snapped, stepping back, and suddenly feeling very uncomfortable being alone with Jeremy. He slipped his coat off, and Jeremy took it with an amused smile.

"Don't be so nervous Andrew," he laughed, enjoying the other man's discomfiture. "I won't bite you, you know."

Andrew looked around the living room as if to find an escape route. "When did Morgan say she'd be back?"

"Any minute now." Jeremy put his arm round Andrew's shoulder and walked him over to the fireplace. "Come and get warm over here."

"I'm fine thanks," Andrew replied, barely resisting the urge to shrug Jeremy's arm off.

"Andrew, for goodness sake, relax. You're so tense. Here, let me give you a shoulder rub."

Andrew moved away from the fireplace. "No thanks."

Jeremy gave him a sad smile. "Why don't you like me, Andrew?"

"I never said I don't like you."

"You don't have to—it's quite evident from your body language. You can't stand me near you."

Andrew shrugged uncomfortably. He had not anticipated this confrontation, and was somewhat at a loss as to how to deal with it.

Where the hell was Morgan?

Jeremy walked over to him and put his hand on Andrew's arm. "Tell me what I can do to make things better between us."

"I don't dislike you Jeremy." Andrew made an impatient gesture. "I just think you should drop this phony routine you have about pretending to be gay, when it's obvious to us all that you are."

Jeremy feigned surprise, then looked at Andrew with an attempt at contrition. "You don't know how hard it is for me to not come out to my friends. Morgan would have an absolute fit if I did. Probably throw me out."

"At least you'd be living the truth, Jeremy. And I'm sure Morgan loves you enough not to let it ruin your marriage."

"It's already in trouble, but I'm sure Morgan has told you that."

"She has mentioned she's a little unhappy, yes, but…" Andrew paused, looking uncomfortably around him. "Look, I don't really want to get in the middle of your personal problems…"

"Of course you don't." Jeremy smiled sadly again. "Why would you care that I am desperately unhappy? Your sympathies lie with Morgan. You're *her* friend. Why would you care that she took from me…someone that I cared for more than anyone else in the world?"

"Morgan is your wife, Jeremy. *That's* who should be caring for. If you're referring to the accident that killed your friend, you can't still be blaming her for that…"

"You just don't get it do you?" Jeremy cut in. "Morgan found out about Kevin and me—and she killed him!"

"That's crazy. How could she possibly have staged something like that? The car went off the road and hit a tree. She could have been killed too."

"But she wasn't, was she?" His face twisted in a grimace of pain and anger. "She got away with just a fractured arm, but Kevin was burned alive."

"Look, Jeremy." Andrew drew a deep breath. "I know this must have been a terrible blow for you, but you can't go on holding it against Morgan and hating her forever. If you can't come to terms with it, and you want out, then *do* that. Make a life for yourself. Live the way you want to, but don't drag Morgan down anymore than you already have."

Jeremy looked downcast as he reached out and touched Andrew's arm, a wistful look on his handsome face. "You really are a good friend to her, Andrew. I wish, somehow, you could be there for me also."

Andrew stared at him with surprise as he saw the man was close to tears. Warm hearted soul that he was, Andrew felt a pang of sympathy for him, and patted his arm to console him. Jeremy leaned forward and laid his head on Andrew's shoulder. Andrew's first instinct to step back from this intimate move was stilled as he heard Jeremy sob quietly. He held him lightly in his arms, then looked toward the door as he heard a key rasp in the lock.

Thank God…Morgan's home, he thought, releasing Jeremy.

But the other man's arms were wrapped around him in a powerful grip from which he could not break free. Taken by surprise, he felt himself being tipped over onto the couch, Jeremy on top of him, his mouth firmly pressed against Andrew's own lips. He lay crushed beneath Jeremy's strong body, who writhed above him, his crotch grinding against Andrew's in mock passion.

"Andrew! Oh my God…Nooo!"

He heard Morgan's anguished cry even as he struggled futilely to throw Jeremy off. Then he heard the door slam.

Jeremy looked deep into Andrew's eyes, a taunting smile playing about his lips. "This actually feels pretty nice, eh?"

"Get *off* me, you asshole!" Andrew yelled, pushing at Jeremy's chest.

Laughing, Jeremy released him and stood up. Andrew jumped to his feet and pushed him roughly away. "You set me up, you bastard!" Andrew raged with impotent fury, wiping his mouth with the back of his hand. "That entire ploy for sympathy so you could use me against her. God, you scuzzball—how can you live with yourself?"

"How can you say that, Andrew?" Jeremy continued to laugh. "I just couldn't control my lust for you."

"Asshole," Andrew muttered, picking up his coat and heading for the door. "You're going to be a sorry fool when Morgan leaves you, and you have nothing and no one to turn to."

Jeremy was still laughing when Andrew slammed the door and ran to the elevator. With any luck Morgan would not have got far. He had to find her and explain to her just what had really happened. As he ran out onto the street, he caught sight of her walking slowly away from the apartment building.

"Morgan, wait!"

She stood waiting for him as he ran quickly to her side. She looked at him from red, tear filled eyes.

"Morgan, let me tell you what happened."

"I saw what happened, Andrew. I was there, remember? I *saw* what happened. I thought you were my friend."

"I *am* your friend Morgan. Your asshole husband set that whole thing up for you to walk in on, and I, like a damned fool, didn't see it coming. I'm sorry, but you must believe me, I had nothing to do with it."

Morgan looked at him long and hard. "It seems I can't trust anyone anymore. Certainly not my husband, and now, not the man I once considered a dear friend. It's Kevin all over again. *You*, ingratiating yourself into my life, pretending to be my friend and all the time—you're fucking my husband!"

"You can't really believe that, surely." Andrew took her arm gently. "Let's go somewhere, out of the cold, so we can talk about this."

"No!" Morgan pulled her arm away from him. "Jeremy told me you wanted him—and I refused to believe him. I trusted you, Andrew. I trusted *you*.

"Morgan, please listen to me…"

"Go home, Andrew. Go home…and never call me again." She turned quickly away from him toward her apartment building, while Andrew stood, miserably hunched against the cold wind, watching her walk out of his life.

Back in Andrew's apartment, Peter and Jeff sat in stunned silence as he recounted the horrendous events of the morning.

"I tried to reason with her, but she wouldn't listen to me. Told me to never call her again." Andrew looked sadly at his friends. "I just can't believe all of this could happen. I mean, I knew Jeremy was jealous of our friendship, but why would he go to these lengths to break us up?"

"Their marriage must have been in worse straits that you thought," Jeff said quietly. "Maybe he thought you were getting too close to his wife and becoming a threat to him."

"How could I threaten him? He's married to her. I'm a gay man in a solid relationship. I don't want to take his place."

"But you were privy to her personal problems. She confided in you. Told you things of a private nature. She may even have been influenced by your opinions and told him so."

"You think Jeremy might have been worried that Andrew could persuade her to leave him?" Peter asked.

"Could be. Let's face it. What guy is going to be pleased about his wife confiding in another man, gay or not."

"But Jeremy's gay too—or bisexual, or *whatever*." Andrew said, impatiently. "He's the one who's been cheating. He's the one who's the cause of the problems in their marriage. She loves him, God knows why, but she does, and she's obviously willing to put up with his shenanigans because of it. She even knew about Kevin, the guy that was killed in the car crash."

"She told you that?"

"Yes, today. She said what happened, was Kevin all over again."

Jeff shook his head in amazement. "So, she knew Kevin and Jeremy were having an affair, and yet she tells all her friends that Jeremy just pretends to be gay."

"Yeah, how sick is that?" Peter muttered.

"The whole thing is really unhealthy," Jeff said, grimly.

"I think you're well out of that friendship, Andrew." Peter looked at his friend and smiled encouragingly. "Ain't you glad we're here to see you through this mess?"

"You've no idea *how* glad I am." Andrew smiled faintly. "Well…" he stood up and shrugged his shoulders resignedly. "Let's go for lunch. There's not much more I can do today. I'll call her tomorrow—and see if she's maybe realized I was telling the truth."

Morgan stood in the center of the living room and glared at her husband. "You have humiliated me for the last time, Jeremy. I will *never* forgive you for involving Andrew in your attempts to destroy me."

"Oh, for God's sake, Morgan. Stop being so damned melodramatic. Your little friend couldn't wait to get in my pants."

"Don't be disgusting. I can't believe you'd sink this low—to take away someone I could feel comfortable with and talk to, when I needed him. You just couldn't see me having someone in my life other than yourself. Your jealousy is sickening."

"Jealousy?" Jeremy laughed. "I wasn't jealous of Andrew. He wanted me—and I gave him what he wanted. That's all."

"And to hell with me, your *wife*. Right? What was it? You thought that I might actually listen to Andrew's opinion of you? Is that what scared you?"

"Scared? Jealous?" Jeremy snickered. "Where do you get these words from, darling? Neither of them applies to me, I can assure you. What's the big deal? You've found out about Andrew's and my little tryst. So, you'll get over it. You always do."

"Not this time!" Morgan yelled at him, walking quickly to the bedroom. "I'm going home for the next few days, over Christmas, and when I come back—you had better be gone!"

"No way, love, no way. I'm not going anywhere." Jeremy followed her into the bedroom, and watched with amusement as she began throwing things into a suitcase.

"I mean it, Jeremy. I shall be suing for divorce as soon as the holidays are over!"

"I know I've heard that somewhere before." Jeremy's tone was mocking.

"This time it's going to happen." She stopped packing and turned to look at him, the smug expression on his face adding to her resolve. "I could forgive you for a lot of things and have done so, many times over the years—but this time you've gone too far. You've destroyed something that was particularly precious to me. Something that I haven't known much of in my life. Friendship, given unconditionally!"

She paused, to give her words weight. "You couldn't bear to see it happen, and I'm sure, poor Andrew was no match for your silver tongue. What did you say to him to make him fall? No, please don't tell me, I don't want to know. Well, this is going to make two people I know very happy. My *parents*. It will give Daddy a great deal of pleasure to throw you out of here, and never to have you spend one more cent of his money!"

Something in her tone was sending alarm bells ringing in Jeremy's mind. The fact that she was clearing out was a good thing. His mind was already racing ahead to this evening when he could have Christopher over. He could call him and tell him he could see him tonight after all, but he would have to deal with Morgan first. He had thought she would come screaming at him like a banshee, her mouth sputtering recriminations and threats. That he could have controlled, physically and emotionally, as he had done in the past. He would hold her tightly against himself to subdue her anger, and when it was spent he would kiss away the tears and cover her protests with his mouth. Then he would carry her to bed and they would have a violent bout of sex.

"Morgan, darling…" he began.

"Don't even *try* to insinuate yourself back into my good graces," she almost snarled at him. "I can't stand the sight of you anymore. You are a disgusting pervert that I should have rid myself of years ago."

"Now, wait a minute…" Jeremy gasped, reaching for her.

"Stay away from me, Jeremy." She backed away from him. "I mean it."

"Stay away from you? Believe me there's nothing I'd rather do." He stood looking at her, his face livid with rage. "For years I've had to put up with your cloying and clinging to me as if I was some kind of possession or prize you could parade in front of your so-called friends. Well, *they* know the truth!" He sneered nastily at her. "They know that I'm here just for the money, certainly not for your looks or your vivacious personality. You're a giant bore, you know that? The only time I feel like I have any kind of life is when I'm not with you! The only time in my life that I was truly happy was when I was with Kevin, and you made damned sure that came to an end—by *killing* him!"

"I did not kill him!" Morgan screamed at him. "But I'm glad he's dead. Glad that he was taken from you. You don't deserve any happiness, Jeremy. You deserve nothing—which is what you'll have when I walk out. *Nothing*!"

Despite his fury, Jeremy paled at her words. He had gone too far this time; he could see it now. She was really going to leave him. He couldn't allow that.

"Listen to me!" he hissed, grabbing her arm.

With all her might, Morgan struck him across the face. Taken off guard, he reeled back with a startled cry, his foot catching on the rug behind him. He went down heavily, his head banging on the parquet floor with a loud thump. For a moment Morgan stood looking down in horror at his prone figure, then she knelt by his side feeling for a pulse. It beat strongly.

"Just unconscious," she muttered. "I better get out of here before he comes to."

Straightening, she lifted her suitcase off the bed, and started to leave the room. Then, she paused and looked back at Jeremy's inert form.

Putting down her case, she walked slowly back to where he lay.

CHAPTER 7

It was Christmas Eve.

Jeff and Peter, the last of their shopping done, strolled into Rockefeller Center Plaza to watch the ice skaters and listen to the carolers. A gentle snow was falling and, despite the cold, the scene was picture perfect. Their meeting earlier in the day with the people who wanted to promote Peter's exhibition had gone extremely well, and a date had been set in the Spring for a gala showing. Now, as they stood at the side of the skating rink, Peter sighed and leaned against Jeff's side.

"I'm so glad we decided to do this—in more ways that one."

"Me too," Jeff agreed. "Having you here is making Andrew feel a lot better about the Morgan situation."

"He's still feeling hurt, though."

"He'll get over it in time." Jeff put his arm round Peter's shoulders. "I'm looking forward to tonight's quiet dinner with just the four of us."

Peter leaned in close to Jeff's side. "I hope she calls him tomorrow. I know it'll make him feel better. I was thinking…"

"No, Peter. Don't go calling Morgan and trying to patch things up between them. It isn't our business."

"What made you think I'd contemplate such a thing?"

"I know you," Jeff grinned. "You have a secret need to be Pollyanna sometimes."

"*Pollyanna*? Couldn't you have thought of something just a tad more butch to insult me with?"

"Not at this moment. Pollyanna suits you just fine!"

"Just wait till I get you home," Peter chuckled. "Seriously though, you don't think it might help?"

"I think we should stay out of it. If Morgan ever comes to her senses and realizes there's no way Andrew would ever have had an affair with her husband, she'll either call him to apologize, or stay silent from embarrassment. Either way, it has to be her decision."

"I guess you're right, O Wise One. I just wish that Andrew and David could come back to Laguna. I know Andrew would be tons happier."

"Well, again, that's up to them, and that's a really difficult situation. David's doing so well with this company. They obviously think the world of him."

"Yeah. Too bad."

"*Too bad*?"

"You know what I mean."

"No, you've lost me." Jeff looked at Peter expectantly, eyebrows raised.

"*Well*, if he wasn't so damned good at his job, they'd fire him and then he and Andrew could come back to Laguna."

"Your logic is a little off," Jeff said, shaking his head and laughing. "'Oh Dave. We hope you get fired so you can come home with us. Forget the humiliation or anything like that. We just want you back in Laguna'."

Peter laughed too, and thumped Jeff on the arm. "You know what I mean."

"That again? I'm not sure *you* know what you mean!"

"I wonder what Jeremy and Morgan are doing right now," Peter mused, in a quick change of subject. "Wouldn't you love to be a fly on the wall over there at this moment?"

"Not on your life. My stomach isn't that strong."

"D'you think they're talking to each other yet?"

"Who the hell knows? She's obviously put up with this sort of mess for years. He must have some winning ways to keep her from leaving him." Jeff stamped his feet suddenly against the cold. "Okay, that's enough of all that. Let's go back to the apartment and give Andrew a hand. He's probably wondering where we are…and a little eggnog and brandy sounds good, right about now."

"Mmm..mm." Peter licked his lips. "What if I poured it all over your body and licked it off, very slowly."

Jeff hugged him close. "Gee. D'you think Andrew would object if we did it in front of the fireplace?"

"I think we could sell tickets!" Laughing at this mental picture, they gathered their packages and set off for Andrew's apartment.

Morgan stood in her bedroom at her parent's home on the outskirts of Hartford. She watched the snow drift steadily by the window, and sighed resignedly. She knew that what she had done would change her life forever. When she returned to New York, she would have to face the consequences of her actions. There was no escaping it now.

"Morgan?" Her mother stood in the doorway, carrying a tray. "I made us some tea. Would you like it up here?"

"Thanks, Mother. That'd be nice." She noticed there were two cups on the tray, and resigned herself to the fact her mother wanted a heart to heart. Her mother set the tray down and busied herself pouring the tea. Morgan watched her spare efficient movements and found herself suddenly envying the quiet, uneventful life, her mother enjoyed. Her parents had been married for almost fifty years, and as far as Morgan knew, were still happy together. She had very rarely heard them row or disagree, and while her father was a man of little patience and strong convictions, he had a great deal of respect for his wife. Her mother smiled at her and sat down opposite her by the window.

"Wretched weather," she said quietly. "They say it'll keep this up for several days"

"Well, I'm not in any hurry to leave." Morgan sipped her tea.

"Have you spoken to Jeremy since…?"

Morgan's hand shook slightly as she replied. "No. There isn't much point."

"Your father's delighted of course. He never could stand the man. But…*divorce*, Morgan? Isn't there any hope you two might reconcile?"

Morgan looked at her mother with surprise. "I thought you weren't that crazy about him, either."

"I'm not. Nor could I ever be about a man who cannot be faithful to his wife." She paused reflectively, for a moment. "It's just that, you're not getting any younger, dear. Do you really want to be alone at your age?"

Morgan tried to control the anger she felt rising inside her. "Sometimes, being alone is preferable to the alternative. Besides, there's no going back now. It's over, for good."

Her mother smiled sadly at her. "A pity you never had children. They would have been a comfort for you now."

Morgan grimaced. "Jeremy would have made the worst possible father, and I am much too selfish to have children. No, that wouldn't have helped one bit."

"Still, it's a pity," her mother said, almost to herself, then fell silent.

"Mother, you don't mind if I stay here for while do you?"

"Of course not, dear. Why would I?"

"Well, you're so used to having just you and Daddy here. I don't want to get in the way."

"Don't be foolish, Morgan. You're our daughter. Your father loves having you here."

"And you?" Morgan looked keenly at her mother. "Do you love having me here?"

Her mother looked back at her with a faintly puzzled air. "Why do ask such things, dear?"

"I don't know. I had a feeling you were a bit put out when I called and said I was coming home after all."

"Nonsense!" Her mother put her cup down.

"Is that why you'd like to see me reconcile with Jeremy? So I wouldn't be a burden to you here?"

"*Morgan…*" Her mother looked at her aghast.

"Oh, Mother, I know you resent me being here. Please don't take me for a fool. You've always resented the fact that Dad doted on me since the day I was born. Always there to pick me up when I made a mess of things. Now it's 'Daddy's little girl' running home again."

Her mother began to gather up the tea things. "Obviously you are still upset about the break up. I had hoped a little talk might help, but I see I was wrong. I'm sorry if you think I am resentful of you. I'm sure you have your reasons—even if they are imaginary. Of course you may stay as long as you like." She stood and picked up the tea tray. "Well, its Christmas Day tomorrow. The Bryans will be here to join us for dinner. It'll be a quiet day." Without another word, she left the room, closing the door quietly behind her.

Morgan sat staring at the door for a long moment. Why had she said those things just now? Now, when she needed all the allies she could get, she had alienated her own mother.

"What a fool you are," she said aloud. "What a time to choose to have it out with her." Impatiently, she rose and followed her mother down the stairs to the kitchen. She'd have to make amends somehow. No point in making things more uncomfortable than they already were.

"Hi guys!" Andrew smiled at Peter and Jeff as they entered the apartment.

"Feels good in here," Peter said, heading for the fireplace. "Boy, it really is Artic-like out there."

Jeff put their packages under the tree, then joined Peter in front of the fire, rubbing his hands to warm them.

"I'm fixing the eggnog. Like some?" Andrew asked.

"You bet. We'll just get out of these coats, and give you a hand."

"David should be home shortly. He's getting off early for the Holidays."

"Excellent," Jeff said, taking his and Peter's coats to the hall closet. "We can really kick back and enjoy the evening—just the four of us."

Peter gave Andrew a hug. "How're you doing?" he asked with concern, as he followed him into the kitchen.

"I'm OK. Still a bit upset about what happened, you know, with Morgan—but I guess she'll come around one of these days."

"Give her some time over the Holidays. She'll have time to sort things out. You know, I've been doing some thinking…"

"Oh, oh." Andrew grinned at him "This could be dangerous to your health."

"Smarty…seriously, I was thinking you should let David know how you feel about being here, in New York."

"Peter, I can't do that. It'd just put a strain on everything. He's so tied up in his work here. I'm sure he would resent it if I told him I wanted to go home."

Jeff stuck his head round the kitchen door and smiled at them. "I'm going to have a quick shower before I partake of the eggnog."

Peter grinned at him. "Don't be long."

"God, he's cute," Andrew sighed, when Jeff had gone. "If it wasn't that I already have David, you and I would have to arm-wrestle over his favor."

"Ha!" Peter smirked. "You'd have no chance. He's mine completely."

"You're probably right," Andrew sighed again with mock despair.

"Anyway…" Peter leaned forward in his chair. "I'm glad he's out of the way—for a little while. We can talk without Mr. Sensible getting his two cents in."

"Did you mention this to him?"

"He knows how I feel about it. Says it's up to you two to work it out, which of course, it is. I was just thinking it might not hurt to push the boat along a bit, you know, *tell* him you're unhappy here."

"I don't know..."

"What do you have to lose? You let him know how you feel, and he either ignores it or does something about it."

"But what if he says, 'Too bad. This is how it has to be. Take it or leave it.'"

"He's not going to say that!"

"You don't know what he'll say, Peter. He loves his work."

"He loves you more."

"I'd like to think that, of course, but I don't know if I want to push the issue. I don't want to back him into a corner over this."

The phone ringing at that moment interrupted them. Andrew picked it up. "This is Andrew." His face brightened. "Well, Hi Eve! How nice to hear from you. Merry Christmas to you too, and to Fred. Peter tells us you're in San Diego. Yes, I called my mother about an hour ago...she said to tell you Merry Christmas if I spoke to you..." They chatted for a few minutes, then he handed the phone over to Peter.

"Hi Mom! Yeah, we're having a great time..."

Andrew wandered out into the living room while Peter spoke to his mother. He stood looking out at the falling snow and thought about what Peter had just said. He had to admit to himself that he was kind of relieved Eve had interrupted their conversation. Peter could be darned pushy at times, and he wasn't sure if he wanted to broach this subject with David quite yet. The situation with Morgan had left him more out of love with New York than ever. Now, it seemed he had lost his one confidant.

Damn that Jeremy, he thought. What a total jerk the man is. As if I were really a threat to his marriage. It would serve him right if Morgan left him because of this...and she should. How much more can she possibly put up with?

Despite her harsh words to him, Andrew could not blame Morgan for her outburst. Of course, it had looked so damning—just as Jeremy had obviously planned it to be.

"Hey, handsome. Penny for your thoughts?"

Andrew turned to find David standing behind him.

"Wow, I didn't hear you come in." Andrew hugged him tightly.

"You were lost in thought, sweetheart," David murmured against his ear. "Are you still blue about Morgan?"

"Yes, but I'm going to put it aside for tonight." He kissed David warmly. "Peter's on the phone with Eve. Hurry and say hello to her."

"Yes, sir!" David laughed. "Where's Jeff?"

"Taking a shower."

"Without Peter?"

"I heard that," Peter chuckled. "Some reputation we have—come and say hello to Eve. Then I have to take the phone to Jeff. He'd be pissed if he misses her. They're all going out for dinner in a minute."

Andrew set their after dinner drinks on the table in front of the fire. The firelight and the reflection of the Christmas tree cast a warm glow over the entire room, and Andrew sighed with satisfaction as he gazed about him. Dinner had been a great success, and now the four friends toasted each other, each one, for the moment, silently appreciating the mellowness of the evening.

"This is definitely my most favorite time of the year," David said, hugging Andrew to his side.

"I couldn't agree more," Peter murmured from the depths of Jeff's arms. "Thank you both so much for inviting us."

"Here here," Jeff agreed sleepily. "Boy, I won't need rocking tonight."

"None of us will," David said. "One last toast. Here's to our two best friends. May you remain so forever."

"Wait…" Peter kept his glass up. "I have a toast too—to David and Andrew, without whom I would never have met the most wonderful man in the world."

"Who the heck is that?" Jeff grinned at him. "Should I be jealous?"

"Only of yourself. What kind of complex would that be?"

"Sort of reverse Narcissus?" Andrew suggested.

"No, that would mean he hated himself," David said.

"How about Oedipal, then?"

"Only is he looks on Peter as his mother."

"Cut it out, you two." Peter scowled at them. "I was being romantic, and you're ruining the moment."

"As long as we haven't ruined your chances!" Andrew laughed.

Jeff grinned at him. "We'll never tell."

"So tomorrow," David announced, "We're just going to kick back, open our gifts, and watch the parade on TV."

Andrew nodded. "Sounds great. We've got loads to eat and drink, so we can just sit around and get fat."

"All right!" Jeff smiled, patting his stomach. "I think I'm already on the right track."

"Oh please," Peter protested. "You are the most in shape man in the world."

"You're only saying that to get on my good side."

"Right...and if these good friends will excuse us, I intend to do that in more ways than one."

"Well, please wait till your bedroom door's closed," Andrew laughed.

The friends hugged goodnight and headed for their respective rooms. Peter sat down on the edge of the bed and rummaged for a moment in the nightstand drawer.

"It's not quite midnight yet—but I wanted to give you this when we were alone."

He handed a small package to Jeff who looked at him reprovingly. "You said no surprise gifts. Only what we'd agreed on."

"I know, I know—but when I saw this, it had your name all over it."

Jeff took the package and opened it quickly. Peter watched him, equally enjoying his anticipation. Jeff gasped as he opened the velvet box under the gift-wrap and revealed a beautiful diamond cut gold bracelet, inscribed with his name.

"Ohmigod, Peter. It's incredible."

"Here, let me put it on you," Peter whispered, and Jeff held out his wrist so that Peter could fasten the bracelet around it. As they admired it, Jeff took Peter in his arms and gave him a lingering kiss.

"Thank you," he murmured against Peter's mouth, then stood up suddenly. "And just because I know you, you villain—I have something for you. I knew you'd come up with something like this, so..." He delved into his toilet bag and pulled out two tiny boxes.

"Look, one for you, and one for me..."

"What in the world...?" Peter asked excitedly.

"Open them at the same time, okay?"

Peter's eyes widened as he saw nestled inside each of the tiny boxes, a gold ring.

"I had them made to match. See? The little scroll design is our initials intertwined."

"Oh, Jeff." Peter could feel tears well in his eyes as Jeff slipped the ring on his finger.

"Now you're mine forever."

"There was never any doubt of that," Peter murmured, as Jeff pushed him gently down on the bed.

CHAPTER 8

Andrew awoke early on Christmas morning. He had not slept well despite the long and passionate love making he and David had enjoyed. He lay for a while listening to David's steady breathing, hoping that he could doze off too, but it was not to be. With a sigh, he swung his legs out of bed and quietly padded from the room. The apartment was still and silent as he gazed out at the snow covered city. Shivering slightly, he pulled his robe around him and went into the kitchen to make some coffee.

As he waited for the coffee to brew, his thoughts turned again to Morgan and the last words she had said to him. Surely their friendship could not end like this? He had to talk to her and make her understand that Jeremy was entirely to blame for the situation in which they all now found themselves.

Under the Christmas tree was a gift he had purchased for Morgan. A small crystal elephant she had told him she thought was cute one day when they had gone window-shopping, after one of their lunch times together. Maybe, if he took it over to her, she would listen to his explanation of what had happened that day when she thought he and Jeremy were making out.

Should he call her first? No, that would give her the opportunity to either hang up on him, or simply tell him he could not come over. If he just showed up on her doorstep, what could she do? Slam the door in his face? What if Jeremy answered the door? Well…that could be a problem. He'd just have to handle that as best he could.

He glanced at his watch. Eight o'clock. Morgan was always an early riser—Jeremy was not. Chances are he'd find her alone, and surely on Christmas morning she would not turn him away. Anyway, it was a chance he was willing to take.

He showered and dressed quickly, without disturbing anyone, then picking up Morgan's gift, he left the apartment. The short two-block walk to Morgan's building was especially difficult due to the wintry weather. Andrew was frozen through by the time he reached the entrance. Henry, the guard, recognizing him, buzzed him in.

"Merry Christmas, Mr. Connor. I don't think Mr. and Mrs. Kennedy are home. Haven't seen them in a couple of days."

"Oh really?" Andrew's disappointment was clearly etched on his face.

"Well, go on up anyway. They may just be lying low over the Holidays."

"I just wanted to drop off this gift for Mrs. Kennedy. I'll leave it with you if she's not home."

"Fine. You know the way."

"Thanks, Henry. Merry Christmas."

Andrew entered the elevator and pressed the button for the fourteenth floor. He should have called first, he thought. She might have gone to her parents to get away from Jeremy. Well, if Jeremy was there alone he could leave right away. That, or punch him on the nose for the trouble he'd caused! He rang the doorbell, then involuntarily stepped back from the door, unsure of the reception he would be given.

He waited a few moments, then knocked and rang the bell again. Still no answer. Sighing, he was just about to turn away, when he instinctively tried the doorknob. To his surprise, it turned in his hand, and he gently pushed the door open.

"Morgan? It's Andrew. Are you home?" Tentatively, he took a step inside the hallway. "Morgan?" he called again. The apartment was stuffy and silent, and a strange sour odor he could not identify, hung in the air.

Worried now, he walked into the living room, then into the kitchen. An open bottle of Scotch stood on the counter, but otherwise everything looked in order. He walked into the hall and saw the bedroom door was open slightly and the light on.

"Morgan?"

The hair on the back of his neck prickled as he walked slowly toward the bedroom door. He suddenly had the worst feeling that something was very wrong. Slowly, he reached out and pushed the bedroom door open a little more. He gasped as it swung open and revealed the naked body of a man lying on the floor.

"Jesus!" Andrew blurted involuntarily.

Jeremy lay on his back, his eyes wide open. His head had been bludgeoned to a pulp, apparently by a bronze horse's head, which lay nearby. The white rug beneath him was stained almost black with his blood. Andrew, although no expert in the matters of life and death, knew there was no need to check his pulse. Jeremy was very dead, and had been for some time. The handsome Jeremy, now reduced to an inert and bloody form. Death had transformed him and taken away his beauty.

Andrew gazed with horror at the sight for a moment, then unnerved by the fact that Jeremy's dead eyes seemed to be looking right at him. He quickly backed out of the bedroom and hurried from the apartment. Henry, the security guard looked up from his newspaper as Andrew ran from the elevator.

"Call the police, Henry. Mr. Kennedy has been murdered!"

While he waited for the police to arrive, Andrew called David and told him what had happened.

"Andrew, why are you there?" David gasped.

"I came over to give Morgan the gift I bought her. I thought, maybe we could talk and work things out."

"Oh, Andrew. Why do always have to be the nice guy? I'll be right over. I'll let Jeff know what's going on. He'll know what to do."

"Okay David, and—I'm sorry. I know I should have talked this over with you first."

"Don't worry about that now. Just sit tight. We'll be right there."

A few minutes after Andrew put the phone down, the hall suddenly filled with police and paramedics. One of them, Andrew guessed to be a detective, marched up to Henry

"Where's the victim?"

"Apartment 1401, fourteenth floor," Henry replied shakily.

"Who found the body?"

"Uh…Mr. Connor here." Henry indicated Andrew weakly.

"I'm Detective Bransky. This here's Detective Fallon." He indicated the tall, dark haired, younger man standing by him who now nodded and looked impassively at Andrew.

"Wait here till we take a look upstairs," Bransky continued. "We'll take both your statements then."

Andrew stood nervously by Henry's desk till the tall detective came back after inspecting the crime scene.

"Nick Fallon." He held out his hand and Andrew shook it warily.

"Andrew Connor."

"You want to sit over here, Mr. Connor?" The detective gestured toward a sofa in the hallway.

"Yes, I guess so."

"You don't look so good. You OK?"

"Just a bit shaken up. Thanks for asking."

"No problem. Come on…sit down. You a friend of the victim, Mr. Connor?"

"A friend of Mor…Mrs. Kennedy, really."

Fallon pulled a notebook and pen from his inside pocket. "Oh, I see. Can I have your address and phone number, Mr. Connor?"

Andrew gave him the information. The detective looked at him appraisingly for a moment. "How did you and Mrs. Kennedy meet?"

"She had an accident. I was her physical therapist. We became friends."

"Uh huh. The husband know about this, Mr. Connor?"

"Of course." Andrew looked up at the detective. "This is not what you're thinking. I'm gay—there was nothing between Morgan and me but friendship…"

"Right, take it easy." Fallon leaned back into the sofa cushions, seemingly unperturbed by Andrew's outburst. "So, why did you come over here today?"

"To give Morgan a Christmas gift."

"But she wasn't home?"

"Right."

"How come you didn't know she wouldn't be home, if you're such good friends?"

"Well, we had a bit of a falling out a few days ago, and I thought I'd come over and try to patch things up."

"What did you fall out about?"

"I'd rather not say, if that's OK. A misunderstanding really. It was rather personal."

Fallon paused in his note taking. "Sure, we'll get to that later. So tell me what happened when you came to the apartment."

"I rang the bell. There was no answer. I was just about to leave, when I thought I'd just try the doorknob."

"You don't have a key?"

"No, of course not," Andrew said, sharply.

"Well, I just wondered. You and Mrs. Kennedy being such good friends."

"Look, I don't like what you're implying here." Andrew flushed with anger. "I've told you, Morgan and I are *friends*. That's all."

"Sorry, Mr. Connor." Fallon's hazel eyes surveyed Andrew keenly. "What about you and Mr. Kennedy?"

Andrew gasped in surprise at the question. "We were…polite to each other."

"Okay. So you turned the doorknob, the door obviously opened. Then what happened?"

"Well, I went into the apartment. I called Morgan's name several times. I got the strangest feeling something was very wrong—then I discovered Jeremy's body in their bedroom."

"Had you been in their bedroom before?"

"No, never. Well, only when Morgan gave David and I a tour of the apartment the first time we were invited over for dinner."

"David?"

"My partner…" Andrew looked over at the lobby entrance as David, Peter and Jeff hurried in. He jumped to his feet to greet them.

"Andrew, are you all right?" David hugged him briefly.

"I'm fine, really. This is Detective Fallon. He's asking me what happened."

Fallon stood up and held out his hand. "You must be David."

"Right, David Angelo. And these are our friends, Peter Brandon and Jeff Stevens. Jeff is a private investigator from California."

"Is that right?" Fallon smirked just slightly as he shook hands with Jeff. "Come to crack the case, eh?"

"Hardly." Jeff looked at the detective appraisingly. "I'll leave that to you."

"Good of you. Well, if you'll just let me finish taking Mr. Connor's statement, we'll be done here."

"Oh sure," David said. "Sorry to interrupt. We were just concerned for Andrew."

The three friends walked over to Henry's desk.

"He's a dry one." Peter looked back at Fallon. "I don't trust him an inch."

"He's just doing his job Peter," Jeff murmured.

"So, Mr. Connor," Fallon continued, flicking his gaze from Jeff back to Andrew. "You saw Mr. Kennedy's body. Then what did you do?"

"I came back down here immediately and told Henry to call the police."

"You didn't touch the body or the murder weapon?"

"God no…" Andrew blurted. "I couldn't go anywhere near him…it was just too awful…"

"Why didn't you call from the apartment?"

"I...I don't know..." Andrew faltered." I couldn't wait to get out of there, I guess."

"Panicked, did you?"

"Sort of. I've never seen anyone in that kind of state before."

"Have you called Mrs. Kennedy?"

"No, actually, I haven't. I really don't know where she is. I'm guessing she went to her parents in Connecticut. I don't know what I could say to her right now."

"Well, we'll take care of all that," Fallon said, standing up as Detective Bransky came waddling over. "Thank you, Mr. Connor. That'll be all for now. We may need you for further questioning. We'll be in touch."

"Further questioning? I've told you everything that happened."

"Yeah..." Bransky looked at Andrew without a trace of a smile. "But like he says, we might need you for further questioning. Don't go on no trips." He looked up at his partner. "Let's talk to the doorman, Nick."

Fallon looked impatiently at his partner, then turned to Andrew. "Right. We'll be in touch, Mr. Connor." With that he walked away toward where Henry stood, still looking decidedly shaken. Bransky trailed after him. Andrew stood watching them, a troubled expression on his face.

"What's up?" Peter put his hand on Andrew's shoulder.

"I think they suspect me of something."

"That's crazy," Peter said, glaring after the two detectives. "Jeff will put them straight. They can't possibly suspect you of Jeremy's murder."

"Calm down, both of you," Jeff interrupted. "They're just doing their job. The police consider everyone a suspect in the beginning. Anyone who had more than a passing acquaintance with the victim, anyway." He looked at his friends and smiled encouragingly. "Let's get out of here. Andrew needs some cheering up, I should think. He's had a rough morning."

"You can say that again," Andrew said, miserably. "God, how is Morgan going to take this, I wonder?"

Morgan sat in the window seat of her room gazing out at the snow, which had fallen steadily for the last couple of days.

"Merry Christmas Morgan," she muttered with a sigh. This was going to be a miserable day. Why had her life changed so radically in such a short space of time? Jeremy and Andrew both out of her life for good. If only Jeremy hadn't been so vicious during that last row, she would probably have forgiven him once more and they would be together right now. She would have gotten over his infidelity yet again, and they would have gone on as before. Not an ideal arrangement perhaps, but better than being alone. Which she was now—and God alone knew when things would get better.

She looked up as she heard her father call her name and knock on the door.

"Morgan?

"Come in, Dad."

Her father entered the room, looking worried and somber. "Morgan, there's a Detective Bransky on the phone. Says they have to talk to you right away. He wouldn't tell me what it was about. Damned rude…"

Morgan rose quickly, cutting her father short as she rushed from the room and ran downstairs to the hall phone.

"This is Morgan Kennedy."

"Mrs. Kennedy, my name is Detective Bransky. I'm here at your apartment in Manhattan with my partner Detective Fallon. We're investigating a homicide. I'm afraid I have to inform you that your husband, Mr. Kennedy, has been murdered."

"Oh, my God," Morgan whispered. "Oh my God, no!"

Her mother rushed to her side.

"What is it, Morgan?"

"It's Jeremy; he's dead—*murdered*!"

She dropped the phone and her mother picked it up.

"This is Morgan's mother. Is this the police?"

"Yes ma'am." Bransky's voice was tinged with impatience. "I'm afraid we'll have to ask your daughter to come identify the body and give us any information she can."

"Well, she's in shock at the moment…and the *weather*…"

"It's all right Mother," Morgan said, appearing to pull herself together and taking the phone from her. "Let me speak to him."

"Can you come right away, Mrs. Kennedy?" Bransky asked her.

"Yes, of course. I'll leave right now. I should be at my apartment in about two hours."

She put the phone down.

"Morgan!" her father blustered. "You can't possibly leave in this weather—and the state you're in."

"I'm fine Dad, really. I've driven in worse weather."

"We'll come with you."

"No, please don't." She stood up and faced her parents. "I have to do this alone. When it's over, I'll come back…I promise."

CHAPTER 9

Bob Bransky looked sourly around the bedroom while Fallon stood watching Jeremy's body being put inside a bag and wheeled from the room. The coroner and the forensic team had done a thorough job, telling the detectives their reports would be available in a few hours. They were now awaiting Morgan Kennedy's arrival.

"Think the fag did it?" Bransky asked him when they were alone.

"He's nervous about something, but I don't see him as a killer, somehow."

"Hey, even sissies can get violent at times," Bransky sneered.

Nick Fallon sighed with impatience, but kept his tone smooth as he replied, "Maybe, but I don't see it in this one."

"According to the doorman, he was over here a lot."

"He's a friend of Mrs. Kennedy's, Bob. That might explain why he was here."

"The doorman says a couple of days ago Mrs. Kennedy went flyin' out the door, real upset, with Connor right behind her. What d'you suppose that was all about?"

"He did say they'd had a misunderstanding. He didn't elaborate, said it was personal."

"Well, he's gonna have to elaborate, Nick" Bransky pursed his lips as if in deep thought. "When Mrs. Kennedy gets here, may be she can tell us what the 'misunderstanding' was all about…" He stopped abruptly as a police officer accompanied Morgan into the room.

"Mrs. Kennedy?" Bransky's eyes blatantly admired the woman in front of him. He pulled himself a little taller and sucked in his belly as he put out his hand for her to shake. Looking foolish when she ignored his outstretched hand, he turned clumsily to look at his partner. "This is Detective Fallon."

Fallon nodded but did not offer his hand.

"And you are?" Morgan asked coolly.

"Oh yeah, sorry. Detective Bransky," he blurted.

"All right, Detectives. It's been a bitch of a day already. My husband is found murdered on Christmas Day and I've had to drive a hundred miles in the worst weather. If you two Sherlocks would make this interrogation as short as possible, I'd be most grateful."

The police officer tried to hide a smile as he said, "We passed the paramedics on our way in. I asked them to hold up. Thought you might want to have Mrs. Kennedy ID the body here. Save her a trip to the morgue."

"Yeah right," Bransky muttered, seemingly annoyed with himself for appearing gauche and clumsy. "That OK with you, Mrs. Kennedy?"

"Yes, let's get it over with."

Morgan's imperious manner slipped a little as they led her from the bedroom into the living room where the paramedics waited. One of them unzipped the body bag to expose Jeremy's face. She gasped at the sight of his once handsome features, now grotesquely contused and discolored from the bludgeoning. Her hands flew to her face as she nodded her head.

"Yes, that's my husband." She turned away and sobbed quietly into her hands.

Bransky cleared his throat. He looked awkwardly at Fallon who stepped in front of him and took Morgan by the elbow leading her over to the sofa. "Can I get you anything, Mrs. Kennedy?"

"Asshole!" Bransky muttered under his breath.

"Would you like a glass of water or something?"

Morgan looked at Fallon blankly. "There's some brandy in the cabinet there. I'd like a glass of that please, if you don't mind."

"I'll get it!" Bransky hurried over to the drink cabinet and poured a large quantity into one of the crystal snifters.

"Can I offer both of you a drink?" Morgan asked.

"No!" Bransky almost yelped. "We're on duty." He handed her the glass gingerly, afraid to slop any on her clothes.

Fallon looked at his partner with some amusement. In the few months he had worked with him, he had never seen him so flustered and out of character. Bob was never the compassionate type. Usually brusque to the point of rudeness, and very rarely caring about how he came across to other people.

"Of course you are," Morgan said. "Well, please sit down, at least."

Bransky resisted the temptation to sit next to her on the sofa, flopping down instead on an armchair close by.

"Do you feel you could answer a few questions?" Fallon asked her.

"I think so." Morgan gave him a small smile.

"So how come it's Christmas…" Bransky blurted, "And you and your husband wasn't together."

Morgan leveled a regretful look at him. "I had left my husband, Detective Bransky. I had gone to my parent's home to spend the Holidays, after which I was going to file for divorce."

Fallon and Bransky exchanged glances.

"On what grounds?"

Morgan was silent for a moment, a pained expression stealing over her face. "I had just discovered my husband was a homosexual."

Bransky's mouth dropped open. "Jeez, that must have been quite a shock!"

"Of course it was, especially as I caught him in the act with a mutual friend."

Bransky leaned forward in his chair eagerly. "Would that friend happen to be Andrew Connor?"

Morgan looked at him with surprise. "Why yes, but how would you know that?"

"Mr. Connor was the one who discovered your husband's body," Fallon explained. "He said he'd come over to give you a Christmas gift. Said you'd had some kind of falling out. He didn't want to enlarge on it; said it was personal."

"It sure was personal!" Bransky cast a triumphant look at Fallon. "How much more personal could it be?"

"It was a terrible blow to me," Morgan continued. "Andrew and I were very close. I had shared some very private things with him. I thought he was my friend, then I find out, the hard way, that he'd been sleeping with my husband."

"How did you find out, Mrs. Kennedy?"

"I walked in on them," Morgan reflected with pain in her voice. "I'd been to the beauty parlor. I got back around noon. Henry, our doorman told me Andrew was visiting and I was…happy to know I'd see him. I was always happy to see Andrew." She paused and looked down sadly. "I guess they didn't hear me come in—they were on the couch…kissing passionately…I ran, and…"

Bransky mumbled, "Don't upset yourself, Mrs. Kennedy."

She looked at him sadly. "It was just such a shock, you know."

"Did you know Andrew Connor was gay?" Fallon asked.

"Oh yes. He and his lover, David, seemed very happy. I never dreamed he was cheating—especially with my husband…" Morgan sipped her brandy delicately while Bransky gazed at her with puppy-like admiration.

"What a terrible thing, Mrs. Kennedy," he commiserated, and Fallon looked at him through narrowing eyes. What the hell was happening to the idiot? Looked like he was falling in love or something equally as stupid. Did he think that for one moment a woman like Morgan Kennedy would take a second look at him—a balding, out of shape sap in a baggy brown suit? Fallon could have laughed out loud if it wasn't so pathetic.

"Do you have any suspects?" Morgan was asking.

"Not at the moment," Fallon answered quickly before Bransky could make a bigger fool of himself. His partner just might shoot his mouth off in order to impress her with his theory of 'the fag' doing it.

"Well, I hope you find the person very quickly." Morgan rose, as if to dismiss the two detectives. "If you'll excuse me now. I have to find a hotel to stay in until I can have the bedroom cleaned."

Fallon stood too, his eyebrows arching in surprise at the coldness of Morgan's statement. Bransky lurched to his feet. "Oh right, Mrs. Kennedy. Don't worry, we'll find the perpetrator."

"One more thing, Mrs. Kennedy…" Fallon paused as they walked to the door. "Was the situation between Andrew Connor and your husband the only reason for you wanting a divorce?"

"Wasn't that enough, Detective?"

"It sure was!" Bransky interjected quickly.

Fallon persisted. "So, that was the only reason?"

"As a matter of fact—no." Morgan's lower lip trembled as she spoke. "I was tired of his blatant reliance on my money. This…this thing with Andrew was just the last straw."

"Don't upset yourself Mrs. Kennedy." Bransky said, glaring at Fallon.

"Thank you Detective." Morgan smiled demurely at him, and Bransky quivered, his forehead breaking out in a rash of sweat beads.

"Well," Fallon said, with a slight laugh as they walked down the corridor to the elevator. "She certainly knows how to jerk your chain."

"Whatdya mean, Nick? She's a real lady, that one."

"A very cold lady, Bob. No remorse for her dearly departed hubby, that's for sure."

"What can you expect? The guy was a homo—and doing it with that Connor guy. I knew there was something fishy about *him*."

"Look, Bob. Before you go off half cocked after Andrew Connor, we better get some facts straightened out. The guy could have a watertight alibi for the time of death, which incidentally, we don't even know yet."

"My gut tells me Connor has something to do with it."

"Your gut could tell you a lot of things if you'd listen to it. Mainly about the abuse it gets from that garbage you call food…"

"Cut it out," Bob snarled, looking down at his ample belly. "We can't all be health freaks, like you. Who the hell has the time to go to the gym like you do, anyway?"

"You could try. If you really wanted to impress a woman like that, you'd have to work on that gut big time."

"Okay, okay. You've made your point. Now let's go find out what the coroner's come up with. Jeez, what a way to spend Christmas Day."

"What a way to spend Christmas Day," Andrew exclaimed angrily, as the four friends walked through Central Park. "I've just ruined the whole thing for all of you."

"What on earth are you talking about?" David took his arm. "You didn't kill Jeremy. You found his body and reported it to the police like you should have done."

"But if I had never gone over there in the first place…"

"It's too late to worry about that now," Peter said. "It's done. It's just a pity it had to be you—*finding* him, I mean. That had to be awful."

"Yes, it was. You know I never liked the guy, but seeing him lying there, all beat up, he looked just pitiful. I could never wish anyone dead, not even someone as devious as him."

"I wonder who it could have been?" David mused. "Who hated him enough to kill him?" He looked at Jeff. "You're awfully quiet, buddy."

"I'm just thinking a few things through—but you're right. Whoever did this had to be really angry. Unless he just happened to surprise a burglar. How did the place look to you, Andrew?"

"OK. It smelled funny, but nothing was out of place."

"So, you don't think it was a robbery?" David asked.

"I wouldn't rule it out altogether," Jeff replied. "Could be the thief or thieves panicked after they killed him and fled the scene without taking anything. Or, it could have been someone he knew."

"What are you thinking, Jeff?" Peter asked.

"Well, Morgan had just found Andrew and Jeremy together in what she thought was a compromising situation. I can't believe she and Jeremy didn't have a few words over that little fact!"

Andrew shook his head. "Oh, Morgan couldn't have killed him. I just can't believe that."

"Plus, the fact that Jeremy was well built and able to take care of himself," David remarked. "She'd have a hard time clobbering him hard enough to bash his brains out."

"Unless she took him by surprise," Jeff said. "Or drugged him first. It's all been done before, many times."

"God, it just doesn't bear thinking about." Andrew paused a moment, then added, "But she wasn't mad with anger when she left me. She just seemed very sad and disappointed in me. That's what made it harder to deal with."

"Well, we'll have to wait and see what the coroner's report has to say. Time of death, autopsy, traces of drugs etc." Jeff smiled at Andrew. "Don't look so sad, Andrew, it'll all be fine."

"I wish…" Andrew began.

"What do you wish, sweetheart?" David asked him, gently.

"I wish we were all back in Laguna right now. Away from all this *mess*, this snow, this city, this…" He stopped, embarrassed by his outburst. "God, David, I'm sorry."

"It's all right." David put his arms round him and held him closely. "We'll talk about all this later."

"I didn't mean to sound like such a bitch," Andrew sobbed. "I think I'm just really upset!"

"And it's no wonder. You've been through a helluva lot today. Come on, let's go back to the apartment and relax. I'll make us all some lunch and we can watch the reruns of the Parade."

Peter smiled at Andrew. "I think we need a group hug." He and Jeff put their arms around their friends and for a long moment the four of them stood among the gently falling snowflakes, beneath the crystallized trees, and took comfort in their friendship and the warmth of their unconditional love for each other.

Nick Fallon leaned backed in his chair and looked at the report on his word processor he had started a few minutes before. Why, he wondered, had Andrew Connor lied to him about his relationship with Jeremy Kennedy?

"We were polite to each other…" he had said, yet according to Mrs. Kennedy, he and the husband had been much more than that. Connor had to have known that this would come up, so why not just confess to the reason why he and Morgan Kennedy had a falling out?

Why was he trying to hide it? If he was having an affair with the husband, why would he kill him? Jealousy? Fear of being found out by his boyfriend now that the wife knew?

Andrew Connor just didn't fit the profile of a killer. At least, not the kind who could bludgeon someone to death. Fallon considered himself a good character reader. It had served him well in the past, and in his opinion, this guy just wasn't the type.

"Finished that report yet?" Bransky was at his side looking over his shoulder at the screen.

"Almost. What's the word from the coroner?"

Bransky peered at the fax he had just received. "Time of death approximately between 4 and 8pm Tuesday night. Death caused by two heavy blows to the head. There was a bruise on his face, left side, and another on his chest. He had ingested some cocaine just prior to his death…and he had engaged in a sexual act." Bransky put the fax on Fallon's desk. "Now here's what I think…"

Fallon winced mentally as he prepared to listen to his partner's theorizing. He folded his arms, leaned back in his chair and closed his eyes.

"Mrs. Kennedy comes home, finds Connor and her husband going at it, storms out of the apartment, comes back, tells him it's all over, she's suing for divorce, then leaves. Kennedy panics when he realizes his meal ticket's out the window. He blames Connor—they fight. Connor kills him and runs, then goes back a couple of days later to "find" the body, with the half assed story about taking a gift to Mrs. Kennedy."

Fallon opened his eyes and looked at Bransky impassively. "Okay, but Connor left the building right after Mrs. Kennedy. Henry, the doorman didn't mention him coming back after that, till the day he discovered the body. If he did kill Kennedy, I think the last place he'd go is *back* to the apartment. He'd want to put a lot of space between himself and the victim. Besides, we don't know for sure it was him Kennedy had sex with. We only have Mrs. Kennedy's take on that."

"You don't believe her?"

"Well, I'm not under her spell like you are. What if *she* offed her old man and is trying to implicate Andrew Connor…"

"What?" Bransky gaped at him in disbelief. "You think that classy woman would stoop to that kind of thing."

"Bob," Fallon sighed. "You need a lobotomy. Mrs. Kennedy strikes me as a woman who could do just about anything if she got crossed."

"Oh, I think you're wrong there, Nick."

Fallon picked up the fax and stared at it for a moment. "A four-hour time span when the murder could have been committed. According to Mrs. Kennedy she found Connor and her husband in the apartment shortly after noon. Say for arguments sake, Kennedy was murdered around six or seven, that gives a lot of time for a lot to happen. How do we know that Mrs. Kennedy didn't come back a second time and confront her husband alone? He smoothes it over, they do some coke, have sex, then they have another row—and she kills him."

"That's stupid!"

"No more stupid than your scenario." Fallon stretched his lean body, looking up at Bransky and grinning at the other man's affronted expression. "Something doesn't add up. I want to talk to Andrew Connor again. Now we know he knew the husband a tad more intimately than he said, I want to know why he lied about it."

Bransky scowled at him. "He hoped we wouldn't find out, probably."

Nick shook his head. "I get the feeling he didn't want to mention it—because he was trying to protect *her*."

"Oh, please!" Bransky hooted.

"It's late Bob," Fallon said impatiently, standing up. "We should talk to the Connor guy again tomorrow, and to Mrs. Kennedy. Have we heard where she's staying?"

"She called a little while ago. Says she's at one of the Marriott hotels in town—she left a number."

"Okay. I'm going now. I promised some friends I'd drop in for some Christmas cheer." Fallon hesitated for a moment then asked. "What are you doing?"

"I'm dropping by my sister's in Queens." Bransky pulled on his coat. "Okay, see you tomorrow. Merry Christmas, Nick."

Fallon mentally breathed a sigh of relief. He really didn't want to have Bob tag along with him. "Yeah, Bob. See you tomorrow—Merry Christmas."

CHAPTER 10

About an hour later, Nick Fallon took the short one block walk from the subway to his friends' apartment, in mid Manhattan. Donna and Jim Hollister had been his friends for as long as he could remember, and he had spent many holidays in their company—usually as one of the several couples they invited to their home. They had all grown up in Pittsburgh together, and he had missed them when Jim's job took them to New York. It was because of their encouragement that he had moved to New York six months ago. They had all been such close friends—the four of them. Now that he was alone, their invitations were even more welcome. He hadn't really relished the idea of going home to an empty apartment on this day. His only hope was that they hadn't invited someone for him to meet. Donna and Jim were unapologetic matchmakers, and had tried on several occasions to fix him up with someone they thought he'd have a lot in common with. Clutching the gifts he had brought for them, he turned up his coat collar against the chill, and looked forward to the warm atmosphere he was certain awaited in their apartment.

He wasn't disappointed.

Donna was a Martha Stewart disciple and had decorated accordingly. As the door opened Fallon could see swathes of garland and lights festooning almost every wall, and the agreeable aroma of cinnamon and pine met his nostrils.

"Nick, so glad you could make it." Donna stood with her arms open, looking elegant and beautiful in a full length emerald green silk dress, a rope of pearls at her throat, her blonde hair swept up in a most becoming fashion.

"Merry Christmas, Donna. You look beautiful—as always," he said, receiving her hug. Looking over her shoulder he saw Jim bearing down on them, also with arms wide open.

"Hey, hey, it's St. Nick himself!" he yelled, putting his arms round Fallon in a tight bear hug. Fallon laughed. He was suddenly glad to be with his friends who, over the years, had shown him there was another world, away from the sad and despairing one he was surrounded by, on a daily basis. Law enforcement could sometimes show a person the worst that humanity could provide. It was good to get away to the company of decent, caring people whenever he could.

"Thanks for inviting me over. It's been a rough Christmas day so far."

"Well, we'll make up for that." Donna took his arm and led him into the living room. "I think you know everyone here."

Fallon looked around at the familiar, smiling faces of the men and women he had met at other parties here. None of them close friends like Jim and Donna, but good company when he needed it. "Yeah…Merry Christmas, everyone."

"Come on," Jim said, an arm round his shoulders. "What'll it be? Eggnog, or a real drink?"

"A real one, I think. Scotch and soda."

"Coming up."

Fallon followed Jim to the bar, stopping to drop his gifts at the designer tree Donna had obviously spent many hours decorating.

"Beautiful tree, Donna." He smiled across the room at her and she waved her thanks. He breathed a sigh of relief as Jim handed him his drink. "Cheers, Jim. I need this."

"Bad day?"

"The usual murder and mayhem." He ran a hand through his dark brown hair as he continued. "But it's my partner, Bob Bransky, who's really getting on my nerves. I don't know how much longer I can put up having to deal with him. It's only been six months, but he and I just don't mesh at all. He's such an oaf at times. Anyway, I shouldn't be bending your ear about this at a party."

"Hey, what are friends for?" Jim grinned at him. "You've listened to my tales of woe often enough over the years."

"What tales of woe?" Fallon laughed. "You've led a charmed life!"

"Well, remember when Donna and I had that big falling out and I was wandering around like a heartbroken idiot? You were the one who kept telling me she'd come around and everything would be OK. I spent a lot of time blubbering like a kid in your company."

"Yeah…" Fallon grinned at his friend. "I remember—and like I told you, it all worked out in the end. You and Donna were made for each other."

Jim's sleepy blue eyes crinkled at the corners as he smiled back. "And what about you? Anyone new in your life?"

"No time for that these days."

Looking round the room he saw, with relief, that everyone was happily paired off. No singles for him to try and make small talk with, after Donna or Jim had dragged them over to meet him. "Even today," he continued, "Bob and I were investigating a murder—not far from here, actually."

"Oh yeah?"

"Some guy, cheating on his wife with other men. He was found dead in their apartment earlier today. The wife was out of town—said she'd left him and was filing for divorce. You should have seen Bob salivating all over this woman, it was pretty sad. He's already got the case all wrapped up. According to him, the guy who found the victim is the perpetrator."

"What do you think?"

"Well, I did talk to him and he withheld some information, but I don't think he's the killer. Probably just really nervous about being mixed up in all this."

Fallon did not generally discuss his cases with friends, but he knew Jim was not about to blab any information he gave him. Over the years, the two of them had confided in each other on just about every level.

"So why does Bob think he did it?"

"Because the guy is gay. Bob is the ultimate homophobe. Thinks every gay guy is capable of just about any crime."

"Sounds like he's not the type you want in law enforcement."

Fallon grimaced. "He's not alone, by any means."

They were interrupted at that moment by the doorbell ringing.

"I'll be right back," Jim said. "Help yourself to another drink."

Fallon freshened his drink, then wandered over to a group of people to say hello. Out of the corner of his eye, he saw Jim re-enter the living room accompanied by someone Fallon did not know. He gave a mental groan as Jim grinned at him and winked. His gaze followed Jim and the stranger as they crossed the room to where Donna was standing with some friends. The two hugged and now Fallon groaned aloud, as this time Donna caught his eye and winked at him. As expected, Jim's next move was to whisk the person over to where Fallon stood trying to ignore what was about to happen.

"Nick…this is Eric Jamieson. Eric…Nick Fallon." Jim beamed at them both as they shook hands.

Fallon had often wondered if he'd done the right thing in coming out to Jim and Donna. They had taken it very well as good friends will, and had been the ones to encourage him to pursue a relationship with Martin. They had been there for him when Martin had been killed, but their mission in life now seemed to be to find him a new lover, often with embarrassing results. He had to admit, however, that this guy was a big improvement on the last two or three Jim and Donna had introduced him to in the last few months. Eric was attractive, just slightly shorter than Fallon, with a good build and a ready smile that included his clear blue eyes. His light brown hair was cut short, almost military style. He was wearing a pale blue roll neck sweater that brought out the blue of his eyes, with startling clarity.

"Nick's a cop," Jim was saying. "So be careful, Eric."

"Jim—cut it out," Fallon protested.

Eric shrugged. "That's OK. I'm a paramedic. I'm used to dealing with cops."

Jim looked across the room. "Oh, oh. I'm getting the high sign from Donna. I'll leave you two to get acquainted."

"Hey…" Eric looked at Fallon keenly, after Jim left. "You were at that homicide on 57th earlier today."

Fallon stared at him with surprise. "Yes I was, but I don't remember seeing you there."

"You were way too busy to notice me."

"I must be slipping…and Jim's slipping as a host. Walked off and didn't offer you a drink. What'll it be?"

"Vodka tonic, with a twist of lime. You the bartender?"

"Only for cute paramedics." Fallon grinned at him. Ouch, he thought, the Scotch must have gone to my head. Eric returned his grin and followed him to the bar. Donna bustled over to them as Fallon poured Eric's drink.

"I see you two have met." She winked at Eric. "Isn't he the best looking cop on the block?"

Fallon rolled his eyes as Eric laughed a trifle uncomfortably.

"Donna, you're tipsy!" He'd wanted to say *drunk*, but thought he'd be kind.

"Well, it's Christmas," she protested. "Now, drink up and have fun." And with that command, she disappeared in a rustle of expensive silk.

"So…" Fallon said slowly, not knowing exactly how to continue.

Eric clinked glasses with him. "The answer is…yes."

"Sorry?"

"She asked if I thought you were the best looking cop on the block. The answer is, yes."

Fallon blinked and colored slightly. "Thank you," he mumbled.

"I knew the murdered guy, you know." Eric looked at him over the rim of his glass.

"You *knew* him?"

"Not well," Eric replied, a shade quickly. "We both went to the same gym. He tried to pick me up once, ages ago. He was good looking and all, but there was something about him I couldn't take." He grinned at Fallon. "I had the feeling he'd been around the block one too many times for my liking. It was a case of not wanting to boldly go, where every other man had gone before—if you'll excuse the misquote."

Nick chuckled. "Good one. He was married you know."

"So I heard. That didn't stop him from trying to make just about any guy in the gym he could."

"Did you know anyone he went with?"

"One or two. Just one night stands from what I understand. He wasn't into long term relationships. A bit difficult with a wife around, I guess."

Fallon was silent for a moment, mulling over this information. If Kennedy was as promiscuous as Eric thought him to be, there could be any number of suspects out there. Jilted boyfriends, angry spouses—and there was always the chance he might have brought back a hustler who demanded payment for favors. This was obviously not going to be the open and shut case Bransky had hoped for. He focused on Eric's face again and smiled.

"Thanks for that information, Eric. Gives me something more to go on."

"You're welcome." Eric smiled at him shyly, and Fallon felt his heart miss a beat.

"Uh..." Fallon said, clearing his throat, "Are you on duty tomorrow night?"

"Don't think so...I'm scheduled days the rest of the week. So, as long as there's no emergency, I have the evenings free."

"Well, unfortunately I sometimes have to work the day and night shifts, but so far, I have tomorrow night free. Would you like to meet me for a drink?"

"I'd really like that."

"Okay...So, barring any emergencies, tomorrow night it is. You have a cell?"

Eric nodded and took the pen Fallon handed him. He scribbled down his number and Fallon gave him his card. They smiled at each other, then Fallon said, "I'll call you tomorrow and set the time. Now, I think we'd better mingle a little, or people will talk..."

"Let 'em!" Eric winked at him as Jim and Donna beckoned them from the other side of the room. Whether it was the Scotch or the touch of Eric's hand on his arm, Fallon couldn't tell, but he definitely felt light headed as the two of them crossed the room to join their hosts.

The day after Christmas, Andrew sat in the kitchen over a cup of coffee and wondered if he should try calling Morgan. She must be feeling pretty bad about now, he thought.

If she and Jeremy had fought over what she thought had happened between him and Jeremy, he was sure she would be suffering feelings of guilt mixed with sorrow. How terrible that the last words they spoke to each other should have been those of anger and recrimination. If only he hadn't allowed himself to be so easily duped by Jeremy. Tentatively, he reached for the phone, then stopped himself. What in the world was he going to say to her?

"Sorry your husband's dead, Morgan…what can I do to help?" Somehow, he doubted she'd want to hear from him after what had happened.

"You're up early." Peter entered the kitchen smothering a yawn with his hand.

"Couldn't sleep. Too much on my mind."

Peter ambled over and gave his friend a hug. "Don't fret, Andrew. Jeff said everything will be all right."

"How can it be all right, Peter? Jeremy's been murdered, for Chrissakes—and Morgan hates me for something I didn't do."

"What I meant was, the police will find out who killed him. You can relax about thinking you might be a suspect…and well, Morgan's bound to come around at some point and realize she'd been foolish to ever think you could betray her like that." He patted Andrew on the shoulder, then poured himself a cup of coffee. "David still in bed?"

"Yes. He's out like a light. I've always envied that capacity he has for sleeping well, no matter what's going on in his life. Why are *you* up?"

"I heard you out here and figured you could use the company."

"Thanks. I was wondering if I should call Morgan…"

Peter frowned. "Not a good idea. I'd give it some time, if I were you."

"You're probably right. I just wish I could be there for her, you know."

"Of course you do, but…" Peter was interrupted by the shrilling of the phone which made both of them jump. "Want me to get it?"

"No, that's OK." Andrew picked up the phone. "Hello?"

"Mr. Connor?"

Andrew's heart sank as he recognized Bransky's gruff voice. "This is Detective Bransky…following up on the Kennedy homicide investigation. Me and my partner, Detective Fallon, would like to come by and ask you a few more questions."

"When?"

"This morning, say around ten o'clock. That OK?"

"I guess so, but I really can't tell you much more."

"We think you can, Mr. Connor. So around ten, then." Bransky hung up without another word, and Andrew looked at Peter with a worried expression.

"That was the cop from Jeremy's investigation."

"The good looking one?"

"No, the other one—Bransky or something. He makes me nervous. I'm sure he thinks I had something to do with it. Anyway, he and the other one are coming over around ten to ask me some more questions."

Peter frowned. "Jeez, we'd better get Jeff and David up and let them know what's going on."

Promptly at ten, Bransky and Fallon were at the door. Bransky looked around the room as Andrew showed them in. It was obvious he didn't like the fact that Peter, Jeff and David were also there. He looked at Andrew sourly. "Is there somewhere we can talk in private?"

Andrew tried to hide his dislike for the man. "I'd rather have my friends here if you don't mind. I have nothing to hide."

"Is that right?" Bransky looked at him grimly, and was about to continue when Fallon interrupted.

"That's OK, Bob. We can talk right here. I'm sure his friends won't get in the way." His impassive gaze went past the friends to the portrait of Andrew hung over the fireplace. He slowly walked over and stood looking at it for a long moment.

"Quite impressive. Who's the artist?"

"That would be me," Peter said dryly, from the couch.

"Really?"

"Peter's going to have an exhibition in town next year," Andrew told him proudly.

"I can see why." Fallon continued to admire the portrait.

Bransky cleared his throat noisily behind them. "Uh…Nick, let's get on with it, shall we?"

"Of course…Sorry guys." Fallon smiled, ignoring his partner's discomfort.

Jeff stood up from where he'd been sitting on the arm of the couch. "We should give these guys some space. We can go in the kitchen till you're through."

"No need." Fallon ignored Bransky's scowl. "Mr. Connor will probably feel more comfortable with you here."

Jeff sat down again and took a long look at Fallon. Was this a game he was playing, or was he really being the nice guy?

"Okay, let's get to the point." Bransky pulled out a tattered notebook. "We talked with Mrs. Kennedy last night, and she told us that you and her husband was having an affair behind her back. Is that right?"

Andrew stared at Bransky with disbelief on his paling face. "She said that?" He sat down on the couch next to Peter and put his head in his hands.

"Is it true, Mr. Connor?" Fallon asked, gently enough. "Were you having an affair with her husband?"

"No, no, of course I wasn't!" Andrew could not hide his anger. "I couldn't stand the guy, if you must know."

"Careful Andrew," Jeff murmured behind him.

"How come then Mrs. Kennedy says she caught you and Mr. Kennedy in the act, so to speak, when she came home, unexpected like?" Bransky asked with a smirk.

Andrew looked up at the two detectives, and shook his head dejectedly. "I can't believe she would have told you this. I tried to explain to her that Jeremy instigated the whole thing for her benefit. I don't know why he did it. Maybe to break up my friendship with her. He called me the day after we'd had a party here in the apartment. Morgan had drunk too much, or something, and had to go lie down in our bedroom. Jeremy said she felt really terrible about it and wanted me to come over, so she could apologize in person. I told him it wasn't necessary and that I'd call her later. He said she insisted on saying sorry in person, so I went over to the apartment…"

"Go on," Fallon urged.

"Morgan wasn't there. Jeremy said she'd be home soon, so I waited. Then he started giving me a sob story about how much he wanted to be my friend. He had me almost believing him. I let my guard down I guess, and when he heard Morgan come home, he grabbed me and threw me down on the couch. That's what she saw."

"And you couldn't fight him off?" Bransky sneered. "Or didn't you want to?"

"Just a minute," David interrupted. "Andrew's telling you the truth..."

"Gee! Were you there?" Bransky looked at David, not bothering to hide the sneer on his face. "No, you were *not* there, Mr...." Bransky glanced at his notes, "...Angelo, is it? So you can't know what happened, really. Now can you?"

"I know Andrew would never have willingly been in that situation, Detective." David forced himself to remain calm, although his instinct was to punch Bransky's smug face. "Like he said, he didn't care for Jeremy Kennedy—and neither did I, for that matter."

"That's as may be." Bransky fixed Andrew with a snake-like look. "The fact is, Mrs. Kennedy says she had no idea her husband was a homo till she found you and him doin' it!"

Andrew jumped to his feet. "We weren't *doing* it, for God's sake!"

"Whoa...calm down, Mr. Connor." Fallon said, glaring at his partner.

Jeff watched the two detectives with interest. Was this the "good cop—bad cop" scenario they were playing? It was an old ploy—one cop would play the heavy, while the other would appear to be more sympathetic and understanding, in order to get the suspect to open up to him. Or was Fallon genuinely angry with Bransky? At that moment, Jeff was not sure.

"Detective Bransky didn't mean to use that term, Mr. Connor." Fallon gave Bransky another fixed stare "He's merely repeating the impression Mrs. Kennedy gave us last night. Please, sit down."

Andrew sat down again, next to Peter who gave his arm an encouraging squeeze.

Bransky glowered at them. "Where were you between 4pm and 8pm on the night of the murder—December 23rd?"

"I...I was right here," Andrew replied. "I had lunch with Jeff and Peter, then they went shopping. I came back to the apartment to do some last minute stuff for Christmas."

"Alone?" Bransky asked. "You came back alone?"

"Why...yes."

"What time would that have been?"

"Somewhere around three, I'd guess."

"Around three? You're sure?"

"No, I just said I was guessing. I really can't remember the exact time."

Bransky looked at Jeff. "So Mr. Connor here was on his own till you came back to the apartment at...?"

"Around five o'clock or so."

Bransky looked as though he thought he had just solved the case. "So, you were alone between 3pm and 5pm," he said triumphantly. "The murder was committed sometime after 4pm..."

Andrew jumped up. "Just a minute—if you're trying to pin this on me, you are way off base. I can tell you that I had nothing to do with Jeremy's death. I may not have liked the guy, but I would never kill him."

David threw a protective arm over Andrew's shoulder. "Are you really accusing him of this? You must be nuts—Andrew wouldn't hurt anyone!" He gave Nick Fallon a searching look.

The detective sighed impatiently as he got to his feet. "Okay, everyone calm down. Bob isn't accusing you, Mr. Connor. He's just trying to get all the facts straightened out and..."

"You don't have an alibi for that time frame, do you?" Bransky suddenly shouted at Andrew, ignoring Fallon totally.

"Bob, for heaven's sake," Fallon muttered.

"You want to treat these fags with kid gloves?" Bransky turned on him. "Well, a killer's a killer as far as I'm concerned."

"Just a minute!" Jeff pushed forward till he was an inch from Bransky's face. "You're way out of line Mister, and you'd better back off before you talk yourself into losing your badge. There are five witnesses here who can testify to your violation of just about every civil right in the book. Now, apologize to Andrew and start conducting yourself with some professionalism...or get out!"

A deadly silence fell on the room as Jeff and Bransky faced off. For a moment it looked like Bransky would explode with rage. His face was livid and the veins on his fat neck stood out like blue cords, then suddenly he stepped back, away from Jeff.

"I gotta get me some fresh air. I'll wait for you in the car, Nick." He turned and lurched from the room without another word. The men watched in stunned silence as the door closed behind him.

"My God," Andrew finally whispered.

"Guys, I'm sorry..." Fallon began.

"That man is a menace," Jeff snapped, looking at Fallon. "You should disassociate yourself from him completely, Detective."

"I don't know what got into him."

"You mean apart from his blatant homophobia?"

Fallon looked at Andrew who stood, pale as a ghost with David's arm around him. "You OK, Mr. Connor?"

"Yes, I'll be fine. I'm just not used to being hated so openly, I guess."

"The man's an ignorant jerk," David declared angrily. "He shouldn't be a cop!"

"Unfortunately, there's a lot more like him," Jeff said, with bitterness. "I can say that from experience."

"I'm afraid you're right," Fallon sighed. "Again, I apologize for my partner's behavior. Can we start over?"

CHAPTER 11

"**Look**, guys," Fallon leaned forward in his chair a little and directed his conversation at Jeff as he spoke. "I've come upon a bit of information about Jeremy Kennedy that opens up a lot of questions, or at least, so it would seem."

"How so?" Jeff asked.

"Seems Kennedy got around quite a bit. He's been seen picking guys up in the gym he went to, for one thing."

"Well, we can attest to that," Peter said, wryly. "He tried to pick Jeff up the first day we were in town."

"Is that right?"

"Yeah, and then he tried to deny it when we met him, here, the following night."

"Well, he was probably still hiding it from his wife," Fallon suggested.

Jeff looked at him intently. "Listen, Fallon…you should know that the relationship between Jeremy and Morgan was a very strange one. She told everyone that Jeremy only pretended to be gay—it was all an act that their friends thought hilarious. She had convinced herself, that the only way to deal with the situation was to ignore what she knew to be true."

"You mean, she *knew* her husband was gay?"

"Right."

"How can you be sure of that? She told Bob and me she found out only when she saw Mr. Connor and her husband together—that it was all a big shock to her."

"She was lying," Jeff said.

"I didn't know for the longest time that she knew," Andrew told Fallon. "But apparently she knew Jeremy had been involved in a serious affair with someone called Kevin. He was killed in a car crash and Jeremy blamed Morgan for his death. They were all big friends for years. When I tried to explain what Jeremy had been trying to do, she wouldn't listen. She said, it was just like Kevin all over again."

Fallon nodded slowly. "Interesting. Well, that certainly gives me more questions to ask Mrs. Kennedy. I'll dig up the report on the accident she and the other guy were involved in. She made it sound as if seeing you and her husband together was the catalyst to make her decide to divorce him. But if she already knew…"

"Perhaps it was the final straw," Jeff suggested. "And especially as it was Andrew, someone she really liked."

"Okay." Fallon rose from the chair. "I have to go see how Bob's doing. Then I think we'll pay Mrs. Kennedy another visit. Find out why she lied. I'll be in touch, Mr. Connor." He looked at Andrew and held out his hand.

Andrew gripped the proffered hand. "Andrew," he said with a small smile. "I hate being called Mr. Connor—it's so stuffy. And you're Nick, right?"

"Right. Okay, Andrew…thanks for your time." He looked at the others as he continued. "Thanks for the info guys. It's been very helpful."

Jeff walked with him to the door. "If I can be of any help, let me know."

Fallon nodded. "I'll be in touch."

Jeff closed the door behind Fallon and looked at his three friends. "Well, that was interesting."

"He's gay," Peter announced. "My gaydar was working overtime."

"No kidding. What was your first clue?"

"Oh, you!" Peter pouted. "He isn't that obvious."

Andrew smiled at them. "I think Jeff was definitely the hero of the hour. You certainly slowed that moron, Bransky, down."

"Yeah, thanks Jeff," David said. "I don't think he's going to want to take you on again."

Peter tried to look menacing. "Well if he does, he'll have to go through me first!"

Jeff grinned at him. "My hero."

"So?" Bransky asked dourly as Fallon got in the car beside him. "Are they going to report me?"

"They should, Bob. What the hell were you thinking, back there?"

"I don't know. I guess I thought I could scare him into a confession."

"Bob, those guys are not wusses. I know you have no time for gays, but they won't be intimidated as easily as you think. I think we should call on Mrs. Kennedy. Her story doesn't quite line up."

"Who says? The guys up there? They're going to cover for their friend, for sure."

"Bob—stop thinking of Mrs. Kennedy as some sort of Madonna figure. If, what they told me is true, then she lied to us about not knowing her husband was gay." He filled Bransky in on his conversation with Andrew and the information the others had given him. "If the guy was that promiscuous and even had a serious affair for a while, doesn't it seem ridiculous that the wife wouldn't know?"

Bransky rubbed his sweaty forehead with the palm of his hand as he mulled over what Fallon had just told him. "Sometimes the spouse is the last to know…"

"I don't think this time that's true, Bob. That accident in New Hampshire…we need the report on that…but right now, let's go see Mrs. Kennedy in her Marriott hideaway, shall we?"

Morgan did not look at all pleased to see her visitors when she opened the door to her suite at the Downtown Marriott.

"I think you could have called first!" She made no move to invite them in.

"Sorry, Mrs. Kennedy," Bransky blustered. "We was in the area, and we have a few more questions for you."

"Nevertheless, you should have phoned me first." She opened the door wider. "Well, I suppose you can come in. Only for a few minutes, though. I'm going out." Morgan stepped back to let the detectives pass into the suite.

"Thank you," Fallon said smoothly. "This really shouldn't take long. There appear to be a few discrepancies we'd like to clear up."

"Oh, such as?" Morgan sat down, but did not offer the men a seat.

"We talked to Andrew Connor and his friends today. They were a little surprised that you claim not to have known your husband was gay, or at the very least, bisexual."

Morgan remained expressionless. "What they think has no bearing on the matter at all. Just because they knew of my husband's proclivities, does not mean I did. I can assure you I knew nothing of his 'secret' life."

Fallon crossed the room and perched on a barstool. Bransky looked around uncomfortably, not knowing where to park himself.

"Oh, sit down Detective Bronsky, for goodness sake," Morgan snapped.

"*Bransky…*"

"Whatever." Morgan looked impatiently at Fallon. "Now, what other untruths did Andrew and his friends tell you?"

Fallon smiled thinly and leaned back on the bar counter. "They said your husband had an ongoing affair with a man called Kevin Anderson, and that Anderson was killed when the vehicle you were driving was involved in a collision. Apparently, your husband blamed you for the accident?"

"Kevin Anderson was a mutual friend." Morgan's tone was terse. "He and his *wife* were friends of ours. His death was tragic. I was driving the car. We were all at a party. Kevin got drunk and I offered to drive him back to the vacation rental property we were sharing. A car ran us off the road and I hit a tree. The Jeep caught fire. I couldn't get Kevin out. He was unconscious and too heavy for me…" Morgan faltered, looked down at her lap and then whispered. "It was terrible."

Bransky coughed sympathetically.

"Why didn't Mr. Anderson's wife drive him home?" Fallon asked, breaking the heavy silence.

"She wasn't there. She and Kevin were divorced the year before."

"So, when you said you were sharing the rental property, you meant your husband, yourself, and Mr. Anderson."

"That's correct. What's wrong with that?"

"*Nothing's* wrong with that," Bransky said, glaring at Fallon.

Fallon ignored him. "And in all that time, you say you noticed nothing intimate going on between your husband and Mr. Anderson."

"Nothing at all. If they were having an affair it was totally unbeknownst to me!"

"I find that hard to believe."

Morgan bristled. "Are you calling me a liar? I think you'd better watch what you say, Detective. My father is a powerful man, with lots of friends—powerful friends who could do your career a lot of damage."

"Okay, Mrs. Kennedy." Fallon got off the barstool and walked slowly toward her. "Have it your way. Your husband's running around town for years, picking up other men, having a long-term affair with a close friend, but you say you knew nothing. I figured you for an intelligent woman, but now I'm not so sure…"

"How dare you! I'm warning you Detective…"

Fallon cut her off. "I'm just trying to get to the truth. I want to know why you're playing this game of pretending to not know what your husband was up to, either behind your back or with your knowledge. All we have to do is talk to some of your friends and find out what they know."

"They know *nothing*," Morgan snapped. "All my close friends knew nothing of Jeremy's perversions. They all thought his gayness was an act, just as I did."

"I don't buy it…"

"Nick, for the love of Mike, calm down," Bransky interjected. "Mrs. Kennedy isn't a suspect in this case."

"I had better not be," Morgan sneered at them. "If anyone's a suspect—it should be Andrew Connor!"

Fallon gave her a long speculative look. "Why do you say that, Mrs. Kennedy?"

"Well, for one thing he was furious I caught him in the act. He probably thought I would tell David what I'd seen. He might have gone back to see Jeremy, after I left, to concoct some kind of alibi. Perhaps Jeremy wasn't keen about letting him off the hook so easily. They argued, fought—and…well…"

"Why would he kill the man you say he was having an affair with?" Fallon said, dismissively. "Just because they were caught red handed? It's not unheard of, you know, for people to be caught in the middle of an adulterous affair—and not try to kill each other afterwards."

"I wouldn't know."

"Wouldn't you, Mrs. Kennedy?"

Morgan glared at Fallon. "I don't like your tone, Detective!"

Fallon returned her menacing look with a steady gaze. "And I don't like your reasoning."

Bransky suddenly lurched to his feet. "And I don't like where any of this is going," he growled. "You're out of line, Nick…"

Fallon turned an angry look on his partner that silenced him. "Just for the record, Mrs. Kennedy, I don't believe Andrew Connor killed your husband, and I don't think you do either. I don't know why you're so eager to pin it on him. You used to be friends, didn't you? He says your husband instigated that whole seduction scene just for your benefit—to ruin your friendship with him. From what I see, your husband succeeded in doing just that."

Morgan's lips tightened slightly. "Andrew tried to tell me the same thing. I didn't believe it then, nor do I believe it now. Jeremy told me Andrew had shown an interest in him for some time."

"Well, it sounds like one person's word against the other." Fallon took in Morgan's haughty expression. "Did you always believe what your husband told you, Mrs. Kennedy?"

"I did, but obviously I was wrong on many occasions."

"And you might just be wrong again, right?"

"I suppose so," Morgan muttered. "But I saw them on the couch. They were kissing..."

"And according to Andrew, your husband duped him into letting his guard down, then when he heard you come into the apartment he used a surprise tactic to force him onto the couch, and make it look like they were engaged in an embrace."

"That's what he told me..."

"Is it not possible he was telling the truth?"

"I suppose so..."

"So if we exclude Andrew Connor as a suspect for the moment, do you have any idea who would want to kill your husband?"

"No, of course not. No one we know...none of our friends, anyway."

"But now you know your husband had a secret life." Fallon sat down on the couch next to her. "Could he have been in the habit of hiring hustlers for instance?"

Morgan gasped. "Detective Fallon, I knew nothing of my husband's secret affairs. As far as I'm concerned, it might have been the man in the moon."

"Okay, Mrs. Kennedy." Fallon moved closer to her. "I'm real sorry for upsetting you earlier. A murder investigation is never easy. We have to explore every possibility. I hope you'll forgive me."

"Well," Morgan said, slightly mollified. "I know you don't have an easy job, but remember I'm the one who is traumatized by all this."

"I realize that, and again, I'm sorry. Now, if you'll excuse us. We'll be in touch when we have some news for you."

Bransky breathed a sigh of relief as Morgan closed the door behind them. "What the hell were you trying to do in there?" he rasped. "You could get yourself suspended...and me along with you!"

"*You're* telling me this, after what you did in front of Andrew Connor and his friends?" Fallon laughed shortly. "That's ironic. At least I apologized." He paused for a moment, then peered closely at his partner. "Bob, where are you in this case? Are you actually on the same page as me? Do you any idea what's going on here?"

"What are you talking about...?" Bransky looked uncomfortable.

"You actually think Andrew has something to do with this, don't you? And the reason you do is because the guy is gay. In your mind that means he's capable of just about anything, right?"

"Well, he had motive—*and* opportunity."

"What motive, Bob?"

"He was found doin' it with the husband. He panicked—didn't want the boyfriend to find out and..."

"Bullshit, Bob. I'm telling you Andrew had nothing to do with it. His story is the real one. The wife's is full of holes."

"Why are so sure?" Bransky grew belligerent. "And what's with this first name crap...? Andrew this and Andrew that..."

"I like the guy, and I believe him."

"*Like* him? He's a homo—how could you *like* him?" Bransky stared at Fallon dully for a moment, then looked away quickly. "Oh my God!" he muttered. There was long silence between them as they walked to their car. "I'm not getting in the car with you," Bransky said.

"Excuse me?" Fallon stared grimly at his partner. "Don't be stupid, Bob." He slid into the driver's seat, and started the car. "Get in."

"No way," Bransky's face twisted in a grimace of dislike. "No fucking way! I'll get a cab back to the station. Then I'll see about gettin' me a new partner."

"Are you nuts? On what grounds?"

"On the grounds that I don't feel safe working with you, no more."

Fallon laughed quietly. "Believe me Bob, you couldn't be safer..."

"I'll be talking to the Chief, when I get back."

"Bob, the Chief knows. He's always known I'm gay..."

"Fuck!" Bransky yelled before walking off, leaving Fallon to pull away from the curb alone.

Jeff stood quietly by the window of his and Peter's bedroom, looking out at the wintry sunshine glinting off the windows of the building opposite. Deep in thought, he did not hear Peter enter the room behind him, until he spoke.

"Hey, good-lookin'. You've been in here a long time."

Jeff turned and smiled. "Just thinking, that's all. Come over here." Peter dutifully did as he was bid, and Jeff wrapped him in his arms.

"Have you got it all worked out?" Peter asked.

"Not yet, but my head is buzzing with the possibilities."

"Mmm, and there's certainly a bunch."

"Well, we know Andrew didn't do it. So that leaves Morgan—or a person, or *persons*, unknown."

"And with Jeremy's extra curricular activities, it could have been anybody."

"Right," Jeff agreed. "How do you feel about Morgan?"

"Well, that day in the restaurant had me worried. You know, when I felt that she was some kind of danger to him. But I'm not sure how that ties in. I don't know if she could actually kill someone, do you?"

"The most unlikely people can be killers…" Jeff led Peter over to the bed. He flung himself down on top of the covers, then pulled Peter down beside him. "Especially when they are driven over the edge. What got me was her eagerness to involve Andrew. The way Nick Fallon told it, she made it sound as if her finding Andrew and Jeremy together was the sole reason for her wanting a divorce, and leaving him to go to her parents."

"Do you think she's deliberately trying to make trouble for Andrew?"

"Yes, I do. But don't worry, she's already failed. Nick doesn't buy it, and it looks as if he's thinking along the same lines as me—that Morgan probably knows more than she's saying."

"You mean she might know who the killer is?"

"She might have a very good idea."

"But wouldn't that put her in danger too?"

"Not if whoever did it, was doing it *for* her."

"You mean someone who knew Jeremy was cheating on her, and wanted it stopped?"

"Something like that. I'm just opening up the possibilities a little more, that's all."

"Someone who loved her enough to kill for her. Wow!" Peter exclaimed. "How many people d'you think she knows who would do that?"

"Not many. Someone very close—a parent, an admirer? We know Jeremy was having affairs all over the place—but what about her? How do we know there wasn't someone else in her life—someone she kept totally secret? We could narrow down the list of suspects to about one, or maybe two. On the other hand, I could be totally wrong about this, and it could be anyone of a dozen guys he'd been seeing and dumped for one reason or another. Maybe one of them got jealous and decided to take revenge—or it could just be little Morgan herself."

"And there we are, back to square one." Peter rested his head on Jeff's chest. "You said a parent. Andrew did mention that Morgan's father disliked Jeremy."

"Enough to kill him though? You have to really hate someone to bludgeon them to death. And Morgan's Dad must be in his late sixties at least. He'd be no match for someone as fit as Jeremy."

"Unless he took him by surprise. You said it was possible that Morgan could have done that."

"True—and just about anything is possible when it comes to murder. I guess we'll just have to wait and see what Nick Fallon digs up." He stroked Peter's hair gently. "How's Andrew feeling?"

"Pretty depressed right now. I think Nick made him feel a bit better, saying he believed his version, but he was upset by Morgan's willingness to throw him to the wolves."

"Having Nick Fallon on our side is a definite plus," Jeff remarked. "Come on…" He ruffled Peter's hair. "Let's go cheer Andrew up a bit."

"Just when we were getting cozy." Peter gave a rueful chuckle, as he followed Jeff to the door.

David was standing in front of Andrew's portrait when they entered the living room. He turned and looked gloomily at his friends. "I was just remembering the Christmas when you gave us this wonderful gift, Peter. It was a much happier occasion. So much has happened since then, and obviously some of it not for the better."

"Come on Dave," Jeff said, taking his friends arm. "It's not like you to look on the bleak side of things."

"No, it's not, but I just hate to see Andrew so darned unhappy. This thing with Morgan has really left him depressed. On top of that, you guys will be leaving in a few days. He's already dreading that…"

Peter looked at Jeff as if for approval of what he was about to say. "Well, I don't think I *can* leave until all this is resolved. If it's all right with Jeff, I'd like to stay on, just to make sure Andrew doesn't feel deserted."

Jeff squeezed his arm. "We'll both stay."

David beamed at them. "That's terrific. Andrew's going to feel a lot better when he hears this news."

"What news?" Andrew asked, coming into the room.

"Jeff and Peter are going to stay on till all this mess is cleared up."

"Oh, you guys…" Andrew immediately choked up. "You can't do that. You've got so much to do in California…"

"Nothing that can't wait," Jeff said.

"You're stuck with us for a while longer, I'm afraid." Peter put his arms around Andrew and they hugged fiercely for a moment.

"That's not all." David took Andrew's hand.

"I can't stand any more good news. Uh…it *is* good news, isn't it?"

"I think you'll like it. When this is over, I'm going to give Graham a month's notice. You and I are going back to Laguna…"

"David!" Andrew flung his arms around him and buried his face against his neck.

"I think that went well," Jeff murmured, smiling at Peter.

"Oh, but you can't do this," Andrew exclaimed. "You're doing so well with Graham's company. He'll be *pissed*."

"He'll get over it. The look on your face tells me I'll be doing the right thing."

"This is great," Peter exclaimed. "We'll all be together again. Hey, this calls for a celebration. Is it too early for champagne?"

"It's never too early for champagne," David said. "Come on, Andrew. Let's crack that bottle we were saving for New Years Eve."

Fallon sighed and watched as Bob Bransky entered the station and went straight to the Chief's office. Probably for the best, he thought, knowing Bransky was about to complain about having to work with a 'homo' and why wasn't he informed of the fact, before agreeing to be Fallon's partner.

Fallon hadn't been too enamored of the idea himself when he transferred to this station six months prior. Right away, Bransky had struck him as a difficult man to work with. Belligerent, tunnel-visioned, bigoted in many ways, Bransky was not the sort of partner Fallon would have chosen—if he'd had a choice.

"Sorry Fallon," Chief Detective Edward Fitzgerald had said when assigning him. "Bransky's partner just retired, so we have to get someone to replace him, and you're it. It won't be easy. Bransky has a bad reputation for jumping to conclusions too quickly—usually the wrong ones."

"*Great*," Fallon had muttered, but he'd put a good face on it, and for a while Bransky and he had managed to get along without too many hassles. But gradually, Bransky's narrow views and bigoted remarks had got on Fallon's nerves and he had made it clear to Fitzgerald that he wanted out. Now, with Bransky in there bad mouthing him, Fitzgerald would be forced to do something.

A few minutes later, the summons to Fitzgerald's office came in the form of the Chief yelling from his office, "Fallon, get in here!"

Fallon ignored the pointed stares from the other guys as they watched him make his way to Fitzgerald's office.

"Come in—and close the door." Fitzgerald did not look happy.

He was an imposing figure of a man. A tall African American who had been an impressive athlete in his youth, Fitzgerald had put on weight in the last few years, but still managed to carry the extra pounds easily. He had been transferred to the precinct only shortly before Fallon himself, and they had almost immediately struck up a relaxed and easygoing relationship. Fallon admired Fitzgerald's professionalism, his ability to make decisions and stand by them. Fitzgerald, an intelligent and open-minded man, had not been at all fazed when Fallon had been open with him about his sexuality from the beginning. He had thought it expedient that it remain his and Fallon's secret, particularly while Fallon was partnered with Bransky.

Now he frowned as he looked at the young detective. "Bob's been in here making all sorts of complaints about you. The one about your sexual orientation I told him he could forget. He'll just have to get over that, but these others about you harassing Mrs. Kennedy, the victim's wife on the case you two are working on—this isn't good, Nick."

"Chief, I'm sorry, but it's like I'm working on my own in this case. Bob hasn't got a clue about what's going on. He's too busy trying to look up the woman's skirt."

"What?"

"He's drooling over her every time she's in the room. He's convinced that Andrew Connor, the guy who found the body, is the killer."

"And you're not?"

"No. He's not the type."

"Because he's gay?"

"Of course not. I'm not stupid enough to believe that because a guy is gay he's incapable of murder, or any other kind of violence."

"Well, Bransky thinks you're protecting him. Almost came out and said it was because all you guys have to stick together."

"You know that's bullshit. If I suspected Connor of the crime I'd be clapping the cuffs on him."

"Right. I know you're a straight cop, if you'll excuse the expression." Fitzgerald allowed himself a wry smile. "So what have you got?"

"Nothing so far. Except the wife is hiding something. I'm just not sure what."

"Well, keep on it. Do you have the forensics report yet?"

"No. I've asked them to put a rush on it. Should have something later today. I'm going to call the New Hampshire station—find out who took the report on the accident Mrs. Kennedy was involved in."

"Okay. Keep me posted."

"What about Bransky?"

"I'm taking him off the case. Reassigning him. Copeland needs some help. His partner Tom Dukakis, is out sick for a couple of weeks. You'll be working on your own for a while till I find you a new partner."

"Suits me."

"Let me have a written report on what you've got so far. Okay?"

"You got it…and, thanks."

Fallon left the office feeling better, despite the dirty look Bransky shot him across the room as he pretended to confer with his new partner. His phone rang as he sat down at his desk. "Fallon here."

"Eric here. Did you forget you were supposed to call me today?"

"Oh Jeez, Eric. I'm sorry."

"That's OK. I know how crazy it can get for you guys." Eric sounded genuinely unconcerned. "Are we still on for tonight?"

"You bet. I'm looking forward to seeing you. It'll take the stress out of the day."

Eric chuckled. "You say the sweetest things, Detective."

Fallon felt his face color, but at the same time he smiled. It had been a long time since he'd had anyone flirt with him. That he'd noticed anyway. "Look Eric, I have to wait here for a forensic report, but after that I can get away. What if we meet at Sullivan's for that drink? You know it?"

"You bet. What time?"

"About six thirty or so. I'll try not to be late."

"Don't sweat it. I'll be there, waiting. See you later."

"Bye." Fallon put the phone, the smile still on his lips.

"Hey, Fallon!" Bransky stood in the doorway of his office. "Fitzgerald give you the good news? I've got me a new partner."

"Congratulations, Bob. I wish I could say it was nice working with you."

"Yeah? Well I could say the same thing. At least with Copeland, I know what I've got!"

"Is that it, Bob? I'm kind of busy here. So if you're through…"

"I'm through," Bransky growled, removing his bulk from the doorway.

Fallon watched him lurch away. "Good riddance," he muttered, then reached for his phone as it rang.

"Detective Fallon?"

"You got him."

"Bates at forensics. We've done a preliminary report and one thing I thought you'd want to know about is, we found two blood types in the samples we got from the scene."

"Two blood types? There was only one body."

"Right. I'm guessing whoever killed the guy got bloodied in the fight. There were traces of the second blood type on Kennedy's body and on the sample taken from the carpet. I'll send you up the whole report in the morning, but I thought you'd want to know this bit of information right away."

"Yeah, right. Thanks, I appreciate it. Anything else unusual?"

"Not really. You'll have my report in the morning."

"Wait…what about the blood on the murder weapon—the horse's head? Was the second type there too?"

"No, just where I described it. Goodbye, Detective."

Fallon put his phone down and leaned backed in his chair. Now, this is a surprise, he thought. Whoever killed Kennedy was hurt in the struggle. That definitely ruled out Andrew, but also Morgan Kennedy. Neither one of them showed any sign of a serious injury. So the perpetrator was someone else entirely. Could it have been one of Kennedy's boyfriends? A street hustler? Or someone with a genuine grudge against Kennedy?

Now, he wished he had someone with whom to discuss these possibilities. That's where a partner could really come in useful—a good partner that is, he thought ruefully as he looked up the number for the New Hampshire police station he needed, and punched in the numbers quickly.

"New Hampshire Police Department."

"Yeah, hi…Nick Fallon, NYPD. I'm trying to reach the investigating officer on fatal accident about six months ago, involving a Mrs. Kennedy and a Kevin Anderson."

"One moment please."

Nick fiddled with his pen while he waited and mulled over an idea that had just come to him. One that might just work out. He wrote down a name—Jeff Stevens.

"Detective Fallon?" The young woman was back. "That would be Detective Frank Mitchell."

"Can I speak with him, please?"

"Sorry, he's on Christmas break for a few days—till the1st actually."

Fallon mentally cursed. "Could you fax me a copy of the report, maybe?"

"Sure, let me have your number."

Fallon gave her the fax number, thanked her and hung up. Then he dialed Andrew's number.

"Hi, Andrew. This is Nick Fallon. How are you?"

"Much better, thanks. We've just been having some champagne."

"Still celebrating the holidays?"

"Something even better. How can I help you, Nick?"

"I wondered if your friend, Jeff was there? I'd like to have a word with him."

"Sure. Just a minute."

Fallon listened to the rustling as the phone was passed over and the murmur of voices in the background.

"This is Jeff."

"Hi, Jeff. Nick Fallon. This may be a little surprising, but I think I'm going to need your help."

"*My* help?"

"Yeah. My partner and I had a little disagreement, and he's been reassigned to another case. I'm working on the Kennedy investigation on my own for the time being, and I really need someone to talk to about it. You know, pass some ideas back and forth, so I don't go too far off in left field, as it were. I know this is a bit unconventional, and whatever I tell you relating to the case must go no further for now, you understand. Would you be interested?"

"Why sure. If it can help Andrew, I'd be very interested."

"Don't worry about Andrew. I'm pretty sure he's in the clear…are you free tomorrow morning about ten o'clock? I can come over and pick you up."

"I'll be here. See you tomorrow then."

"Right. Thanks, Jeff."

Nick walked over to the fax terminal and waited for the New Hampshire Police report on Morgan Kennedy's accident. As soon as it came through he tore it from the machine and read it through quickly. It looked like a standard accident report, nothing unusual—except at the bottom a note had been added in long hand. *Father of Mrs. Kennedy—Mr. Joseph File—has requested any further interviews be conducted by NYPD.* It was signed, Frank Mitchell.

"Huh!" Fallon looked at the banks of filing cabinets. Should be a report filed here somewhere, he thought. He checked the 'K' drawer and found nothing relating to Morgan Kennedy. Ditto under 'F' for File. Returning to his office he fired up his computer, but after searching for several minutes, he came up empty handed. Could be the ball had been dropped and no one assigned to the follow up interview. He'd just have to wait until Mitchell came back to work on the 1st.

Fallon glanced at his watch. Six-fifteen already.

"*Damn*," he muttered. He'd wanted to go home and change quickly before meeting Eric, but now there would not be enough time—he'd just have to clean up in the men's washroom, and hope he'd look presentable enough.

⁂

Jeff put the phone down and looked at his friends who were gazing at him expectantly.

"Well?" Peter asked. "What did Nick want?"

"A date."

"*What*? I thought I saw him show a deal of interest in you…"

"No, silly." Jeff leaned back and laughed. "Seems he and his partner have had a parting of the ways. Bransky, or whatever his name was, has been reassigned to another case. Nick wants to run some ideas by me, see what I think. The good news is he's pretty sure Andrew's off the hook."

"That's great," David said fervently.

Andrew looked skeptical. "But can he do this? I mean, use you as a partner?"

"Only totally unofficially. It can go no further than this room. My guess is he's doing this because I have the experience and I'm close to the case, being your friend. But he is taking a chance of being reprimanded."

"I wonder what happened between him and his partner?"

"Well, they didn't seem very compatible when they were over here."

"You're right," David remarked. "Starsky and Hutch they were not."

"Well, he's certainly being a big help to us. He seems determined to clear my name."

"That's the easiest part…" Peter grinned at him. "You didn't do it."

"Yes, but he doesn't know me from Adam. For all he knows, I could be just putting on this young, *cute*, innocent guy act for his benefit, when all the time I'm a serial killer having sex with my victims, then bashing their brains out."

The three friends looked at Andrew in amazement, then simultaneously they all burst out laughing. David wiped his eyes. "Yeah, Andrew. That's you all right…' The Mass Murderer of Manhattan' come to rape and kill us in our sleep!"

"Oh God, Andrew." Peter hugged his friend. "You are a hoot. I'm just glad to see your sense of humor has come back."

"You know," David said, smiling happily. "I think we should go out on the town tonight. There's a little bar and restaurant not too far from here that does an incredible lasagna."

"Great idea," Jeff exclaimed, jumping to his feet. "It'll be our treat. Come on, Peter. You'll need a good scrubbing before we go out." Peter gaped at him with mock affront, then squealed as Jeff threw him over his shoulder and made for the bedroom.

"Help!" Peter yelled. "Wait, on second thoughts, don't bother…"

"Scrubbing?" Andrew laughed. "Is that a new word for it?"

David shook his head. "New to me. Those two are insatiable."

"It's only been two years. They're not an old married couple like you and me."

"Well, let this old married man show you what he's still made of."

"You're just determined to make me the happiest man in the world, aren't you?"

David nuzzled Andrew's neck as he whispered, "It's my life's work and sole ambition."

CHAPTER 12

As he pushed open the door to Sullivan's bar, Fallon caught sight of Eric sitting alone at a table, and he felt his heart quicken. God, he's cute, he thought, as he walked quickly over to where Eric sat.

"Hey, Eric."

"Hi there." Eric stood and held out his hand.

Nick took it and enjoyed the pleasant tingle he felt at the touch of Eric's warm skin. Eric had taken off his coat and scarf and was wearing a beige knit shirt, open at the neck. He looked fresh and, Fallon thought lasciviously, good enough to eat.

"Good to see you," he said, sitting down and trying not to look too much on edge.

"I ordered you a Scotch and soda. Is that OK?"

"Perfect." He picked up his glass at the same as Eric. "Cheers." His hand shook slightly as he raised his glass to his lips.

Eric caught his eye and grinned. "Relax, Nick. You seem tense."

"I don't do this very often." Fallon tried to smile. "I guess I'm a bit rusty at the dating game."

"Is this a game, then?" Eric said, somewhat teasingly.

"No, no. I didn't mean it that way…"

"I'm kidding, Nick. Look, relax. We're going to have a nice evening getting to know one another. That's what the first date is all about. I'll ask you very personal questions—and you'll decide whether it's any of my business or not."

Fallon looked at Eric's smiling face and found himself mesmerized by the dimples on each side of his mouth.

"Okay, so let's start," Eric was saying. "How old are you?"

"Uh…thirty-four."

"I'm thirty-one."

"You don't look it. I thought you were younger."

"Is that why you asked me out?" Eric chuckled. "You like 'em young?"

"No, no. I didn't…oh Jeez. You're kidding again, right?"

Eric's smile got broader as he nodded.

"Okay," Fallon said. "Let me ask you one. Where are you from?"

"Cincinnati, Ohio. And you?"

"Pittsburgh. I've only been in New York six months."

"Like it?"

"Not really, but I wanted a transfer out of Pittsburgh, and this came up."

"Why did you want to leave?"

"Personal reasons."

"Aha!" Eric leaned forward and looked into Fallon's eyes. "You see, you can't give that answer, my friend. It's the personal stuff I'm interested in."

Fallon looked away uncomfortably. "Not on the first date."

"Sorry. Touched a nerve have I?" Eric looked at him, an apology in his light blue eyes.

"Somewhat. It's just not something I want to talk about just yet."

"Got it. Hey, I have a suggestion," Eric said, his smile returning. "This place is a bit too public. If you're hungry, I know a nice little restaurant close by. The owners are friends of mine, and the atmosphere is a bit cozier than this. Interested?"

"Sounds good." Fallon downed his drink and stood up, glad of the change of subject.

"Let's go then." Eric threw on his coat as they left. The cold night air took their breath away after the warmth of the bar. "It's not far," Eric said, through chattering teeth. "Just a block or so." They walked briskly together, their shoulders occasionally touching with an intimacy that Fallon found exhilarating.

"Here it is." Eric indicated a frontage so small Fallon would have missed it had he been on his own. Eric held the door open for him and the warmth and aromas of good cooking overwhelmed Fallon's senses as they entered. He looked around at the dimly lit restaurant, with its intimate discreetly lit tables occupied mostly by couples, deep in conversation. Soft music played gently in the background lending a comfortable and welcoming atmosphere.

"This is *great*," Fallon whispered.

"Isn't it? I love this place." Eric put his hand on Fallon's arm. "Let's sit down over here."

"Shouldn't we wait to be seated?"

"Uh uh. Steve and Jimmy kind of have this table reserved for me. I come here a lot." He smiled as two men appeared from the back of the restaurant.

"Eric..." one of them exclaimed. "We wondered if you'd be by tonight."

"Uncle Steve, Hi. This is my friend, Nick Fallon. Nick, these are my best buddies in all the world. My uncles, Steve and Jimmy."

Fallon extended his hand and it was warmly shaken by both men.

"We're delighted to meet you," Steve said.

"We've got something special tonight," Jimmy said, eyes twinkling. "Your favorite—Mama's Meatloaf."

"Oh, you have to try it, Nick." Eric grinned at him. "It's the greatest."

"How can I resist?" Fallon smiled back at him. "It's the greatest!" He was beginning to feel relaxed in this atmosphere of warmth and bonhomie. He sat down and let the two men fuss over them.

Eric handed him a menu. "Nick and I will have a couple of Scotch and sodas first, guys."

"Coming right up." Steve and Jimmy disappeared in tandem to fetch the drinks.

"They run this place all by themselves?" Fallon asked, noting the absence of any other employees.

"Yep, Jimmy does the cooking. Steve's the server and the host, and they both clean up after. They have a guy comes in the morning to set up the tables. I sometimes come by and help them close up on my way home after the late shift. I eat here so often and they refuse to charge me, so I help out as much as I can."

"They're your uncles?"

"Not really. They were friends of my folks in Cincinnati. They lived just down the street with Jimmy's mother. They ran her restaurant in town for years. When she died, they decided to come here and open their own place. Something they always wanted to do—live in New York. They love it here."

"They seem really nice."

"They're like family to me." Eric's voice was warm with affection. "They love to mother me. They're very protective—so watch out..." He laughed to let Fallon know he was kidding again. Fallon looked at Eric smiling at him across the table and once again felt that tug in his heart.

"I promise I'll be good," he said huskily.

"Not *too* good I hope." Eric gave him a sly look as Steve approached their table.

"Here we are." He placed their drinks in front of them. "Is it going to be the meatloaf, then?"

"I think so," Eric said as Fallon nodded. "But give us a little while. We're in a talkative mood."

"No problem." Steve disappeared again.

"So..." Fallon took a gulp of his drink. "Are your parents still in Cincinnati?"

"Oh yeah. Still hail and hearty. I visit a couple of times a year. Never miss Thanksgiving, of course. What about you?"

"My mother died when I was a kid," Fallon said slowly. "My father had left some years before that. My big sister raised me. She's ten years older than me."

"Where is she now?"

"She still lives in Pittsburgh with her husband."

"Are you still close?"

"Very. She was kind of pissed at me when I moved away, but we talk on the phone every week. I would have gone to see her at Christmas but I couldn't get the time off. You know how that is."

"Oh yeah. Me too. My folks wanted me home this Christmas, but I had to tell them, no can do."

"So, thanks to Jim and Donna, here we are."

Eric smiled at him. "I'll drink to that..."

They looked up as Steve appeared before them carrying a basket of warm breads.

"Thought you might like something to nibble on," he murmured, then left quickly.

"He has to report back to Jimmy every now and then," Eric chuckled.

"You mean as to how we're getting along out here?"

"Right...this is the first time I've ever brought an attractive man here since my breakup."

"Breakup? How long were you together?"

"Too long..." Eric's expression was rueful. "By about a year."

"I'm sorry," Fallon said sincerely.

"Oh, it was my fault I guess. Couldn't bear to let go. I kept thinking we could work it out, when all we were doing was beating it to death."

"Are you still friends?"

"We were, until about a year ago. He met someone and I just didn't get along with the guy. John, my ex, had to make a choice, and it was goodbye Eric. Just as well really. It made me face the truth at last. Something I should have done ages before." He looked straight into Fallon's eyes and smiled. "Made me grow up finally and realize that life is something you have to work at. It's not just all handed to you on a plate. When you're young, you think life owes you something. You take a few hard knocks—and *pow*, you're waking up and smelling the coffee."

"Anyone since then?"

"Nothing serious. Oh, there's been the odd one night stand." He grinned. "Sometimes, very odd—you know, you meet someone in a bar—you think you've gone home with Brad Pitt, and you wake up with Pee Wee Herman."

Fallon was still chuckling when Steve showed up again, this time to take their order.

"Definitely, the meatloaf," Fallon said.

"Make that two, Uncle Steve."

"Jimmy and I want to treat you to a bottle of wine," Steve said in a stage whisper. "Don't let it get around though," he added, with a wink at Fallon. "Can't have the patrons thinking we're an easy touch."

Fallon smiled at him. "That's very nice of you both."

Steve produced a bottle of French Cabernet and poured them both a glass. "Skol," he whispered and disappeared once more.

"He likes you," Eric said, raising his glass. "And so do I," he added, with a shy smile.

Fallon clinked his glass against Eric's and said as their eyes met, "I'm very glad you agreed to meet me tonight, Eric. You've really helped make this a much better day."

It was a little after ten when they left the restaurant. Steve and Jimmy waved them goodbye at the door.

"Great guys," Fallon remarked as they walked away.

"The best," Eric agreed. He looked sideways at Fallon. "Walk me home?"

"That was my intention."

"It's not far."

"Doesn't matter how far it is. I don't even feel the cold anymore, do you?"

"No." Eric linked his arm through Fallon's as they walked in a comfortable silence through a gently falling snow.

"I'm sorry I was rude earlier," Fallon said, breaking the silence.

"You weren't rude."

"Yeah, I was...when I told you I didn't want to talk about my personal reasons for leaving Pittsburgh."

"Oh that, that's OK." Eric squeezed his arm.

"I *will* tell you."

"When you're ready."

"Right."

Eric slowed his steps. "Here we are—told you it wasn't far. Like to come up?"

Fallon hesitated. This was the moment he had been both anticipating with excitement, and at the same time, dreading. He would have been disappointed had Eric not asked him, but what was expected of him if he accepted? It had been so long since he'd been in this position. In fact, he'd never been in this position. All those years with Martin—he'd been out of the loop for so long.

Eric was looking at him expectantly, hopefully. How could he turn him down? What the hell. He could go up, surely. It didn't mean anything was going to happen. Just a continuation of their conversation—a goodnight kiss and a promise to call. No harm in any of that. So why was he so damned nervous?

"I promise I won't tie you to the bed and keep you captive for months on end," Eric laughed lightly, as if he felt Fallon's reticence.

Fallon brushed a few snowflakes from Eric's light brown hair. "Then I'm not coming," he said, his grin belying the apprehension he felt.

"C'mon." Eric took his hand and led him up the steps. The apartment was small, with a comfortable lived in feeling. Fallon looked around at the overstuffed couch, the pile of magazines on the coffee table, the tasteful lithographic prints on one wall.

"Nice," he said quietly, comparing it with his own Spartan-like quarters he had never been interested in sufficiently to furnish properly. "It feels like home."

"I like it," Eric replied. "Here, take off your coat. Like some coffee?"

"Coffee sounds great." He followed Eric into the tiny kitchen and watched as he prepared the coffee. He found himself smiling as he admired the easy, deft movements of the young man.

"What?" Eric asked, noticing Fallon's smile.

"You look…nice."

"You use that word a lot."

"Only when it's warranted."

Eric stepped closer. "You should smile more," he murmured. "It totally turns me on." He put his arms around Fallon's neck and kissed him firmly on the mouth. Fallon jerked back in surprise. "Wait…" he gasped awkwardly, but

Eric did not release him. Instead, he kissed him again, this time forcing Fallon's lips apart, his tongue probing the inside of his mouth. Fallon could feel the blood drumming inside his head. He gasped as he felt every fiber of his body come alive with sensual desire. Roughly, he pulled Eric into his embrace, pressing himself hard against the other man's willing body.

Their kiss deepened. Time seemed to stand still. They remained locked in each other's arms, their mouths demanding more of each other. The scorching heat of their passion threatened to consume them. At last they broke apart, panting and breathing heavily.

"Wow, Detective. Where did you learn to kiss like that? Eric asked, shakily.

Fallon smiled but could not speak. He knew he had no words to express how he felt at that moment. Instead, he touched Eric's face gently with his lips and sighed happily. Eric's fingers were working at undoing Fallon's shirt buttons. He slipped his hands inside the shirt and caressed the smooth skin that covered Fallon's muscular torso. They undressed each other, standing there in the kitchen, their clothes strewn haphazardly on the floor. Eric sank to his knees, taking Fallon's erection in his mouth.

He should stop it now, Fallon thought, before they reached the point of no return. He should leave, before what was happening became too powerful for him to resist—but it was already too late. The fates had determined that he should be with this man, and he felt powerless to resist. His body arched with ecstasy as Eric's lips and tongue brought him close to the brink.

"Not yet." Gently, he pulled Eric upright and held him close against his body. With a sensual smile, Eric took his hand and led him to the bedroom.

"We have all night," he said softly as he pulled Fallon down onto the bed.

CHAPTER 13

At nine thirty the following morning, Fallon called Jeff and asked if he could meet at him somewhere else other than the apartment.

"Sure," Jeff replied. "Where do you have in mind?"

"There's a coffee shop called Katie's not far from Andrew's apartment. He can probably tell you how to get there. Say around ten?"

"You got it. I know where it is. Peter and I had bagels there yesterday."

"See you there, then."

Fallon was already seated at a table when Jeff showed up slightly before ten. He looked up as Jeff entered.

"I ordered you some coffee. Like a bagel or something?"

"No, the coffee's fine," Jeff replied, noting that Fallon looked a little tired. "Rough night?"

"You could say that." A smile creased the corner of Fallon's mouth. "Jeff, I appreciate you meeting me here. I'm in a bit of a bind, what with Bransky being such a jerk. I don't mind him not being around anymore. In fact, I prefer it, but it does pose its problems."

"Well, I'd be glad to help you out, like I said."

"Good. I don't think I have to remind you this has to be totally between you and me." Jeff nodded his understanding and Fallon continued. "Here's what I got so far. I picked up a copy of the forensic report on my way over here. Something interesting has shown up. There were two blood types at the scene. On Kennedy's body and from the sample taken from the carpet."

"He must have wounded his attacker," Jeff suggested.

"That's the most likely reason," Fallon agreed. "He'd also had sex just prior to his death."

"So what if he'd hired a hustler? I'm presuming he had sex with a guy here, of course—and they fought over money or some kind of sex act the hustler wasn't into."

"That's possible. From what I understand, Kennedy was pretty promiscuous."

"I'd say that was an understatement."

"Okay, but the report doesn't mention anything about signs of a struggle. No hair or skin under Kennedy's fingernails. He must have been taken by surprise."

"But how did someone else's blood get on his body, if there was no struggle?"

The two men were silent for a moment as they both thought over the possibilities. An idea suddenly occurred to Jeff, and he voiced it carefully.

"Is it possible that there might just have been a third party in all of this?"

"Go on."

"Let's suppose Kennedy had someone over to have sex with—a hustler, a lover—someone…and the killer was watching or walked in on them, and they all got into a fight."

"Then there *would* be signs of a struggle," Fallon said. "And, if someone else killed both Kennedy and whoever he was with, where's the other body?"

"Right—and the doorman would surely notice someone trying to sneak a dead body out the door!"

"*If* he came out through the lobby, which is kind of unlikely." Fallon looked at Jeff thoughtfully. "Maybe we should check and see if the building has back door access that the residents can use. In fact, let's do that. We can take another look at the apartment too, at the same time. You should visit the scene of the crime. It might just help get you even more inspired."

Morgan's apartment was still sealed with police tape, but there were no longer any police officers on duty. Jeff and Nick stood in the master bedroom and looked around them. The large bloodstain on the white rug was the only sign that anything violent had taken place in the room. The murder weapon—the bronze horse sculpture, had been removed for evidence.

"We should have brought Peter here."

Fallon looked at Jeff, surprised. "Why?"

"Peter's extremely psychic," Jeff explained. "Has been ever since he came out of his coma over two years ago. He's helped me a couple of times on cases with his 'feelings' as he calls them"

"Uh huh," Fallon muttered.

"I'm serious, Nick. You don't know the story. His lover was murdered, and Peter was in a coma for nearly three years as a result of the beating he took."

Fallon stared at Jeff for a long moment. "I had no idea," he said finally. "That's a tough break."

"Yeah, it was. But, here's the thing. Ever since he came out of the coma, he's been susceptible to these, uh…psychic kinds of feelings when someone close to him is in danger."

"Wow, you really believe this?"

"Yes, I do. I didn't before, but it's hard to discredit the evidence of your own eyes."

"Well…" Fallon remained skeptical. "I know the department sometimes works with psychics on cases, but I've never had any of that kind of help. Blind luck, sometimes, but never any ghosties telling me what to do!"

"Okay, forget it." Jeff turned away, impatiently. "Let's check out the other exits to this place."

"I didn't mean to piss you off," Fallon apologized, as they rode the elevator back down to the lobby. "I'm just not into that kind of thing."

"Nick, like I said, I wasn't either. Seeing is believing, as they say."

They walked into the lobby and approached the doorman's station.

"Hey Henry," Fallon asked the doorman. "Is there another way in or out round here?"

"Not on this floor, Detective—you have to take the elevator to the basement. There's a door to the alley down there."

"What if there's a fire?" Jeff asked.

"Well, there's an emergency stairwell that goes all the way down there too. See, there's the door to it at the other end of the lobby."

"Thanks Henry." Fallon walked towards the unmarked door. "Let's take a look, Jeff." They ran down the two flights of stairs and found themselves in the basement of the building.

"There's the exit," Jeff said, pointing. He pushed the door release, and it opened up into the back alley.

"So," Fallon murmured. "Someone could have carried a body down here, using the stairs—and got out unseen."

"Only if that someone knew about this exit. It would have to be somebody familiar with the building."

"Or someone who was *told* about this exit in advance."

"Well, what if Jeremy used this as the way in and out for some of his visitors? It would keep Henry, or whoever was on duty at the time, unaware of what was going on all the time."

"That's also a possibility." Fallon smiled at Jeff. "I knew this was a good idea—asking you for you insight. Too bad you don't live in New York. I could use a good partner."

"I have to admit I'm enjoying this. Private investigation in Laguna is mostly divorce and insurance claims."

"Well, if you ever need a change, you could move here…"

Jeff laughed shortly. "Peter would have a fit. Especially now as Andrew and David are planning on moving back to California."

Fallon frowned. "They are?"

"Yeah. David told us last night he's handing in his notice. Once this case is wrapped up they'll be on their way."

"Too bad. I like those guys."

"Hey, if you ever come to California…"

"Nah, not likely." Fallon looked around the basement impatiently as he spoke. "Not with the shitty time off we get. I've had more vacations canceled since I joined the force. You can never plan very much ahead." He started climbing the stairs back to the lobby floor. "We've seen enough here. Let's go talk to Henry some more."

Jeff followed him, bemused by Fallon's change of tone. A lonely guy, he thought, and not one to make his true feelings show. He wondered if there was anyone in Fallon's life. They entered the lobby area and walked over to the security desk. Henry was not there. He had been replaced by a young man who sat, feet up on the desk, reading a magazine.

"Where's Henry?" Fallon asked without ceremony.

"Takin' his lunch break."

"You his relief?"

"Sometimes. I generally work the night shift, but today Bill called in sick, so they asked me to fill in."

"Bill?"

"He's the one who works the break schedule. Who're you guys?"

Fallon flashed his badge briefly. "Detective Fallon, NYPD. This is my partner, Detective Stevens. We're investigating the homicide in apartment 9D."

The young man pulled himself up in his chair and looked sadly at Fallon. "Oh yeah—Mr. Kennedy. That was terrible."

"You knew him?"

"Yeah…only 'cos he was real friendly every time he went in and out. He'd stop and shoot the breeze sometimes, you know. Real nice guy."

Fallon gave Jeff a sharp look, then turned back to the young security guard. "What's your name?"

"Brad. Brad Schenk."

"Did Mr. Kennedy ever invite you up to his apartment, Brad?"

"As a matter of fact, he did. A couple of times." Brad smiled innocently. He had the fresh wholesome look of a Midwest farm-boy about him. "But, I had to tell him that just wasn't allowed. I'd be fired if it was found out I'd been up there during work hours."

"So you never went up to the apartment?"

"No sir!"

"Why do you think he invited you?" Jeff asked.

"Well, like I said—he was a really nice guy. Just to be friendly. Said he and his wife liked to have company."

"Did they have a lot of company?"

"Oh yeah. They had dinner parties and the like. They'd always call down and tell me how many couples to expect."

"Did Mr. Kennedy ever entertain on his own?"

"Not really. Anytime he was home alone, I never had anyone on my list. Oh wait…once or twice someone would show up, and I'd call to see if it was OK to send them up, and he'd say, yeah."

"Were these callers male or female?"

"Both times it was a guy."

"Thanks Brad, you've been very helpful." Fallon gave Jeff a nod and together, they walked toward the exit. Outside, the wintry sunshine was struggling, and failing to make itself visible through a steel gray sky.

"Okay, Jeff. We've ascertained that Kennedy could have visitors when he wanted without the security guy knowing. They could come in, unseen, through the basement and up the elevator and out the same way."

"Right. And obviously the guys on duty were not at all suspicious of any callers Jeremy might have—he was such a nice guy!"

Fallon frowned. "How the hell could Morgan Kennedy not have known what was going on?"

"But she had to know, Nick. She knew he'd been having an affair with this Kevin guy—the one in the car crash. Surely, she must have guessed it didn't stop there?"

"According to her, none of that happened."

"That line sounds more hollow every time I hear it." Jeff shivered slightly as the cold air seeped through his wool coat.

Fallon held out his hand. "I've taken up enough of your time. All this has given me a lot to think about. I need to talk to my boss and bring him up to date. Can I call on you again for help?"

"Of course," Jeff said, as they shook hands. "Like I said, I'm enjoying this."

"Great. I'll be in touch." He paused, then looked gravely at Jeff. "I'm real sorry to hear Peter's story. It's something I can relate to, in a way..." He broke off and looked away quickly, clearing his throat.

"Something you want to talk about?

"Maybe some other time." Fallon's voice took on a gruff edge. "Tell the guys I said 'Hi.'"

Jeff stood for a moment watching as Fallon strode off, then he turned and headed back to the apartment.

* * *

"So what do you have so far?" Fitzgerald asked Fallon as he signaled for him to close the office door.

"Forensics came up with two different blood types at the scene, for starters." Fallon laid his report on Fitzgerald's desk. "Funny thing, there's no sign of a struggle. There's another person's blood on Kennedy's body and on the floor, but no sign that they were engaged in a fight."

"Hmm." Fitzgerald cupped his hands under his chin. "What do you think happened there, then?"

"I think it's possible someone else killed Kennedy—and whoever was with him at the time."

"But they'd have to dispose of the other body."

"Right. I checked out the building. There's a basement door out to the alley at back."

"Okay, but then the perp would still have to lug the body some ways to get rid of it. We haven't found any corpses in that alley have we?"

"No," Fallon laughed. "But what if the perp had all this planned out? What if he'd parked his car in the alley so he wouldn't been seen, come in through the basement door, and went out the same way, carrying the body."

"Can the door be accessed from the outside?"

"No."

"Then how could he get in? Unless..."

"Someone let him in."

"So all this could have been premeditated? Someone set all this up?" Fitzgerald looked at Fallon skeptically. "Seems a bit far-fetched."

"That's what I don't know as yet," Fallon conceded. "There're too many holes in all of this so far, but I think I'm on the right track. If I could only find who Kennedy had with him that night…"

"What about Andrew Connor? If the wife's right about him and her husband having an affair…"

Fallon looked steadily at Fitzgerald. "Chief, you can kick me all round this office if I'm wrong, but I'll bet just about anything that, other than finding the body, Andrew Connor had nothing to do with Kennedy's murder."

Fitzgerald nodded, a wry smile on his face. "Well, keep on it Nick, and keep me informed."

"You got it." Fallon stood up to leave.

"By the way…" Fitzgerald began slowly, and Fallon waited for him to continue. "Bransky's been making noises about how no one will want to work with you. I've told him to cut it out, but…"

"Don't worry about it. Bob's all hot air and besides, he's not that highly thought of out there."

"Okay, Nick. I know you can handle it. I could get one of the officers to give you a hand, if you need it."

"I'm fine—really." He couldn't tell Fitzgerald about Stevens being his unofficial partner just yet…maybe when they finally cracked the case. "Is that all, Chief?"

"That's it. Good luck, Nick."

"Thanks." He left Fitzgerald's office, and could hear his phone ringing as he walked down the hall. He quickened his pace and picked up the phone hurriedly.

"Fallon here."

"It's Eric, Nick." The now familiar voice brought a small smile to Fallon's lips.

"Eric. Good to hear your voice."

"Yours too." Eric sounded genuinely pleased. "How's your day going so far?"

"It's going. Still working on the Kennedy case."

"That's why I called, actually."

"It is?" Fallon said, surprised.

"Yeah. This may be nothing, but a friend of mine's roommate has disappeared. Nathan, my friend, went home for Christmas. He just got back last night and it looks like Chris, his roomie, hasn't been in the apartment for days. Nathan's really worried. He asked me to check with the hospitals, which I've done, but I've found nothing. So I thought maybe you could check your missing person's database."

"Sure, I'd be happy to. But…what has this to do with the Kennedy homicide?"

"Well, like I said, this may be nothing—at least, I'm hoping it's nothing, but before Nathan left to go home, Chris told him he was going over to Jeremy Kennedy's apartment."

"What?" Fallon blurted. "You're sure about that?"

"Totally. Nathan wasn't happy about it. He knew Jeremy's reputation like I did, but Chris wouldn't be talked out of it. He said he really liked the guy and that Nathan was just jealous. They had a fight about it, and Nathan ended up telling him to go do as he pleased, if you know what I mean."

"How old is Chris?"

"About twenty-six, I think."

"And his last name?"

"Swenson. He's about my height, five eleven, brown hair…green eyes, I think, yeah green, good looking guy, good physique. Works out quite a bit."

"That how he met Kennedy?"

"Probably. Like I told you, Jeremy used that gym as his personal pick up palace."

"Uh huh," Fallon muttered, as he entered the facts Eric had just given him into his computer. His finger hit the 'search' button and he sat back to await the results.

"Nick?" Eric sounded worried. "You don't think Chris could have killed Jeremy Kennedy, do you?"

"Hardly…" Fallon paused as the image of a young man's face appeared on his screen. The grainy photograph had been taken in the morgue. "Are you a close friend of Chris's, Eric?"

"Not really. I don't know him that well. Just as Nathan's room mate."

"Okay, because this is bad, Eric." Fallon's eyes scanned the report quickly "Someone, matching the description you just gave, was taken out of the East River two days ago. Cause of death was not drowning. He'd been shot in the back of the head."

"Oh my God," Eric gasped

"Eric, this is very important. If Chris turns out to be the person Kennedy had in his apartment, you've probably saved me hours, maybe days of work trying to find out who the second person in the room was."

"You *knew* he was there?"

"No, I didn't, but forensics came up with something which made me think that a third party might be involved. I'm going down to the morgue to check on what they've got on Swenson. Do you think your friend, Nathan, would be up to identifying the body?

"I'll ask him." Eric's reply was subdued.

"Give him my cell number and have him call me. If he can meet me at the City morgue, that would be good." He was just about to put the phone down when he stopped and asked, "Eric? You OK?"

"Yeah, Ill be fine. It's poor Nathan. He's going to be really upset. I think he liked Chris more than he let on."

"It's a tough break," Fallon muttered. "I'll call you later, Eric."

"Thanks Nick. Talk to you later."

Fallon put the phone down wishing he could have comforted Eric some more. He was never very good at expressing his feelings like some other people.

Like Eric, for instance.

As Fallon drove slowly through downtown toward the City morgue, he found himself reliving those moments of the previous night, when Eric had shown him affection, mixed with a tenderness and passion he had not experienced in many years. Their lovemaking had been simple and straightforward—mostly kissing, touching and exploring, but it had made Fallon very aware of just what was missing in his life. That closeness, that caring, that intimacy. They had fallen asleep in each other's arms, and Fallon had dreamed of Martin and the last time they had made love.

What a strange thing to dream about, he thought—locked in the arms of another man. Or was it because of where he was that the dream had come to him? At least the dream had not included the last fight they'd had.

The day of the accident, when they had bickered over the fact that Martin had accepted an invitation to a weekend party without first consulting him. He had driven Martin to the airport in silence, and had not given him even a cursory hug before he had disappeared into the terminal—never to return. The private plane his company had charted so that he could attend an emergency board meeting in Atlanta, had gone down a half hour after take off. All on board were killed.

Fallon's life almost came to a sudden stop too. Jim and Donna were caring and compassionate, but nothing could fill the void that loomed ahead no matter where he turned. Over and over, he had cursed himself for letting Martin get on that plane without telling him he loved him. To let a stupid quarrel get in the way of how they really felt for each other. Even now, Fallon's fist punched the steering wheel as he remembered. Three years had done nothing to soften the guilt he still felt. Three years without ever touching another man.

Till last night, with Eric.

The sound of a car horn startled him from his reverie. The lights had turned green and he hadn't noticed. He lifted his hand in apology and accelerated through the intersection.

The clerk at the City morgue looked at Fallon's badge without expression. "How can I help you?" he asked, drumming his fingers on the keyboard of his computer.

"You have a John Doe here. Here's the particulars and the ID number."

"Ah yes, here he is. Fished out of the East River two nights ago. Not a Merry Christmas for him!"

"What did the coroner find?" Fallon ignored the clerk's attempt at levity.

"Let's have a look-see. Ah yes, severe trauma to the back of the skull, caused by a single gun shot from a small caliber handgun. Most evidence washed away of course, but a small sample taken from his fingernails showed traces of carpet fibers. Conclusion is, he'd been killed on dry land, then dumped in the river."

"Was he wearing clothes?"

"Let's see. Ah yes…" The clerk's repetition of that phrase was getting on Fallon's nerves but he said nothing as the clerk continued, "Jeans and a white shirt. Wallet and ID were gone. No money. No shoes or socks. No watch or any other jewelry. Suspected mugging and robbery."

"Had he had sex just prior to his death?"

"Let's see…"

Fallon gritted his teeth.

"Ah yes, evidence of seminal discharge indicates he'd had sexual intercourse…"

"Who's in charge of the case?" Fallon interrupted.

"Let's see. Ah yes. Detectives Copeland and Bransky."

Fallon groaned inwardly. He'd have to deal with that idiot again. "*Damn*," he muttered.

"Something wrong, Detective?" The clerk smirked at him.

"Wrong? Let's see. Ah yes, just about everything." He grimaced as his cell phone rang. He turned away from the desk to answer it. "Fallon here."

"Nick, it's Eric. I'm on my way over with Nathan. He wanted me to come with him. Is that OK?"

"That's fine. I'll wait for you here." He looked at the clerk. "I think we may have a name for your John Doe. I have someone coming over to ID the body."

Fallon sat on a bench outside the morgue and waited for Eric and Nathan to show up. His heart quickened just a little when he looked up and saw Eric and his friend approach the entrance.

"Nick, Hi." Eric smiled gravely as they shook hands and their eyes held for just a beat longer, then Eric turned to his friend. "Nick, this is my buddy Nathan." Fallon shook hands with the young man who had obviously been crying. He was about Eric's age, slightly taller, with sandy blond hair and a slender physique. Attractive in a very vulnerable way.

"Hello Nathan." Nick was gentle. "Sorry, this isn't going to be easy for you."

"I'll be all right," Nathan replied, without conviction. "I just can't believe it can be him."

They walked into the reception area; Eric holding Nathan's arm tightly as if he was afraid his friend might fall over. The clerk opened the doors to the morgue and Nathan gasped at the sight of rows and rows of refrigerated cabinets that lined the walls.

"I can't believe this. I just can't believe this," he kept saying. He was visibly trembling as the attendant pulled open one of the cabinets, and the platform on which a corpse lay slid into view. Tears squeezed out from his closed eyes and Eric took his arm to support him.

"Is this Christopher Swenson?" Fallon asked Nathan, who let out a long shuddering sigh as he finally looked on the body of his dead friend.

"Oh, my God," he wailed. "It *is* Chris…it is!" He fell into Eric's arms, sobbing grievously, and the clerk gave Fallon a raised eyebrow glance, which he ignored. He watched as Eric led Nathan away.

"I'll get the information you need so you can contact his parents," Fallon told the clerk, who merely nodded.

But Nathan was unable to give Fallon any of the information he needed. "I don't think he had any family," he said between sobs. "His mother raised him alone, and she died a couple of years ago. That's when he came to New York. He never mentioned any brothers or sisters or anything like that."

Fallon looked at Eric over the top of Nathan's head and gave him a sympathetic smile. His new friend was going to have his hands full for the next few days.

"Eric, I'll be here if you need me."

CHAPTER 14

Morgan snapped shut the book she had been reading and nervously paced the floor. Today would be the first time she had left the hotel room since she had arrived back in the city. Today was Jeremy's funeral, and of course she had to attend. She would have to endure the looks and whispers of the other attendees, some of whom used to be her friends.

Strange, she thought bitterly, how not one of them had called her since the news of Jeremy's death. Were they ever really her friends? Were they Jeremy's friends? Or was it just her social standing and wealth that had attracted them? Were they too embarrassed now to call her, and to simply sympathize over her loss?

"God, what bastards," she muttered viciously. But the people she knew automatically veered away from death, particularly murder. Especially one as lurid as Jeremy's.

"Damn him!"

He had ruined her life. For the second time Morgan found herself excluded from the social circle she needed to thrive. First, after Kevin's death—and now after Jeremy's.

A knock at the door heralded the arrival of her parents. They had insisted on coming to the funeral.

"Only for your sake sweetheart," her father had told her. "As far as I'm concerned Jeremy got what he deserved." Her mother was less vocal, but Morgan could tell the scent of scandal truly offended her and her patrician upbringing.

Morgan sighed as she opened the door to let her parents in. Morgan's father, Joseph File, was a tall man with silver gray hair and a military bearing. He hugged his daughter as he entered, but her mother merely patted her arm as she passed into the hotel suite. Morgan knew her mother had not quite forgiven her outburst on Christmas Eve. All of that seemed so long ago, and so unimportant in the face of what she now had to endure.

"I thought we'd have a drink before we go," Morgan said, looking at her father.

"Good idea," he agreed. "Keep the cold out. I'll have a brandy."

"Mother?"

"You two go ahead, if you must." Her mother looked at them with disapproval. "I don't wish to have anything, thank you."

Morgan shrugged and poured two large brandies. She handed one to her father.

"Hardly the time for a toast, I suppose. Absent friends, perhaps?"

"Morgan, really!" her mother snapped.

"Oh, she's just trying to keep her spirits up, Margaret." Her father can quickly to his daughter's defense. He knocked back his brandy. "Cut the gal some slack, will you?"

Margaret was having none of it. "It's cutting the slack that's brought us to this. If Morgan had been a little more selective in her choice of a husband, we wouldn't be in the middle of this…this unpleasantness."

"Don't talk like I'm not in the room, Mother, if you don't mind. I didn't ask you to come today. I would have preferred to have done this alone!"

"Now, now," her father interrupted. "I can't have my two best girls at odds. Not today, or any day, for that matter. Come on now. Let's not cast blame anywhere."

Margaret sniffed. "The blame will lie where it should."

"Let's go." Morgan threw back the rest of her brandy and started to put on her coat. "Let's get this charade over with."

Margaret glared at her and her father shook his head wearily. This would not go down as one of his better days!

"Andrew…" David looked worried as he watched his partner pull on a freshly laundered shirt. "You're not really thinking of going to the funeral, are you?"

"As a matter of fact, yes I am."

"But *why*? You didn't even like the guy."

"I know, but Morgan will be there. I thought it would give me a chance to talk to her. I've tried calling, but she puts the phone down when she knows it's me."

"All the more reason to stay away," David advised. "If she really wanted to talk to you, she wouldn't be acting like such a bitch."

"David, she thinks I was having an affair with her husband!"

"But you told her you weren't. If she were really your friend, she would give some credence to your side of the story. How the hell could she believe that louse, when she knows he'd lied to her for years?"

"I don't know," Andrew sighed, looking miserably at him. "I just hate the way our friendship has ended. I'm really fond of her, you know?"

David put his arms around him and kissed his cheek. "I know you are sweetie, but this is not a good idea. You, going to the funeral I mean."

"I'll just sit at the back and try to catch her eye. If she ignores me, I won't go any further. I promise."

"Then, I'm going with you."

"Oh, David. You'll hate it."

"Yes, I will. But I'm not having you go alone. You go, I go!"

"I love you," Andrew said, hugging David tightly.

Jeff was in bed, listening to Peter crooning in the shower, when his cell phone rang.

"This is Jeff Stevens."

"Hey Jeff, it's Nick. What're your plans for today?"

"Nothing much, at the moment. What's up?"

"Well, it's Jeremy Kennedy's funeral today. I thought I'd make a back seat appearance. Check out who shows up. Some interesting people can show at funerals."

"You mean like the murderer, perhaps?" Jeff asked wryly.

"It's been known to happen. Like to join me?"

"Can't think of anything I'd rather not do," Jeff laughed. "But count me in."

"I know it's not the greatest invitation you could have while you're on vacation, but I'd appreciate if my partner could help me out."

"Your *unofficial* partner, you mean. And, as I am unofficial, I may have to bring a friend along."

"You mean Peter."

"Right. There's no way he'd be left out of this."

"Okay. Just let him know we have to be low key."

"Oh, he can be great at that," Jeff chuckled.

"All right. I'll pick you guys up in about an hour."

"See you then." Jeff turned off his cell phone and lay back on his pillow.

"Who was that?" Peter asked, appearing in the bathroom doorway, toweling himself off.

"Nick Fallon. He wants to take us out."

"You're kidding." Peter jumped on the bed and pressed his still damp body against Jeff's. "Where to?"

Jeff grinned. "A funeral."

The small chapel the funeral home had suggested for Jeremy's service was less than half full when the five men entered together and sat in the back row. Jeff had called Fallon back when he found out Andrew and David had also planned on going and had suggested they all go together. Whether Fallon had minded or not he had not said, but agreed to pick them up and drive them to the chapel.

"Not much of a turn out," Peter whispered to Andrew as they sat down.

Andrew nodded, then whispered back, "That must be Jeremy's brother down at the front." He pointed out a young man sitting in the front row on the opposite side from Morgan and her parents. He was alone.

"Must have left the wife and kids at home."

"Not many friends here," Peter observed.

Andrew grunted, but did not reply. His eyes were fixed on the back of Morgan's head as though willing her to turn round and acknowledge his presence. David sat next to him, his arm lightly resting protectively on his shoulders.

Jeff and Nick sat silently side by side watching as one or two more people drifted in and took seats far from the family members. Two familiar faces suddenly appeared. Bob from David's office and his partner, Michael. They smiled a greeting and sat down in the row in front of them.

"Didn't think we'd see you guys here," David whispered.

"It was Bob's idea," Michael said, with a grimace. Bob was about to say something when the service began, and everyone fell silent as the minister started intoning his sermon.

"Who're those guys?" Fallon said into Jeff's ear, indicating Bob and Michael.

"One of them works with David. The other is his lover."

"They friends of the Kennedy's?"

"Not close, but they knew about Jeremy's pick up habits."

Just then, the minister introduced Jeremy's brother who stood up to give the eulogy. Daniel Kennedy was every bit as tall and imposing as his brother had been, but with a gentler air. He spoke in a quiet, controlled manner, and Peter found himself listening intently to the grief of a loving brother, who was totally unaware of his sibling's devious side. He and Andrew exchanged glances as Daniel drew a picture of a caring and benevolent brother, husband and uncle.

What on earth can be going through Morgan's mind listening to this? Andrew wondered.

An uneasy silence fell on the assembly as Daniel Kennedy resumed his seat. The minister cleared his throat and concluded the service. The pallbearers took their places by the casket and eased it slowly up the center aisle, followed by his brother, Morgan and her parents. Morgan looked neither left nor right as she walked stiffly behind the casket. She gazed stonily in front of her, declining to catch anyone's eye as she left the chapel. The graveside service was to be family only, and Andrew watched dejectedly as Morgan climbed into her parent's limo and drove away.

Fallon stood to one side watching everyone leaving the chapel. Of the dozen or so people in attendance no one seemed especially interesting to him.

"I thought the brother seemed very nice," Bob was saying to David and Andrew.

"I bet Morgan was grinding her teeth all through that eulogy," Michael remarked, without a trace of a smile..

Andrew nodded. "It was like he was talking about a totally different person. Someone I would like to have known."

"They were obviously very close," Peter remarked. "Jeremy must have gone to great lengths to ensure his brother never knew about his 'other life'."

Jeff walked over to where Fallon stood. "So, what do you think?"

"I think I wasted your time—but to bring you up to date, I got a tip that a young guy, who had a date with Kennedy on the night he was murdered, turned up dead in the East River a few days ago. I've got a positive ID on him."

"Wow! That's a bit of a break for you, isn't it?"

"It could be. Only problem is, Bob is investigating that case and he won't be helpful about passing on any information he gets. He's regarding it as a mugging and robbery."

Jeff looked at Fallon intently. "Of course, he wouldn't know the guy was killed in the Kennedy's apartment. Anything unusual about the body? Had he been tied up or anything?"

"No, he'd been shot once in the back of the head. Small caliber gun. Any traces of Kennedy's blood were washed off in the river."

"So there's nothing to connect him to the Kennedy murder. How do you know he had a date with Jeremy?"

"A…a friend of mine called me. Someone he knows roomed with the dead kid and wanted him to check with the hospitals."

"Your friend's a doctor?"

"No, a paramedic. Anyway he couldn't find out anything, so he called me asking me to check out our missing persons list."

"So what's your next move?" Jeff asked.

"I'm going to have to talk to the Chief. Let him know there's a connection between these two killings. I'm going to need access to the investigation."

"Right. Well, if I can be of any more help…"

"Oh, don't worry." Fallon allowed himself a smile. "You'll be hearing from me." He glanced over to where the rest of their group was still engaged in conversation. "We'd better break up that coffee clutch so I can drive you back."

When they joined the friends, Andrew introduced Fallon to Bob and Michael. "We're having a little get-together on New Year's Eve, Nick. Would you like to join us?"

For a moment Fallon hesitated, then he nodded. "That would be great." He looked a little uncomfortable for a moment, then he asked, "Uh, would it be all right if I brought a friend? I mean, I'm not sure if he's available, but if he is, I'd like you guys to meet him."

"Of course," David said. "It's a date, then. Say around 10 o'clock? We can all see the New Year in together."

Bob and Michael said their goodbyes and walked off to their car.

"Nick…" Andrew looked at Fallon quizzically. "Would it be a great inconvenience to ask you to stop at the cemetery? I'd still like to see if I could talk to Morgan today."

"Andrew…" David looked at him with an exasperated expression..

"I know I'm being obsessive, David. I just want to clear this up between her and me."

"Now is not the time, Andrew." Peter took his arm. "She's not in any mood to listen to reason today. Why don't you wait a couple of days, then call her."

Andrew looked at his friend for a moment, then sighed with resignation. "I guess you're right. Let's go home, then."

"Let's eat!" Jeff exclaimed. "I'm starving. C'mon, I'll treat."

"I'll drop you guys off," Fallon said. "I have to get back to work."

As they drove through the heavy afternoon traffic in Manhattan, Peter decided to take Andrew's mind off the gloomy day by lightening the atmosphere a little. He winked at Andrew sitting beside him, then tapped Fallon on the shoulder. "So who's the mystery friend we're going to meet New Year's Eve, Nick?"

Surprised, Fallon looked at him through the rear view mirror. "Uh, someone I met Christmas Day…at a party…at a friends' apartment."

"He's a paramedic," Jeff said.

"How do you know?" Peter asked, surprised.

Jeff grinned at him. "I'm a private eye, that's how."

"He's guessing," Fallon chuckled.

"But I'm right—right?"

"Uh huh."

"I'm impressed," Andrew said, getting into the conversation. "A cop and a paramedic—there's a fantasy for you."

"Andrew!" David exclaimed. "What's got into you? It's usually Peter who says that kind of thing."

Peter gasped with mock affront. "David, how could you be so mean to me? Are you suggesting that I'm a bad influence on Andrew?"

David laughed. "Well, he's got a lot pushier since he met you."

"I shall ignore that." Peter looked at him with disdain.

Andrew giggled. "Me too. So Nick, tell us about this paramedic. Does he have a name?"

Fallon colored slightly and shook his head. It had been a long time since he'd been in the middle of this kind of banter, and he wasn't quite sure how to handle it. He liked these guys very much and wanted to be a part of their easy-going camaraderie. He knew Eric would fit in just fine, but it wasn't easy for him to let his guard down so soon.

"Uh…yeah, his name is Eric and he's uh…he's very nice," he managed at last, his voice sounding strange to his own ears.

"That's it?" Andrew looked at him, the teasing smile still on his face. "Just nice?"

"Well, you'll meet him in a couple of days. So then, you can see for yourself."

"Tell him to wear his uniform."

"*Andrew*," David yelled. "Just wait till I get you home!"

Fallon laughed out loud. "You know, that isn't such a bad idea. Only thing is, he looks even better out of it."

Andrew fell silent, and the other guys chuckled quietly as they imagined where his mind had just gone.

Later, when he returned to the station, Fallon tapped on Fitzgerald's office door.

"Come in Nick. Got something new?"

"I think so. A young guy's body was taken out of the river the other day. Name of Christopher Swenson. I got a tip he'd been with Jeremy Kennedy the night he was murdered."

"Yeah…?" Fitzgerald stared at Fallon intently.

"Swenson was shot in the back of the head, then dumped in the river."

"Sounds like there *was* a third party involved."

"Right." Fallon leaned forward in his chair. "Bransky and Copeland have the case. They're looking at it as a robbery motive. I need access to that investigation, and I'll need your help. Bob isn't likely to just hand anything over right now."

"Gotcha." Fitzgerald raised his considerable bulk from his chair and walked to the door. "Bransky, Copeland. My office, now."

"What's up, Chief?" Bransky asked as he and Copeland entered the office. He was unable to mask the look of dislike he threw Fallon's way.

"You're investigating the murder of a John Doe found in the river, right?"

"Right," Copeland answered.

"Anything on that yet?"

"Not really," Bransky said slowly. "Looks like a mugging that got lethal. Guy was robbed of everything except his shirt and pants. There were no witnesses and no one's come forward."

Copeland eyed Fallon cautiously. "Well, we haven't actually done much in the way of follow up. Bob here, seems to think it's open and shut robbery."

"Is that right?" Fitzgerald looked grim. "Have you talked to the coroner or the morgue since your preliminary investigation?"

"Uh, we was going to get on that today," Bransky muttered.

"Well, looks like Nick here saved you the trouble. He knows who your John Doe is, and possibly just where he was murdered."

"Shit!" Copeland mumbled under his breath.

Bransky glared at Fallon. "You could have come and told us, instead of running to the Chief behind our backs!"

"Cut it out Bob," Fitzgerald snapped. "I told Nick I wanted him to keep me informed on all aspects of the Kennedy case."

Bransky sniggered. "The Kennedy case? What the hell has this got to do with the Kennedy case?"

Fallon stared coolly back at Bransky. "I think the guy they took out of the river, his name is Chris Swenson by the way, was murdered in Kennedy's apartment, and then dumped in the river."

"*What*? What possible link is there between the two cases?"

"I got a tip," Fallon said.

"A tip? From who? I want to talk to whoever gave you that tip!"

"All you need to know, Bob, is that the body was positively I D 'd by a friend of his who said he'd had a date with Kennedy the night he was murdered."

"Nick, we'll need to get a statement from Swenson's friend," Fitzgerald said.

"I know that, Chief. I was hoping you'd reassign the case to me so I can do that."

Bransky stood up so suddenly he almost knocked his chair over. "No fucking way you're taking this case away from me and Copeland, here. We're in charge of this!"

"*I'm* in charge of it!" Fitzgerald snapped. "And I want you to handle this in a fair and professional way. I'm not taking you off the case, Bob, but you have to let Nick in on any new developments—right away!"

"Chief," Fallon moaned, standing up. "I know I can get more out of Swenson's friend…"

"Why?" Bransky interrupted, seething with rage. "Because he's a faggot too?"

Fallon went white with anger as he faced Bransky. "You stupid bigoted asshole…you haven't got the first idea how to handle this case, or any other I've seen you involved in. Your preconceived ideas and jaundiced views of human nature make you the worst kind of cop there is!"

"Why you f…" Bransky raised a ham like fist, but Fitzgerald stepped between them.

"Stop this now, both of you, or I'll suspend the pair of you!"

Copeland stood, his mouth open, at the scene in front of him.

"I'm sorry, Chief." Fallon stepped back, still shaking with anger.

"You *should* be sorry," Bransky yelled.

"I'm not apologizing to you, Bob." Fallon cast his ex-partner a contemptuous look.

"That's enough, both of you," Fitzgerald commanded. "Bob, you and Copeland get out of here for a minute. I'll call you back in when I want you."

"But, Chief!" Bransky spluttered. "I don't want him messin' in our investigation…"

"I said, out Bob…now!"

Fitzgerald sighed heavily as he watched Bransky slouch out of his office, closely followed by a speechless Copeland. "Sit down Nick." He waved to the chair in front of his desk and peered at Fallon keenly. "We have a problem here. I can't have my detectives at each other's throats."

"This I know," Fallon agreed. "But you saw what Bransky's like. He's an ignorant jerk!"

"That he is, Nick. I can't deny that. But if I take him off this case he would have every right to file a complaint, and you know he would. That won't get any of us what we want. I can direct him and Copeland to include you in anything they find out, and I'll help in any way I can. But that's it."

Fallon drew a deep breath. He knew that what Fitzgerald was saying was correct, and he hated the fact that he had just lost his temper in front of him.

"Again, Chief, I'm sorry I lost it there. I'm afraid Bransky just brings out the worst in me. He's so fucking heavy handed. I know he's going to scare the living daylights out of Chris Swenson's friend."

"Okay…" Fitzgerald shifted slightly in his chair. "I'll have the kid brought in here to make his statement and I'll sit in on it. That make you feel better?"

"A lot better. Thanks Chief."

"Right, so go solve the Kennedy murder," Fitzgerald said with a tight smile

Fallon returned the smile with one just as serious, then got up and left the office.

CHAPTER 15

Jeff was restless after they returned to the apartment. David had decided to go to his office and get some work done. Andrew and Peter were playing chess in the living room. Jeff had tried to settle down with a book, but his mind was working over time.

"Damn!" he muttered, throwing aside the book and pacing around the bedroom. He walked out into the living room and stood for a moment watching Andrew and Peter involved in their game.

"I'm going to take a walk."

Peter looked up at him and frowned. "Are you OK? Would you like some company?"

"No. You guys go on with your game. I just need to think a little. The fresh air might help." He bent and kissed the top of Peter's head and smiled at Andrew. "Won't be long."

Peter grinned at him. "Don't do anything I would."

Jeff didn't know why, but he knew he had to go back to the alley behind the Kennedy's apartment building. Ignoring the biting cold of the late afternoon, he quickly covered the few blocks that lay between the two apartments, and soon found himself in the deserted space outside the back door of the apartment building. Slowly, he began to make his way down the alley, his eyes sweeping the ground for any kind of clue. A couple of derelicts watched him with toothless grins as he approached them. He stopped and stared at them for a moment. Could they have seen anything unusual going on that night?

"Hi guys."

"Hi, yourself." One of them gave him a wary look. "You a cop?"

"You don't look like a cop," the other said, hunching himself into a tight ball as if to protect himself from attack.

"No, I'm not a cop. You guys spend a lot of time here?"

"As much as we can. It's our home away from home." They both cackled at this attempt at a joke. Jeff stared at the first derelict's feet. Incongruously, he was wearing a very new pair of light beige loafers.

"Nice shoes." Jeff crouched down on his haunches to get a good look at them.

"You wanna buy 'em?"

"I might. How much?"

"Twenty bucks?"

"Hey," the second man yelped. "You wanna buy a watch?"

"That depends. Where did you get it?"

"Right here!" He thumped his fist on the dumpster he was leaning against. "Where we found the shoes. The guy who was helping the drunk guy the other night threw everything in here. He must have been mad at him or something!"

"What else did he throw in there?"

"Oh, I dunno. Couple of other guys got in there along with us. They was laughin' about hittin' the jackpot, so I guess they found some money. Whatever, they wouldn't let us in on it…the bastards. So, you want the watch?"

"Let me see it." Jeff held out his hand.

"It's a good one. Worth at least a couple of hundred."

Jeff looked at the watch the derelict handed him. He turned it over and drew in a sharp breath as he read on the back…*For Chris, Happy 21st. Love, Mom.*

"I'll give you fifty, for the watch…and the shoes."

"We'll take it." The derelict's dirty hand was thrust in front of Jeff's face. Jeff handed over the money, then looked at the first man as he removed his shoes.

"Aren't you going to have cold feet?"

"Nah. I got my trusty old boots right here. Wouldn't throw these away. I reckoned those shoes weren't going to last very long anyway."

"Did either of you get a good look at the man who was helping his friend?"

"Not really," the first man said, pulling his boots on over filthy socks. "It was dark, the lights never work here."

"Did he have a car?"

"Yeah, but don't ask me what it was. I'm no good at that kind of thing."

Jeff looked at the other man. "What about you?"

"Nope. It was a dark color—black or dark green or something."

Jeff sighed, then stood up. It was too much to hope for that these men would be able to give him a viable description. They struggled to their feet, already planning to hit the nearest liquor store with their newfound wealth.

"Thanks guys," Jeff murmured as they scurried off. He looked at the watch he held in the palm of his hand, and read the inscription again…*For Chris, Happy 21st. Love, Mom.* He felt himself filled with a deep sadness for the young man who had owned it. He pulled Fallon's card from his wallet and quickly punched in the numbers on his cell phone. Fallon answered immediately.

"Hi, Nick. It's Jeff. I've got something here you'll want to see."

Fallon met him in the lobby of David and Andrew's apartment. Without a word, Jeff handed him the watch with the inscription facing up.

"Too late for prints, I'm afraid. Someone else has worn it for the last few days."

Fallon blew a low whistle threw his teeth as he read the inscription. "Where did you get this?"

Jeff related the story of his meeting with the two homeless men, then he produced the shoes from his coat pocket. "By themselves they didn't mean much. It was just strange to see them on that guy's feet. A homeless man wearing Gucci shoes was just wrong somehow."

Fallon smiled at the thought. "But the watch clinches it," he said. That definitely puts Swenson in Kennedy's apartment. We're ahead of forensics with this one. I was waiting for the results of Swenson's blood type matching the sample found in the apartment." He paused. "What about the guy putting him in the car? Did they get a look at him?"

"They say not. It was too dark. They couldn't even describe the car."

"Damn." Fallon frowned for a moment, then brightened. "But this is good, Jeff. Thank you. You sure you don't want to work with me?"

"I'm sure," Jeff chuckled. "You'd be living dangerously if you even breathed a word of that offer to Peter." He looked over Fallon's shoulder as the elevator door opened behind him. "Speak of the devil."

Peter and Andrew got out of the elevator and walked toward them with quizzical looks on their faces.

"Where are you guys going?" Jeff asked

Andrew smiled at them. "To the deli. We're getting some munchies for tomorrow night." He looked at Fallon. "Is your friend going to make it?"

"I don't know. I haven't had a chance to ask him yet," Fallon replied uneasily. Peter was looking at him as though he had just become an adversary.

"So," Peter said testily, looking now at Jeff. "Did you just bump into each other on your walk?"

"No. I found something I thought would be useful to Nick, so I called him and he met me here."

Fallon nodded. "Jeff's being a big help. What he found today gives me a lot to go on."

"That's terrific." Peter's tone was cool. "Okay, Andrew. Let's go shopping. Catch you later."

"Bye guys." Andrew gave Jeff a puzzled smile as Peter tugged his arm and pulled him toward the exit.

"Uh oh…" Fallon looked at Jeff worriedly. "I think Peter thinks I'm up to no good here."

Jeff chuckled. "Pay no attention. Peter just likes to ripple the surface sometimes. It's when he causes waves you have to watch out."

"Well, I don't want him to get the wrong idea."

"He won't. I'll make sure of that."

"I'd better get going," Fallon said, looking at the watch again. "I want to show this to the Chief before I have to hand it over to Bransky and Copeland."

"Good idea. Keep me informed, won't you?"

"You bet I will."

"And Nick, make sure you and your friend come over tomorrow night."

"You don't think Peter will mind?"

"That's why I said, 'You and your friend'…just kidding," he added, laughing at Fallon's worried expression.

"What did you make of that?" Peter asked Andrew as they walked to the corner deli.

"Make of what?"

"You know what…Jeff going for a walk, and meeting that cop."

"He told you how that happened. He called him because he'd found something he thought Jerry could use. I'm presuming in the Jeremy investigation." He gave Peter a sideways glance. "You're not jealous are you?"

"Of course not!" Peter snapped, tartly. "I just don't like the way he looks at Jeff sometimes. Like he'd jump him any minute."

"What? You're crazy. Hey, Jeff is a gorgeous looking guy. I'm sure there's lots of people who'd like to 'jump him' as you so eloquently put it. But I think Nick Fallon is not the type to go around stealing other people's boyfriends."

"Why do you say that? You hardly know him."

"Gay intuition. Don't you get the feeling that he's been really hurt by someone or something? I think he'd be really slow to make overtures to anyone. It would have to be someone really special."

"Like Jeff," Peter exclaimed.

"Oh, for heaven's sake Peter…" Andrew glared at him. "Don't forget Jeff would have a say in this too. And if anyone is crazier about you than that man, I want to meet him—and give him my condolences."

Peter stopped in his tracks. "Andrew! Do you think I'm that hard to get along with?"

Andrew looked at his friend's despondent expression and smiled as he took his arm, and they walked on again together. "No, I don't think that. You're my best friend, and you wouldn't be if you were hard to get along with."

"Thanks," Peter said, feeling mollified. "So you think I'm just being silly?"

"Totally silly, my friend. Hey, you're the psychic one. You should know Jeff would never dream of looking at anyone else. Besides Nick just got through telling us he's seeing someone 'very nice', as he put it."

"You're right. I should apologize to Nick for being rude back there."

"Oh, I'm sure Jeff has smoothed it all over by this time. Here's the deli. Damn, I forgot my list. Oh well, we'll just have to wing it."

Fallon grimaced with disappointment when he looked into Fitzgerald's office and found it empty. He knew by rights he should hand over the watch and shoes to Bransky and Copeland as soon as possible. It was their case after all, but Bransky would, of course, be resistant to anything Fallon brought to change his mind about Swenson's death being just the result of another unsolved robbery. He definitely needed the Chief to know about this first. He put the watch and the shoes in the bottom drawer of his desk and locked it. He looked across the hall to see if Bransky was in his office, but the room was empty.

"Good," he muttered. He could stall for the time being. He picked up the phone and dialed Eric's number.

"Hello?" Eric's voice was muffled.

"It's Nick. How are you?"

"Exhausted. I had to pull an all-nighter. One of the guy's kids was sick and he couldn't work, so they called me in. Then, this morning, I had to go with Nathan so he could give the police his statement."

Fallon frowned. "You went with him?"

"I had to. Nathan was a nervous wreck after they called and said they wanted him to come downtown. He begged me to go with him, so what could I say?"

"How'd it go?"

"All right, I guess. That fat cop is a real moron, but your boss was there. He was real nice, and the other guy there, he was cool too. Nathan liked him."

"Did they ask you any questions?"

"No. I guess Nathan didn't mention me in his statement. So anyway, I came back home and crashed."

"I'm sorry I woke you."

"No, that's OK. I'm glad you called. Want to come over?"

"You've no idea how much I'd like that, but I can't. I have to wait and talk to my boss about the Kennedy case."

"I understand." Eric sounded disappointed. "When do I get to see you again?"

"Are you free tomorrow night, or are you baby sitting Nathan?"

"He's going back to his folks for a few days, so I'm free."

"Great. These guys I know have invited us to their apartment to see the New Year in. Would you like to go with me?"

"I'd rather be alone with you." Eric's tone of seduction made Fallon smile.

"We can do that too," he murmured, slightly amazed at how intimate their conversation had become. "We don't have to be there till ten."

"Well, come over here at eight. We can have our own private celebration first."

"Sounds great. Okay, you go back to sleep now."

"I will, and I'll dream of you."

Fallon was still smiling when a shadow loomed over his desk. He looked up as Bransky glowered down at him. Fallon came back to earth really fast.

"What do you want Bob?"

"I just wanted you to know what a shit I think you are. Hiding behind the Chief like that, and trying to take over my investigation!"

Nick looked at him blandly. "Well, that way something might get done. God knows, you don't want to be bothered finding out why the kid was killed."

Bransky's lips twisted in a sneer. "You think you're so smart trying to tie the kid and the Kennedy murder together. Well, his little friend couldn't be sure if Swenson had a date with Kennedy that particular night. All he knew was Swenson was going to call Kennedy that day to set something up. He might never have been over at the apartment at all."

"Oh, he was there all right." Fallon unlocked his drawer. He reached in and pulled out Chris Swenson's watch and shoes. Bransky looked at them dumbly for a moment.

"Look at the back of the watch, Bob."

Bransky picked up the watch, then flipped it over. His face became bright red as he glared at Fallon. "Where the hell did you get this? And how? You've been withholding evidence from me and Copeland. I'll have you suspended for this…fired!"

"Calm down, Bob. I just got them an hour ago. You weren't here when I got back to the station. Well, here you are. The evidence you need to place the kid at the murder scene."

Bransky looked like he was about to implode. "*Where* did you find this watch?" he rasped.

"I bought it from a bum in the alley behind the apartment building. He and his buddy saw two men leave the building, the night of the murder. It was dark; they couldn't give any descriptions. One looked like he was carrying the other, he said. He figured they were drunk. Then they saw the one guy throw away Swenson's belonging, the shoes, the watch, probably his billfold. The two bums didn't find that. They were beaten to it by some other bums." He had deliberately left Jeff out of the story. That he was using him as an unofficial partner in his investigation would really blow Bransky's mind.

Bransky, meanwhile, was staring at the watch as if he could not believe it was in his hand.

"Don't thank me, Bob," Fallon said lazily, amused by his ex partner's flummoxed expression. He got up from his desk and picked up his coat. "I'll let you tell the Chief you've got yourself a break in the case. See ya."

He left Bransky, standing silently in his office, still clutching the watch in his meaty hand.

When Andrew and Peter returned from the deli, Jeff was sitting warming himself at the fireplace.

"Hi!" he greeted them, smiling. "Get everything you needed?"

"Sure did." Andrew beamed at him as he made for the kitchen. "Anyone call?"

"Yes, as a matter of fact. Bob called to say he and Michael can't make it New Year's Eve. Michael has a stinking cold, so they're going to take it easy till he feels better."

"Oh, that's too bad. Well, I hope Nick doesn't cancel. We'll be eating appetizers for the rest of the week!"

Peter was quiet as he took off his coat and hung it up. Jeff gave him a stern look. "Come over here, you."

Peter did as he was bid, and stood looking down at Jeff, a suitably innocent expression on his face.

"Did I get the impression you were hinting at something inappropriate earlier today?" Jeff allowed just a touch of a smile to tug at the corner of his mouth.

Peter flung himself into Jeff's arms and laid his head on Jeff's chest. "I'm so sorry. I was behaving like a total jerk."

"Yes, you were." Jeff could not resist teasing him. "A total jerk."

Peter raised his head and looked Jeff in the eye. "Well, there's no need to agree so *readily*."

Jeff smiled benignly at him and repeated. "A *total* jerk."

"Well, he does look at you with a gleam in his eye," Peter pouted. "I've seen him."

Jeff laughed and gave him a playful tap on the chin. "He's only interested in me professionally. You know he's seeing someone. They've only been out on a couple of dates, so I hardly think he's going to get the wandering eye already. And besides…" he tightened his arms around Peter. "It takes two to tango, and my dance card is filled with just one name—yours."

Peter smiled contritely. "Andrew said I was being a nut. He thinks Nick has a dark and painful past."

"I'm inclined to agree with Andrew. I think Nick's been lonely for a long time."

"Well, I really am sorry for being a boor." Peter snuggled into Jeff's arms. "I wouldn't blame you if you wanted to give me a good spanking."

"Spanking's too good for you." Jeff chuckled deep in his chest. "You'd enjoy it too much."

"Oh, oh!" Andrew exclaimed, coming out of the kitchen. "I heard that. Does this mean I'll be sitting out here on my own till David gets home?"

Peter smiled at him smugly. "'Fraid so."

"Off with you then. I'll knock on your door at the cocktail hour, if you'll excuse the expression." Andrew smiled to himself as he settled down to read his book. The phone rang suddenly. Probably David, he thought, saying he's on his way home.

"Hi, this is Andrew."

There was a pause and then, a voice he'd thought he would never hear again murmured in his ear, "Andrew, this is Morgan."

"Morgan?" Andrew gasped.

"I saw you at the funeral yesterday."

"Yes, I was hoping to talk to you then, but you seemed so distant…"

"It's been a terrible time, Andrew." Her voice trembled, and she seemed close to tears.

"Is there anything I can do, Morgan?"

"There's nothing anyone can do…You used to be my friend…"

"I'm still your friend, Morgan. You know I would never do anything to hurt you. You have to believe me."

"I think I do believe you, Andrew. Jeremy lied to me so many times. I should have known that what I saw was all a set up, planned by him."

"Where are you Morgan? Can I come and see you?"

"Not tonight. My parents are still here, driving me crazy. They're leaving early New Year's Day. I could meet you for lunch after they leave if you like. It would be like old times."

"That would be terrific…"

"Why don't you come by the hotel? I'm at the Downtown Marriott. Say around noon? We can have lunch here and have a good long talk. I've missed that, Andrew."

"Me too."

"Till then. Bye, Andrew."

"Bye Morgan, and thanks so much for calling. He put the phone down slowly. "Wow!" he said aloud. "*That* was a surprise."

Morgan cradled the phone in her lap and turned to face the man who sat on the opposite side of the room from her. "Well, it's done. He'll be here the day after tomorrow at noon."

"Good. Don't forget to get him to leave a good set of prints on this." Her visitor got up and crossed to where Morgan sat on the couch. From his pocket he drew a handgun and gave it to her. Morgan handled it gingerly. She'd always been afraid of guns.

"Remember," her companion said. "He has to suspect nothing."

"Oh, he won't." Morgan smiled coldly up at the man. "He's going to be so protective of poor little me; he'll go along with anything I say."

"Make sure he does." The man turned to go. "I'll call you later."

CHAPTER 16

Around ten o'clock the next morning, Fallon sat in Fitzgerald's office going over the link between the murders of Jeremy Kennedy and Chris Swenson.

"What about the gun used to kill Swenson?" Fallon asked.

Fitzgerald looked at the forensics report. "Small caliber hand gun. There was no exit wound. The blood they found on Kennedy's body matches Swenson's. Probably seepage from the ears. According to this, the gun's not army or police issue. Small enough to hide in your pocket."

"Or purse?"

"I suppose. But it wasn't a *woman* the bums saw in the alley putting the dead guy in a car."

"Right. I just keep coming back to thinking Morgan Kennedy's involved in all of this, somehow."

"Well, she couldn't have lugged a dead body that far, Nick."

"True, not without help." Fallon was silent for a moment.

"What are you thinking?"

"That she had someone else murder her husband."

"Jeez, Nick!" Fitzgerald exclaimed. "There's absolutely no evidence for that. None!"

"No, but there's motive. The wronged wife syndrome."

"She'd have had to have someone in her pocket, ready to come at the drop of a hat. The time frame between her leaving Kennedy and his getting killed, is only two three hours at most. Not a lot of time to find a hit man."

"Okay…but if she's not involved, is this then just a random killing? Someone walking in to rob the place, finding Kennedy and Swenson and taking them out—all without a struggle?"

"She didn't have to be involved, Nick. If the two guys were unaware there was someone else in the apartment, they could have been taken completely by surprise. Swenson was shot in the back of the head. Boom, he's out of the way. Before Kennedy can react, he's cracked on the head."

"So why go to all the trouble of removing Swenson's body?" Fallon mused. "Just to confuse us? Whoever did this was sloppy. Get rid of the body but leave traces of his blood at the scene?"

Later, sitting at his desk, Fallon had to admit he was getting frustrated with the whole thing. He had thought linking Swenson to the murder would have been a break through, but now it just seemed there were more pieces of the puzzle to fit. His phone ringing interrupted his thoughts.

"Nick?"

He smiled when he heard Eric's voice on the other end, and instantly thought how amazing in such a short space of time, Eric had begun to feel so important to him. He, who had tried so hard for so long to stay out of personal relationships. Donna had always said it would just take the 'right one' to change all of that. She might just be right about that.

"Hey Eric," he said warmly.

"I just wanted to make sure you were coming over before we meet your friends."

"You bet. I'm looking forward to it."

"Me too." Then his voice turned serious. "Any progress on finding out who killed Chris?"

"Not yet, but we know for sure he was with Kennedy when he was murdered. We just have to find out who wanted Kennedy dead."

"Probably his wife."

"What makes you say that?"

"Well, let's face it. She'd had to put up with a bunch of shit from him over the years. I'm not saying she actually *did* it, but she must have wished him dead several times, when she found out what he was up to behind her back."

"My feelings exactly," Fallon muttered.

"Then what about all those guys he used, then dumped. Could have been anyone of them…"

"Hey!" Fallon laughed. "Quit being so helpful. You're piling up the suspects too quickly."

"Sorry, but you know what I mean."

"Yes I do. Eric, I gotta go. I'll see you later."

"Bye, Detective Fallon," Eric said teasingly. "I'll be waiting."

❧ ❧ ❧

David looked at Andrew across the table as they busied themselves, laying out plates and glasses for the New Year's Eve snacks they planned on serving, when their guests arrived. A frown creased his brow as he considered how he was going to pose the question without upsetting Andrew.

"What's wrong?" Andrew asked him.

"I'm concerned about something."

"Tell me."

"This meeting with Morgan tomorrow. Are you sure this is a good idea?"

"This again?" Andrew looked at him impatiently. "We've been over this. You *know* I want to see her and make things right between us."

"Well, it's not just me. Jeff and Peter think you should go easy on this. Don't pin your hopes too much on you and Morgan being the buddies you were, before all this happened."

Andrew shook his head. "Look, David. A lot of terrible things have gone down in the last week or so. Morgan's been through a lot. You can't blame her for being strung out and defensive, and feeling like no one cares about her. I'm her friend. She says she wants to see me. I'm going to be there for her. End of story."

David smiled gently at him. "I just hope she appreciates the kind of friend you are. You are without a doubt the most loyal, unselfish man I have ever known." He came round the table that separated them and put his arms around Andrew, holding him closely. "Two of the reasons I love you so much, of course."

Andrew kissed him on the chin. "I know all you want to do is protect me from getting hurt, but I don't want you to worry about this. If my friendship with Morgan isn't the same as it was, I'll accept that—but I have to try."

"Of course you do." David nuzzled his neck. "You wouldn't be Andrew if you turned your back on her."

"You think I'm a softie don't you?"

"Yes.... but I've been glad to take advantage of that many times." They kissed long and sweetly, then jumped as a discreet cough sounded behind them. Peter and Jeff stood watching them, amused smiles on their faces.

"Should we leave?" Jeff asked.

"No no," Andrew laughed. "We're done, for the moment."

"Can I get you something to drink?" David asked.

"I'll wait till the guys get here," Peter said.

"Good idea," Jeff told him. "Don't want you getting unruly too early."

"I thought you liked me unruly."

"Not in front of relative strangers though," Jeff taunted him. "Andrew and David know you, but the other guys…"

Peter gave him a haughty look. "I shall be the model of decorum."

"Let's not get too ambitious," Andrew laughed. "Just be your sweet and sunny self."

"That's me, all right. Okay, maybe just a teensie drink to get the ball rolling. It *is* New Year's Eve after all."

Eric smoothed the hair back from Fallon's forehead, smiled and kissed the tip of his nose. "Can I ask you something?" he murmured, his lips gently touching Fallon's mouth.

They were lying on Eric's bed, their naked bodies entwined in a post coital embrace.

"You can ask me anything."

"Where did you learn to make love like that?"

Fallon raised an eyebrow as if in surprise. "I thought I was pretty rusty. It must be you who inspired me."

"I'd love to think that, because it *was* pretty wonderful."

"Yes, it was. I could stay here with you in my arms all night, making love to you, till you begged me to stop."

"I'd never ask you to stop." Eric laid his head on Fallon's chest and gently worried at a nipple with his teeth. Fallon shuddered with desire at this sensation. He stretched himself out, holding Eric's smooth and pliant body tightly against himself in a crushing embrace. Eric moaned in ecstasy as he writhed rhythmically beneath Fallon. His face took on a wanton expression as he smiled into Fallon's eyes. He reached behind him, then slipped a condom into Fallon's hand.

"Here, I want you inside me," he whispered, his voice thick with passion.

Fallon fumbled for a moment with the condom, then he knelt over Eric, and let him guide him into that most tempting of places. Eric's eyes flew open in surprise for a moment as Fallon entered him, gently at first, then thrusting more firmly as their passion grew. Eric clung to him as their sweating bodies moved together in unison. He cried out Nick's name as he came, then yelled in triumph as he felt the other man's own shuddering orgasm, deep inside him. They collapsed in each other's arms and lay silently for a long time, their only movements the occasional caress from hands or lips. They must have drifted off to sleep, for suddenly Fallon was aware of Eric gently shaking him.

"It's almost nine thirty."

"Damn. Does this mean you're going to throw me out of bed?"

"Only to take you to the shower, unless you want to renege on the invitation from your friends."

"Better not. Although…" he smiled at Eric, "You make it a tough choice."

"We can come back here afterwards." Eric hopped out of bed and headed for the bathroom. Fallon lay back in bed listening to the shower water splash into the tub. Eric stuck his head round the corner.

"Come on, Detective. It's more economical to shower together—and way more fun." As he climbed into the shower, Fallon had to agree. Eric, adorably covered in a soapy lather, wrapped his arms around him and slithered against him seductively.

"Now, this is what I call a body wash…" Eric sighed.

Fallon held him tightly; feeling a rush of such emotion that he almost could have wept with joy. "Eric, Eric," he whispered in the young man's ear, and he, overcome by that same emotion, clung to Fallon silently as the water cascaded down on them and enveloped them both in it's steamy warmth.

CHAPTER 17

At ten thirty, they arrived at Andrew and David's apartment and Fallon gave David a slightly embarrassed smile as he apologized for being late.

"No problem, Nick. Come on in." David grinned at him and waited for him to introduce the handsome young man who stood beside him.

"This is Eric. Eric, David."

"Hi, Eric." David shook his hand warmly. "Welcome. Come on in and meet everyone else. These are our friends from California, Jeff and Peter." As he shook hands with Eric, Peter was quick to notice the intimate looks he and Nick shared.

"They have that 'just fallen in love' look," he whispered to Jeff as Andrew led Nick and Eric to the bar. "I remember what that felt like, don't you?"

"Can't say I do," Jeff drawled, then dodged a punch from Peter. "You'll have to remind me later." His smile faded as he saw the pained expression on Peter's face. "I was just kidding," he protested, taking Peter's arm comfortingly. Peter sagged against him. "What's wrong, Peter?"

"Oh God, Jeff. One of those damned feelings again. I feel really sick!" Jeff held him to stop him from falling over and was alarmed as he felt Peter's body spasm as if in pain. David, noticing the problem, crossed quickly to their side.

"Jeff. What's wrong with Peter?"

"He'll be OK in a minute, I think. It's one of those nauseous things he gets from time to time."

"I'll be fine." Peter tried to smile. "Sorry about that, David."

"Don't be silly." David squeezed his arm. "Why don't you sit down? You're shaky, still."

Peter allowed Jeff and David to lead him over to the couch where he gratefully sat down. He looked up at Jeff and David apologetically. Jeff sat next to him and put his arm round his shoulders.

"You'll be OK. Just rest a moment." Jeff was getting used to these, what used to be alarming moments, living with Peter. "What do you suppose brought that one on?"

"I haven't a clue. I was just watching Nick and his friend going to the bar with Andrew, when there it was. God, I hope it wasn't a portent of something nasty happening to them."

"In their line of work there's always an element of danger, Peter. Eric's a paramedic; Nick's a cop—ergo, danger."

"But it involved Andrew too. Look, Andrew's coming over. Let's drop it."

"Peter, what's up? David just told me you felt sick."

"I'm fine now, thanks—and I'm not about to let it dampen this evening. So let's forget it." He stood up, smiling, determined to change the subject. "Let's drink a toast to our hosts. The lovely David and Andrew who have provided us with a very interesting stay in New York City."

"*Too* interesting, if you ask me," Andrew said wryly. "Murder, police investigations, funerals—you name it. Hardly what you came for."

"But, on the plus side, we've made some new friends," Jeff said, indicating Nick and Eric. "What better way to start a new year?"

"I'll drink to that." Fallon raised his glass and put his arm around Eric's waist. "It's going to be a very good year."

Everyone raised their glasses, but Peter caught Jeff's eye as he drank and the two felt a pang of misgiving even as they joined in the toast.

"Okay," Andrew was saying. "There's lots to eat on the table. So help yourselves, please."

Eric touched Peter's arm. "Nick tells me you painted the portrait over the fireplace. It's awesome."

"It's only Andrew," Peter kidded.

"Well, he's a good-looking guy, but you've given him a really different look, you know. Very sexy. Were you and he lovers?"

"No…" Peter almost choked on his champagne. "We're the best of friends. I have to admit I found Andrew very attractive, but he and David were together when we all met."

"Well, it looks like it was a labor of love."

"Believe me, it was. You're very right about that. If it wasn't for Andrew I might not be here today."

Eric looked at him with surprise. "What do you mean?"

Peter briefly related the story of his years in a coma and how Andrew supported him physically and mentally during his long recovery.

Eric listened intently, then said, "That's what good friends are all about. Being there when you need them." His eyes glistened as he looked from Peter to Fallon.

"You like him a lot, don't you?" Peter asked gently, still worried about the strange feeling he'd had earlier.

"Yes, I do. He's a much sweeter guy than you'd think on first meeting. There's a lot there he doesn't let you see, but I saw a side of him tonight that touched me in a way I'll never forget."

Peter smiled at Eric's earnest expression. "I know what you mean. What is it about cops, I wonder?"

"Jeff's a cop too?"

"A private investigator. He used to be a cop in LA. And you're a paramedic?"

Eric nodded.

"Is that how you met Nick?"

"No, actually we were introduced by mutual friends. But I had seen him earlier when he was called in on the Jeremy Kennedy murder." Eric smiled at the memory. "I looked at him and thought, Wow, there's someone I'd like to know better. He didn't even give me the time of day."

"He seems very fond of you now," Peter said slyly, watching as Fallon approached them.

The detective's eyes gleamed as he looked at Eric. Eric took his hand and smiled at him. "We were talking about you. Hope you don't mind."

"It was all good stuff," Peter said quickly, and Fallon laughed.

"Then you don't know me very well." He grinned at them both as he squeezed Eric's hand. Fallon could not remember when he had enjoyed himself more. Just being with Eric would have been enough, but now he felt completely relaxed in this friendly atmosphere, among a group of men with whom he had so much in common. The stress of the day seemed to melt away.

"I intend to get to know you a whole lot better, Nick," Eric said after Peter had excused himself and gone off to help Andrew in the kitchen. Fallon smiled at him and hugged him lightly, slightly amazed at how quickly all this intimacy had come about. He had never allowed himself to get so familiar with another person so soon. Martin had always joked about how hard he'd had to pursue him before he got the first date.

"We've got all the time in the world for that," he murmured in Eric's ear, causing the young man to shiver with excitement.

"Behave yourself, Detective, or I'll be hauling you out of here before midnight—and that wouldn't be polite."

"You sure you're all right?" Andrew looked at Peter as he helped him line up the champagne bottles for the midnight toast.

"Perfectly sure." Peter was trying to convince himself that his earlier nausea had not been one of his 'feelings', but merely a reaction to something he'd eaten earlier. The last thing he wanted to think was that something bad was going to happen to his best friend. He'd been through quite enough in the last few days. At the same time he knew it was never wise to ignore those moments of premonition. He wished Andrew wasn't going to see that Morgan woman in the morning. He still had bad feelings about her. He couldn't put his finger on a reason, anymore than he could about this latest bout of nausea.

"Andrew?"

"Yes?"

"About tomorrow…"

"*Peter*. Don't start on me like David did. I'm going to see Morgan, and that's that."

"Yeah, I know." Peter looked at him with what he hoped was a cute expression. "How about if I come too?"

Andrew looked at him, momentarily at a loss for what to say. "*You* come with me?" he finally managed.

"Would you mind that much?" Peter feigned a hurt tone.

"Well, no…Actually, yes. I mean it would be better if Morgan and I were alone. We have so many things to talk about."

"And I'd be in the way?"

"Well, I didn't mean it that way. You'd never be in the way, Peter…but Morgan might be a bit intimidated if you showed up too."

I just bet she would, Peter thought. Aloud he said, "Well, it was just a thought."

"Are you worried she might beat me up or something?" Andrew laughed. "I can handle myself quite well you know. There's not a woman I can't beat at arm wrestling!"

"No, silly. I wasn't worried about that."

"Well, what then?"

"Andrew, I don't know. I just hope you're not opening yourself up for an even greater hurt."

Andrew sighed. "Morgan was the one who suggested we get together, Peter. I didn't call her. I think she's realized I could never betray her like that, and she wants us to be friends again. That's all."

Peter could see there was no way he was going to talk Andrew out of this, so he smiled at his friend and hugged him. "You're the best friend a person could ever have."

"Stop getting maudlin all over me. I know it's New Year's Eve and we're supposed to get sentimental, but what with you and David telling me what a wonderful person I am, it might just all go to my head."

Peter chuckled. "Not you. Didn't I mention modest too? A wonderfully modest best friend."

They both laughed as they carried the bottles into the living room. Everyone gathered round to have their glasses filled with champagne to toast the approaching New Year. David switched on the TV and they watched the ball in Time Square climb to its zenith in readiness for midnight. As always, the excitement that the crowd generated was contagious, and the six friends stood closely together as the count down began.

"THREE, TWO, ONE!" they all joined in and then yelled, "HAPPY NEW YEAR!"

Eric smiled shyly as Fallon looked into his eyes and whispered, "Happy New Year. It's just the beginning for us." He kissed him gently on the lips, then tightened his embrace as he felt Eric's tongue probe between his lips and caress the inside of his mouth. He felt a jolt like an electric shock course through his body, and for a moment he thought he'd blacked out. When he opened his eyes again, Eric was looking at him, a little smile playing at the corners of his mouth.

He knows he's got me, Fallon thought…and I don't mind at all.

"Let's walk back to your place, shall we?" Fallon suggested as they exited Andrew and David's apartment building. Despite the harsh cold of the night he felt exhilarated. He flung his arm around Eric's shoulders and hugged him to his body.

"Sounds good." Eric agreed. "The cold air will clear my head—all that champagne—I'm not used to it. You didn't have to get me drunk to have your way with me, you know."

"Well, at least it was on the house." Fallon grinned at him. He wanted to kiss Eric right there in the street. He could not remember ever feeling this way before. He kept looking at Eric as they walked at a brisk pace through the now almost deserted streets, returning the greetings of a few, still celebrating stragglers, wending their way home. They walked with their arms around each other, recounting the hours they had spent together

"Come on up," Eric said, when they finally reached the small brownstone he lived in. "I'll fix us some coffee."

Inside the apartment it was warm and inviting, and Fallon sighed contentedly as he pulled off his coat. Eric kissed him on the cheek. "Make yourself comfortable while I get the coffee going."

"I don't want to let you out of my sight for a moment," Fallon growled.

Eric took his hand. "Okay. You can watch."

Fallon followed him into the kitchen, the scene of their first intimate moment. He leaned against the counter watching as Eric made the coffee.

"Your friends are great guys," Eric said. "I really enjoyed tonight."

"I did too, all of it."

"Well, if you're referring to the earlier part of the evening, I have to say that was *my* favorite."

"I hoped you'd say that." Fallon smiled at him.

"Nick?"

"What is it?"

"There's something you and I should talk about." He paused for a moment and Fallon looked at him expectantly. "I don't want you to think I jump into bed with any guy I start dating."

"I didn't think you did."

"Well, you know...I kind of forced the issue with you, because I wanted you so badly, but I want you to know I have been very careful since my ex and I broke up. I kidded about it a bit that first night with you—but really, I have been. I don't want to you to think there's any kind of risk in making love to me."

Fallon smiled gently at him. "Thank you for telling me that, but I had you figured as a pretty honest guy—or should I say pretty *and* honest guy?"

Eric returned his smile. "So here's the next part. I know there's a part of your life you didn't want to talk about the other night, and I respected that, but I'm beginning to have very strong feelings for you, and..."

"You're worried there's a big dark secret I'm hiding." Fallon tried to hold his smile in place.

"Tell me if you think it's none of my business."

"No, I won't tell you that. Truth is…I'm having the same feelings for you. I never believed that could happen to me, again."

Eric pushed a mug of steaming hot coffee toward him as he listened.

"Thanks," Fallon muttered. "Okay…where to begin?" He sipped the coffee slowly.

"Let's go sit on the couch." Eric led Fallon by the hand into the living room. "Take off your shoes, be comfortable." Eric sat beside him, one hand resting on Fallon's thigh.

Fallon put his arm round Eric and pulled him close. "His name was Martin and we lived together for ten years," he began. "He was the first man I ever really fell in love with, and after him I never wanted anyone else. He was everything to me, and he spoiled me rotten."

"Was he older than you?" Eric laid his head on Fallon's shoulder

"Only by two years, but he was much more mature than I was. I was twenty-one and still fumbling around with career choices. He was already a financial officer for a huge corporation. By the time he was thirty he was their most valuable employee. He earned big bucks. We lived in a beautiful town house—something I never could have afforded on police officer's pay, but he never made me feel I wasn't pulling my weight."

"Because he loved you," Eric said, simply.

"Yes, because he loved me. And I loved him with all my heart. Not in the beginning, though…" Fallon paused, smiling as he remembered. "God, I led him a merry dance for months before I went out with him on a date. I just knew he was the settling down type, and I wanted none of that. I wanted to run around and sample everything, and get high."

"*You* did drugs?"

"Very briefly," Fallon laughed. "Martin ran into me one night in a bar. I was high as a kite and ready to do dumb things. He took me home and read me the riot act, or at least he said he did. I don't remember much about it. What I do remember is waking up in his bed, in his arms—with just a vague recollection that we'd had sex. I accused him of taking advantage of me while I was wasted, but he laughed and said it was really the other way around. I'd been all over him and he hadn't had the heart to turn me down! Anyway, we made love again that morning…and I never left."

"You lived happily ever after."

"For ten years anyway." Fallon's tone was bitter.

"What happened?"

A painful silence ensued before Fallon spoke again, his voice thick with emotion. "He died in a plane crash three years ago."

"God, I'm sorry," Eric whispered.

"The worst part is, we'd had a fight that day and he died with that miserable memory, instead of knowing how much I loved him. If I could take back all the stupid, shitty things I said to him. I would give *anything*, if only I could!"

"Nick, you can't torture yourself with this. He wouldn't want you to..."

"How the hell would you know what he'd want?" Fallon glared at Eric, his eyes dark with anger. Eric recoiled as if Fallon had struck him.

"I'm sorry, Nick," he gasped, moving away.

Fallon looked at him, the anger dying in his eyes. He reached out and took Eric's hand. "Jesus, Eric. Now I'm doing it to you. Me and my asshole temper. I don't deserve any second chances."

Eric stared at Fallon for a long moment. God, how he loved this man. He wanted to hold him and comfort him.

"Nick..."

"I'm sorry Eric. I've ruined it haven't I? I've let you see the jerk I was hiding from you. It didn't take long for me to blow it."

Eric sighed and stood up. Fallon looked up at him miserably.

"Stand up..."

Reluctantly, Fallon got to his feet. "You want me to go..."

"No. I want you to put your arms around me while I tell you something."

Hesitantly, Fallon did as he was told. Eric slid his arms around his neck putting his mouth close to his ear. "I love you, you big jerk!" His lips fluttered against Fallon's skin.

Fallon groaned with relief and his arms tightened around Eric's supple body. "You mean it?" he gasped.

"Yes, I mean it, dummy!" Eric laughed. "I love you, warts and all."

"Hey!" Fallon pushed him back gently. "Who's got warts?" He was grinning from ear to ear.

"That's better," Eric snuggled into his arms again. "I want to see you smile like that every day."

"I love you Eric." Fallon kissed the soft skin below Eric's ear.

Eric smiled up into Fallon's eyes. "I know," he said.

CHAPTER 18

New Year's Day dawned gray and wet in New York City. The snow in the streets turned into a soggy slush, from which the vagrants and homeless people fled to the warmth and security of the city shelters.

High above those streets, Peter stood looking out of the bedroom window. Jeff was still asleep, and though Peter longed to waken him and share this feeling of unease that had gripped him since the early hours of the morning, he did not disturb him. Instead he padded silently from the room and headed for the kitchen to make himself a cup of coffee. He was worried, and had been since his 'feeling' of the night before. Even though he had tried to push it to the back of his mind, it kept resurfacing and reminding him that it should not be ignored.

If only he knew what it meant…

He tried to rationalize it by reminding himself that he'd had this same strange feeling when he met Morgan and nothing terrible had happened to Andrew, but rather to Morgan's husband. Now this feeling was back, involving Andrew again—but this time, with Nick. Did it mean that they were both in danger? As Jeff had pointed out Nick's very profession put him in the path of some danger everyday. Perhaps it was related to something that had already taken place. A past danger, from which he had obviously come through all right.

Peter raked his hands through his thick hair in frustration and wished he had the answer. He poured himself a cup of the now brewed coffee, and sat at the kitchen table trying to concentrate. A shadow fell across the table and he looked up, startled. David stood looking down at him.

"You're up early," he remarked giving Peter's shoulder a friendly rub.

"What about you?" Peter asked.

"I tried sleeping in, but it wasn't on the cards today."

"Can I pour you some coffee?"

"I'll get it."

David looked at him as he poured his coffee. "You're worried about Andrew, aren't you?"

"Yes, frankly, I am. I don't like the idea of this visit with Morgan."

"Neither do I." David took a sip of his coffee. "I think Andrew is going to be very disappointed with the outcome. I have a feeling Morgan's bitchy enough to really let him think she's forgiven him, and then, laugh in his face."

"I just hope that's the worst of it," Peter muttered, almost to himself.

"What do you mean?"

"Oh, nothing. I'm just being a paranoid queen, I guess. That sickly feeling I had last night, I haven't been able to shake it completely."

"You mean, one of your psychic turns?"

"Yeah, something like that. I just can't figure out what they mean most of the time!"

David looked at him worriedly. "I wanted to go with him, but he won't let me."

"I offered too." Peter gave David a small smile. "No wonder he thinks we're both overreacting. Both of us running around like mother hens."

"Well…" David came to sit at the table. "There's no point in trying to dissuade him any further, I guess. We'll just have to be there to pick up the pieces if it doesn't go well. He thinks the world of her, you know. And I'm not sure why. I mean, he hasn't known her that long, and the woman isn't even honest. All that bull shit about Jeremy not being gay!"

"She's a strange bird for sure," Peter agreed.

David sighed heavily. "It's all my fault really."

"What?"

"If I hadn't been so wrapped up in my work, to the point of neglecting him and leaving him on his own for hours and hours, he might not have felt the need to see so much of her."

"Oh, come on, David. Andrew's a big boy. Yes, he was lonely, but he should still have been able to discern whether she was just using him or not. They were probably using each other, in a way. Hers was a troubled marriage…he was lonely…they just needed to kibitz a bit, to get over their frustration."

"Is that supposed to make me feel better?" David asked ruefully.

"What I'm saying is, it's not your fault, and besides, you're both coming back to California, so that's made him feel tons better."

"Still, I wish I had been more there for him. We might never have got tangled up in this mess in the first place."

"Now, you're just being silly," Peter said. "There's no way anyone can know what's going to happen. Even me, with my so-called psychic ability—more like a disability, really. If I could just work out what these feelings mean when they happen, it might save us all a lot of grief."

When Nick arrived at the station around ten o'clock that morning, Bransky was loitering in the hall outside his office. He tried to ease his way past the man's considerable bulk, but his ex partner wanted to talk.

"Hey Fallon, Mrs. Kennedy was on the phone for you earlier. She wants you to call her at the hotel. On her cell she said. She wanted to talk to me actually, but I had to tell her I was off the case and *you* was in charge now." He added the last part with a sneer.

"I'm sure she was devastated to hear that, Bob."

"She wasn't too pleased. Wanted to know why I couldn't help no more. I told her I couldn't discuss it with her, as it came from my superior."

"Very diplomatic of you, Bob. Thanks for the message. I'll give her a call." So saying, he closed his office door and smiled to himself as he heard Bransky muttering as he walked away. Fallon sat at his desk and closed his eyes for a moment. God, he was tired…but he smiled as he remembered the incredible hours he had just spent with Eric. Part of him was still nervous about what had happened.

It had all been so fast—in just one week he was head over heels in love with someone he hadn't even known existed, before Christmas Day. The other part however, exulted in this heady feeling of love and lust that was almost intoxication. Now, the vision of Eric's seductive smile and willing body swam before his eyes. He could almost smell his fragrance and feel the smooth skin that stretched like silk over his supple muscles. Fallon shook himself, as he felt himself becoming aroused at the memory of their last lovemaking.

His hand shook slightly as he reached for the phone and quickly punched in Morgan Kennedy's cell number. He came firmly down to earth as he heard her brittle voice on the line.

"Yes?"

"Good morning, Mrs. Kennedy. This is Nick Fallon. You wanted to talk to me?"

"Oh yes, Detective Fallon. I wondered if you could meet me in my hotel room around noon today? There's something I want to show you. It may help in your investigation."

"Can you tell me what it is?" Fallon asked, keeping the surprise he felt out of his voice.

"I'd rather not discuss this over the phone if you don't mind," Morgan replied icily. "Can you be here or not?"

"I'll be there, Mrs. Kennedy. Around noon you said?"

"Make it about ten after. I'm expecting a phone call, but have reception call my room when you arrive. I'll have them send you up."

"Okay. I'll see you later, then."

"Goodbye, Detective."

Fallon put his phone down and sat for a moment thinking about what had just happened. What could she have to show him that she did not have before? She hadn't been in the apartment since the day they summoned her from Connecticut. Or had she? Maybe, when her parents were in town for the funeral, they had gone over there and found something she thought might be of interest. A diary maybe, or a photo of someone. Well, he'd just have to wait to find out. He looked at his watch. Ten thirty.

He grimaced as his phone rang, and he answered, "Fallon."

"Detective…Frank Mitchell, New Hampshire Police Department. You called when I was on vacation. You got everything OK?"

"Oh yeah…thanks for calling. I got the faxed report on the Kennedy accident. I just have one question."

"Shoot."

"You signed off saying Mrs. Kennedy's father had put in a request that any follow up was done here in New York. Any idea who might have handled that here?"

"Don't you guys keep records, Detective?"

"I knew you were gonna say that," Nick chuckled. "Yeah, we do, but I can't seem to find 'em. Must have fallen into a black hole or something."

"Well, hang on a minute. Let me check my file. I think I jotted down the name of the guy who they said would interview Mrs. Kennedy."

Fallon drummed his fingers on his desktop as he listened to Mitchell rustling papers.

"It was just a courtesy thing of course," Mitchell said. "The investigation was pretty well put away, just the way she described it, you understand. But the father's a bit high profile—friend of the Mayor's, and all that—you know how it is. Gotta keep them happy."

Fallon's drumming got a bit more impatient as he listened to Mitchell's rambling.

"Right, here it is…" Mitchell said finally. "Detective Robert Bransky was the one who did the follow up."

Fallon almost dropped the phone. "*What*? You're sure?"

"'Course I'm sure. It's there in black and white—Det…", but Fallon had already hung up.

He leaned back in his chair as the implications of what he'd just heard whirled through his head. "Bransky…" he muttered. "That son of a bitch. He knew from the first day…" Why had Bob not told him he knew Morgan Kennedy? Why had they *both* pretended not to know each other?

He got up and strode over to the office Bransky shared with Copeland. "Where's Bob?" he asked sharply.

"He stepped out for a while," Copeland replied glumly. "Said he had some business to attend to. Hey," he added as Fallon turned to leave. "You want him back as a partner? He's driving me nuts."

"No thanks, Copeland. He's all yours." Fallon looked at the other detective grimly. "But if it's any consolation, I feel your pain."

Returning quickly to his office he dialed Jeff's cell number and listened to the message telling him the cell phone's owner was not available. He gave a disappointed grunt, then quickly dialed Andrew's number. He sighed with exasperation as the answering machine clicked on and he listened to David explain they could not come to the phone, but please, would the caller leave a message?

"Yeah, hi guys. It's Nick Fallon. Had a great time last night. Could you have Jeff call me on my cell when he can? Tell him it's important." He sat for a moment, looking at the gray walls of his office, then as realization unfolded itself upon him, he said aloud,

"*That son of a bitch.*"

Jeff and Peter were at the gym with David. Andrew had shooed them out of the apartment earlier, saying he was tired of their efforts to cancel his appointment with Morgan.

"I'm telling you all for the last time—give it up, guys. I mean it…!" he had finally yelled at them. "If it's a disaster, I only have myself to blame. Then you can all say—'I told you so.'"

So they had let him be to get showered and dressed for his lunch with Morgan. Their workout had left them feeling elated and invigorated after the slow start to the day. Now as the three of them sat in the whirlpool, David could not refrain from, once again, voicing his worries about 'the meeting'.

"He should be just about there by now. I hope it's going to go well."

Jeff sighed. "David, *relax*. He'll be all right."

"I'm not so sure about that!" Peter spluttered, just before he disappeared under the bubbling water.

"Peter, stop fooling around." Jeff said, as he and David stared resignedly at the top of Peter's head, watching as his blond hair weaved and bobbed just below the surface of the whirlpool. "Wait a minute…" Jeff exclaimed, as Peter remained under water for what began to seem as way too long a time. "Peter!" Jeff grabbed him under the arms and pulled him upright.

"Oh, my God," David cried, seeing Peter's white face emerge from the water. "He's ill!"

"No, it's one of those damned attacks again," Jeff panted, lifting Peter out of the whirlpool. He laid him gently on the tiles. "Peter, sweetheart. Can you hear me?" He massaged Peter's chest as he spoke.

"Should I call 911?" David hovered anxiously over them.

"Wait just a moment. I think he's coming to."

Peter's eyes fluttered open and slowly focused on Jeff's face.

"Jeff," he whispered.

"I'm here." Jeff lifted him into his arms.

"It's Andrew. We have to help him…" Peter now looked at David. "David, Andrew's in terrible danger!"

"What do you mean?"

"We have to go…" Peter started to struggle within Jeff's arms. "We have to go to him."

"Okay, okay…" Jeff tried to calm him. "We'll all go to the hotel soon as you feel better."

"No, *now*." Peter yelled. "Before it's too late!"

Andrew knocked on the door of Morgan's hotel room and breathed out a long sigh to relax himself. No point in denying he was nervous of this meeting, no matter how much he wanted it. The door opened and Morgan, looking her usual elegant and regal self, stood smiling at him.

"*Andrew.*" She opened her arms to him. "How wonderful to see you." She grabbed Andrew by the arm and pulled him into the room, hugging him tightly and kissing his cheek. Andrew hugged her back, glad that she was so pleased to see him.

"I've missed you so," she said in his ear, then stepped back to look at him. "You look thinner!"

"I shouldn't, after all that Holiday overeating," Andrew laughed. "You look wonderful, Morgan."

"Thank you, darling. Come on in. I have some champagne to celebrate our reunion."

Andrew followed her into the suite and took the glass she offered him.

"Here we are," she murmured, filling his glass from a bottle of Taittinger's. "Sit down, darling and kick your shoes off. We have a lot to talk about!"

Andrew smiled at her as he sat on the couch. "I've missed our lunch hours together."

"And me, sweetie. We certainly have to make up for lost time."

"How are you coping now your parents are gone?"

"Better." Morgan laughed a trifle shrilly. "They mean well, but they really were getting on my nerves. My mother especially. I was getting very tired of her sanctimonious looks and criticism. God knows, I haven't exactly been a saint in my time, but I certainly don't intend to end up a shriveled up old fossil like her."

Andrew gaped at her in surprise. "Morgan, you don't mean that."

"Oh yes, I do." Morgan laughed again. "She's never approved of a damned thing I've ever done. You should have seen her face when I showed her my latest purchase."

"What is it?" Andrew asked, a tad uncomfortably.

Morgan delved into her purse and produced a handgun. "This!" she said, flourishing it under Andrew's nose. "This is my protection from whomever it was killed Jeremy, and is now out to get me."

"What?" Andrew exclaimed. "You think you're in danger?"

Morgan snickered. "A girl can't be too careful—and besides, it's quite pretty, don't you think. Here…" She held the gun out to Andrew. "Take it. Feel how smooth and light it is."

Andrew carefully accepted the gun, weighing it in his hand.

"Don't worry, sweetie, it's not loaded. Hold it by the handle. That's right. Finger on the trigger. See how easily it handles."

"I hope you never have to use it." Andrew shuddered and handed it back to her. Morgan took the gun from him, holding it lightly by the barrel. "Oh, me too." She placed the gun on the sofa by her side.

Just then the phone rang. "Excuse me, darling." She picked up the phone. "Yes? Oh yes, send him up."

"You're expecting someone else?" Andrew asked, surprised. "I thought we were having lunch—just the two of us."

"Oh, we are. It's just that tiresome detective wanting to ask me some more questions. He called earlier. I told him I was busy, but he insisted."

"You mean Nick Fallon?"

"That's right. Of course, you know him, don't you…?"

"Yeah. As a matter of fact he celebrated the New Year with us last night."

"How nice…" Morgan smiled at him, but Andrew felt a distinct chill in her words.

"What's wrong?" he asked her as he heard Fallon knock at the door.

"Why, nothing, darling." She gave him a little smile as she got up to open the door.

"Detective Fallon…" Andrew heard her greet Nick. "Do come in. You know Andrew of course?" Andrew noticed that Fallon did not seem too surprised to see him there.

"Hi, Nick. I hope I'm not in the way."

"Not at all." Fallon smiled at him. "I'm sorry to interrupt. Soon as Mrs. Kennedy shows me what she says will be helpful in my investigation, I'll be on my way."

Andrew looked at Morgan questioningly, but she seemed not to notice. She was looking over Fallon's shoulder as the door to the bedroom opened and Andrew saw with surprise that Fallon's ex partner, Bransky, had entered the room. Too late, he saw what the man was about to do.

"Nick…look out!" he yelled, as Bransky drove the butt of his gun into the back of Fallon's head, who went down like a dead weight at Andrew's feet.

"What are you doing?" Andrew dropped to his knees beside Nick's inert body.

"We're setting you up, Andy boy," Bransky sneered. "You see, the way we see it, Mrs. Kennedy here called her brave detective because you were coming over and she was afraid you meant her some harm, seeing as how she knows it was you bumped off her old man. So he shows up to protect her, you slug him from behind, then put a bullet in his brain from the gun you so carelessly handled earlier. Mrs. Kennedy, of course, tries to stop you, you rough her up a little and that's when I come in. Worried that my ex-partner might have gotten himself in trouble, I follow up on the call I took from her earlier in the day. I bust in here and find you with gun in hand and shoot you in self-defense. How does that sound?"

"You're *insane*," Andrew shouted at him. He looked desperately at Morgan. "Tell me you had nothing to do with this, Morgan. You can't be a part of this."

Morgan looked down at him coldly. "I'm afraid you're wrong about that, Andrew dear." She smiled superciliously, as she continued, "Actually, this was my idea. Someone has to take the blame for poor Jeremy's murder, and it might just as well be you."

Andrew looked at her in horror. "But why? Why are you doing this?"

"Because I despise what you are Andrew, and what you stand for."

"What I stand for?" Andrew gaped at her incredulously.

"What the lady means…" Bransky sneered, "Is that she hates homos like you and your friends. People like you are what turned her hubby into a faggot."

"My God!" Andrew felt anger growing inside him. "You surely don't believe that? That's the most ignorant thing I've heard. *You* might believe it," he rasped at Bransky. "But Morgan, you're far too intelligent for that kind of crazy thinking."

"Shut up," Morgan snarled at him. "Don't forget I caught you seducing Jeremy."

"*Seducing* him?" Andrew gave a shout of derisive laughter. "Jeremy was a full-blown, card carrying homosexual long before I ever met him—and you damned well know it."

"Quiet," Bransky growled. "It doesn't matter anymore. The gun you left your prints on for us is the one that shot the Swenson kid. Mrs. Kennedy will testify that you confessed to the murders to her—and to poor Nick here, before you shot him in cold blood."

Beside him, Fallon groaned softly as he appeared to regain consciousness. Bransky kicked him as he tried to sit upright. Andrew moved in front of Fallon to protect him and Morgan struck him a stinging blow to the side of his face.

"Pervert…" she hissed at him "You have no idea how much I hate you and your kind." She looked at Bransky. "Finish them now."

Andrew gazed at her in horror as the full weight of what she was saying sank in.

"Wait a minute, wait a minute," Bransky chuckled. "Before I have that pleasure, I want Nick here to know why he's going to die."

Fallon peered at him through dazed eyes as he gingerly touched the back of his head. His fingers came away, sticky with blood. He looked at Andrew. "You OK?" he mumbled.

"Isn't that touching?" Bransky sniggered. "He's worried about his fag friend."

"What the hell's going on, Bob?" Fallon growled. "Killing Jeremy Kennedy wasn't enough for you?"

"Oh, you figured it out?" Bransky glared at him. "Fucking smart aren't you?"

"Not really." Fallon met Bransky's eyes coldly. "I wasn't a hundred per cent sure till about an hour ago. All I had to go on was the fact that you and this bitch knew each other before her husband's homicide. I couldn't figure why you wouldn't have told me that, or why the two of you pretended not to know each other—unless you were hiding it for a very good reason. That reason being, of course, that you killed Jeremy Kennedy and Chris Swenson."

"Bob!" Morgan barked. "He knows everything—kill them *now*."

"I'd be very careful what you say, Mrs. Kennedy." Fallon struggled to his feet and opened his jacket slightly. "You're on the air, so to speak."

"He's wearing a fucking wire!" Bransky screamed.

"What do you mean?" Morgan 's voice rose in panic.

"A *wire*, you stupid bitch!"

Fallon smiled wryly at Morgan. "It means that the police have been listening to everything you and Bob said in this room since I arrived." He yelled in the direction of the door, "Okay, guys.. you can come in now…"

Morgan looked at him as though stunned for the moment. Then the look turned to one of venom and hate. Moving with lightning speed, she grabbed Bransky's gun from his hand and leveled it at Fallon. "They're too late to help *you*," she screamed insanely, pulling the trigger. Bransky grabbed for the gun, and at the same time Andrew pushed Fallon out of the way. The blast from the gun knocked Morgan off balance. Andrew grabbed her arm and threw a wild punch, catching her squarely on the jaw. She went down like a sack of potatoes.

At that moment, the door crashed open and Jeff, Peter and David rushed into the room. Bransky stared at them dully, not quite understanding what had just happened.

"You all right, Andrew?" David panted, running to his side.

"Yes, except for sore knuckles." He shook his hand ruefully and looked down at Morgan who still lay sprawled on the floor. "David!" Andrew's voice was filled with indignation. "She called me a pervert!"

Fallon picked up Bransky's gun. "Bob, I'm arresting you for the murders of Jeremy Kennedy and Christopher Swenson and for attempting to murder me and Andrew Connor…"

"Like hell!" Bransky yelled, turning to escape, but Jeff leaped on him, twisting one arm behind his back and forcing the fat man to his knees.

"You're not going anywhere," Jeff said in Bransky's ear. "Except to jail."

Morgan moaned faintly as she came round. She started to splutter epithets as Andrew and Peter yanked her to her feet and Fallon slipped handcuffs on her. "You can't do this to me…my father will destroy all of you!"

Fallon gave a short bark of laughter. "I think it's your father who'll be destroyed, when he finds out what his darling daughter has been up to."

She glared balefully at them, till Andrew stepped close to her and said quietly, "I never thought I would feel this much contempt for any one I once liked and respected. I should feel sad to see what you have become, Morgan, but what I really feel is a great anger for the lives you have destroyed. Jeremy wasn't much, but he didn't deserve to die, and that poor kid he was with. What had he done to you? You're a miserable excuse for a human being…and to think I once called you my friend."

Morgan's body sagged as her pent up rage suddenly ebbed and the knowledge of defeat swept over her. She looked away from Andrew's intense stare and said nothing.

"Okay, let's go," Fallon snapped. "I want to deliver you both personally…and, by the way, Bob…" He grinned at the others as he added. "How do you like my back up? All gay guys, just for you."

After he had handed Bransky and Morgan over to the police outside the hotel, Fallon turned to Andrew. "I have to thank you for saving my life back there."

Andrew smiled at him. "I think it was just a reflex."

"Maybe, but if you hadn't pushed me out of the way, I'd have caught that bullet." Fallon held out his hand, but Andrew brushed it aside and hugged him.

"You're one of us now," he said, emphatically. "We don't shake hands, we hug. I hope it doesn't embarrass you."

"It might have, once upon a time. I can't thank all you guys enough for being there when I needed you."

Just then an ambulance pulled up and Eric and his partner jumped out. "Hey," Eric exclaimed, "What's going on? We got a call that someone had been hurt here."

"That would be Nick," Jeff said. "He got clobbered pretty hard on the head. I don't think he knows yet just *how* hard!"

"I'm OK," Fallon muttered.

"Let me take a look." Eric ignored Fallon's protests and examined his head. "Nick, for God's sake…you're going to need stitches in this."

"Am not!" Fallon jerked his head out of Eric's hands.

Eric looked at him sternly. "Listen to me, mister. You'll have major problems if you don't let me take care of that."

"Oho," Peter laughed. "Better not argue with the medic, Nick."

"Okay, okay." Fallon gave in with a sigh. "But I have to get over to the station right away."

"Get in the ambulance," Eric ordered him. "We'll drive you over there."

Fallon rolled his eyes and looked at his friends imploringly. "Somehow, I'm getting the idea that my life is no longer my own."

"You've got that right…" Eric grinned at him. "Aren't you the lucky one?"

The four friends chuckled as they watched Fallon being bundled into the ambulance.

"You guys meet me there?" he pleaded.

"We'll be there," Jeff assured him. They watched as the ambulance pulled away.

Peter looked at his friends expectantly. "Well, can we have anymore excitement today—or, is that it?"

"Lord, I hope that's it," David said, fervently. He looked at Andrew with concern. "You all right, babe?"

"Yes, I'm fine, though I really can't quite believe any of this. If anyone had told me that Morgan was such a cold and calculating bitch, I'd never have believed them. I thought her problem was she loved Jeremy too much—not that she planned to murder him and pin it on me. What a fool I've been. I should have listened to you and Peter." He looked at them all questioningly. "How did you manage to get here when things started to get ugly, anyway?"

"It's a bit of a long story," Jeff said. "Let's get a cab over to the police station, and we'll fill you in on the way."

"So, Peter came through again with another psychic attack?" Andrew had listened intently as Jeff related the story of what had happened to Peter in the spa.

Jeff nodded. "He was so sure you were in trouble, I decided to call Nick at that point and found *he'd* been trying to get hold of me. He told me he'd found out that Morgan and Bransky had known each other for several months, and never mentioned it to him. He was naturally suspicious as to why Bransky hadn't told him, and then when I said you were on your way over to see Morgan, he got worried. Morgan had asked *him* to come over to her hotel room at roughly the same time you were going to be there. He said he figured it had to be some kind of set up. So we rushed over to the hotel and met him there."

"She told me Nick had arranged the meeting with her," Andrew interrupted. "She even got me to handle her gun so my prints would be on it when they shot Nick with it. God! I still can hardly believe she'd do something so terrible. But how did she get Bransky involved?"

"Apparently they met when Morgan was involved in the accident that killed Jeremy's friend, Kevin. Bransky did a routine follow up for the New Hampshire police, and he was smitten by her immediately."

"She must have confided in him about her unhappy marriage," David added. "The man obviously would do anything for her—even murder."

Peter nodded. "And the fact that Jeremy was gay, just made it all the easier for him. As far as Bransky was concerned he was just doing Morgan, and society, a favor."

"So they set the whole thing up between them?" Andrew asked

"Seems that way. We're still a bit hazy on all the facts. Her statement should be illuminating…and Bransky's!"

Fitzgerald looked grimly at Bransky as the disgraced detective stood, still handcuffed, in front of him. He glanced at Fallon and signaled for him to sit down.

"How's the head?"

"Better. The medics took care of it on the way over here." Nick smiled slightly at the memory of Eric fussing over him in the back of the ambulance. After he had bathed it with antiseptic he had announced it didn't need stitches after all. "I guess everyone's right about me being hard headed," he'd managed to joke, even as he winced at the effect of the stinging antiseptic.

"Just take it easy, please Nick," Eric had whispered in his ear applying a dressing to the wound. "I didn't find you, just to lose you this quickly."

Fallon came back to earth with a guilty start as he heard Fitzgerald growl, "Sit down, Bob."

Bransky sat down heavily. "I want a lawyer!"

"You'll get one," Fitzgerald said, with contempt. "Your girlfriend's in there with her attorney now, and from what I gather she's nailing you for the whole thing. Says it was all your idea."

"She wouldn't do that. She wanted me to…" He stopped suddenly. "I ain't saying nothin' without my lawyer here."

Fitzgerald looked resignedly at the police officers that stood, flanking Bransky on either side. "Okay, take him down and lock him up. We'll get a statement from you when your lawyer gets here." He watched as Bransky shuffled out, glaring balefully at Fallon. Fitzgerald rubbed his eyes then fixed Fallon with a look.

"What's this I hear about you using civilians as your back up?"

Fallon smiled ruefully at him. "It seemed a good idea at the time."

"You could have got them killed, Nick. That was totally irresponsible, not to mention stupid. Why the hell didn't you call for police back up?"

"I did…sort of," Fallon protested. "The other guys just got there first."

"But how did they know what was going on?"

"Well, one of them, Jeff Stevens, the ex-cop, called me and said his friend Peter had had a psychic premonition that their friend Andrew Connor was in imminent danger. He's had these feelings before, and according to Jeff they're pretty reliable. Connor was over at the hotel at Mrs. Kennedy's invitation—to patch up their friendship she'd said. I thought that was strange as she'd called me and wanted to give me some help with the investigation. I told Jeff this and we wondered why she'd want us both there at the same time. Then my devious mind got to thinking *set up*, particularly as I'd just found out that Bob and the Kennedy woman knew each other and had never mentioned it to me."

"Wait a minute," Fitzgerald growled. "You're telling me this hunch first came from a guy's psychic intuition?"

"Well not exactly, Chief. But it confirmed in my mind that something fishy was going on, and sure enough, when I got to the hotel, the Kennedy woman had already set Andrew up by getting him to handle the gun they were going to use to shoot me."

"Go on," Fitzgerald said, grimly.

"Bob was hiding in the bedroom, and when I came in he snuck up behind me and clobbered me with his gun. I wasn't completely out, so I could hear him telling Andrew they'd set him up for my murder. I'd rigged a phony wire inside my jacket, and when Bob saw it he went to pieces." Fallon grinned at the memory, then continued. "The other three guys came crashing into the room at that point. Mrs. Kennedy tried to shoot me but Andrew pushed me out of the way and socked her one."

"Christ," Fitzgerald muttered. "How come the police back up was late?"

"Well…" Fallon looked anxiously at his boss.

"Yes?"

"I didn't actually get around to calling them in until that moment."

"What? You said you called for back up, and the other guys just got there first!"

"Well…" Fallon reddened as he continued with his explanation. "I didn't want to call for back up without knowing what it was I was in for. If I'd gone in there and I'd been wrong about everything, I'd have looked pretty stupid."

"Better looking stupid than looking dead!"

"And besides, you don't know these guys. Once they knew Andrew might be in danger, there was no stopping them from getting involved. They didn't want him to go there in the first place. Peter, the one with the psychic ability, had tried to talk him out of it several times."

"There you go with that psychic stuff again."

"I think you should meet these guys, Chief."

"Well, I do want to read Andrew Connor's statement. Who's dealing with that?"

"Police Officer Daniels, Chief. She's got them all at her desk right now."

Fitzgerald rose slowly from his seat. "Okay, let's go talk to them," he muttered reluctantly. Fallon followed him out into the main office where a pretty blonde police officer was talking and laughing with the four friends. They looked up, still smiling, as Fitzgerald and Fallon approached them. Fallon made the introductions.

"I have to apologize for getting you in harm's way!" Fitzgerald looked reprovingly at Fallon. "I hope you're not considering a lawsuit."

"We enjoyed it too much for that," Peter was the first to exclaim.

"Uh, which one's the psychic?" Fitzgerald asked, somewhat uncomfortably.

"I'm not a psychic." Peter grinned at him. "I just get these strange feelings, sometimes, when things are about to go wrong."

"He's being unusually modest," Jeff told Fitzgerald.

"Yeah," Andrew chuckled. "Go on, Peter, be yourself."

Fitzgerald allowed himself to smile at the friend's obvious camaraderie. "I'm just glad it all turned out right, and no one got hurt," he said, gruffly. "All right, gentlemen. We won't waste anymore of your time. You do understand, however, Mr. Connor, that you'll be called as a material witness when this goes to trial."

Andrew nodded, looking at the Chief seriously. "What's happening to Morgan?"

"She's talking to her attorney. A hearing will be set to determine if she can get out on bail."

"And Bransky?" Jeff asked.

"He'll be assigned a public defender, but I doubt if there will be a bail hearing. He'll be in custody till the trial."

"Well, that's the good news." Jeff stood up. "Okay, guys. Let's go."

"Nick?" David looked at the detective inquiringly. "Why don't you and Eric stop over tonight when you're free? We can have a drink and kick back. After all this excitement you could probably use some "R and R."

"That'd be great—thanks."

Fitzgerald shook his head. "I don't know about you guys. He puts you all in mortal danger, and you still want to have him as a friend. Me? I'd stay clear of him if I were you!"

Fallon grinned at his boss and wondered what he'd say if he knew Jeff had been a part of this since Bransky stopped being his partner. Better he didn't find out.

"Uh, just one thing," Fitzgerald looked at Peter. "My wife's crazy about all those psychics on the TV. Are they for real, do you think?"

"Oh, absolutely." Peter tried not to grin.

"You think so eh?" Fitzgerald shrugged uncomfortably. "She spends so much money on that stuff. They keep telling her she's coming into a fortune, but it's *them* that's getting rich."

CHAPTER 19

Fallon entered the interrogation room alongside Fitzgerald and Bob Perkins the Assistant DA. Bransky looked up bleakly as the men sat at the opposite side of the table from him. His look fixed on Fallon and turned to one of anger.

"I ain't saying anything in front of that faggot!"

Perkins glanced at Fallon who remained impassive. "I obviously have to remind you that you're under arrest for murder Bob, and that Nick is the investigating detective on the case. He has every right to be here—in fact, he *must* be here. So, are you prepared to make a statement?"

"Not until I have a lawyer here."

"Bob," Perkins continued. "Mrs. Kennedy tells us that it was your idea to murder her husband. That she tried to dissuade you and you threatened her in return."

"She's a goddamned liar!" Bransky screeched. "She called me after she and him had a fight. She reminded me I'd said I'd do anything for her when we first met..."

"And *would* you do anything for her?"

Bransky looked at Perkins miserably. He seemed to deflate like a balloon with a slow leak. He slumped deeper in to his seat before he continued. "When I first met her, she was really upset. She'd been in a car accident and the guy with her was killed. Her old man, she said, blamed her for everything and had left her. Then she told me, he and the dead friend were homos and had been screwing around for months right under her nose. I couldn't believe it! That a beautiful woman like that could be cheated on by guys doing it with each other. I mean, what the fuck is that?" He looked balefully at Fallon. "Well, I suppose you could tell us all about that, right *Nicky*?"

Fallon sighed, but sat back in his seat and remained silent.

"Go on, Bob," Perkins urged.

"I don't know—where's my lawyer?" Bransky looked around him nervously.

"He's on his way, Bob. It might be easier for you if you just tell us what really happened." At that moment the door opened and a pale young man sporting a buzz cut and goatee entered.

"I'm Bill Evans." His statement was addressed no one in particular. "Detective Bransky's counsel."

"Oh great," Bransky moaned. "They sent me some kid straight out of rookie school. Can I request someone else?"

Evans looked at him sourly. "At least give me a chance, Detective. Have they read you your rights?"

"Of course they have," Bransky sneered. "Whatdya think, we're amateurs here?"

"I'll need a minute alone with my client," Evans said tersely, again not looking at anyone in the room.

"Okay." Perkins got up. "Let us know when you're ready." He, Fallon and Fitzgerald left the room. They met Jeff in the hall and Fallon pulled him to one side.

"This is going to take longer than we thought, Jeff. Why don't you guys go on home? I'll come over later and let you know how it's gone down."

"Sounds good," Jeff said. "What about Eric?"

"Oh, right." Fallon shook his head distractedly. "Thanks Jeff. Do me a favor." He quickly scribbled down a number. "Here's his cell. Would you call him and tell him to meet me over at your place?"

"Sure." Jeff smiled at him. "How's it going in there?"

"He's rattled 'cos Morgan Kennedy's blaming him for the whole thing, saying he threatened her as well."

"Wow! Hell hath no fury, as they say…" He patted Fallon's shoulder as he turned to go. "See you later, buddy."

"Right." Fallon returned his smile, then walked over to where his Chief and Perkins stood in deep conversation.

"Let's pay Mrs. Kennedy and her attorney a visit, shall we?" Perkins said as Fallon joined them. "Her father's on his way over here. I'd like to see if we could cut a deal before he gets here."

"Good idea," Fallon said. "He sounds like a member of the old school that believes in power plays. He'll probably never agree to his daughter making deals with the police—other than us dropping the charges."

"Yeah," Fitzgerald growled. "Like *that's* going to happen. He's probably trying to get the Mayor over here right now."

Perkins knocked on the door then quickly entered the room where Morgan and her attorney Ralph Payton were seated.

"So," Perkins said loudly as they entered. "What do we have so far from your client?"

Ralph Payton, who looked to Fallon to be at least a hundred years old, blinked rapidly at them, and announced in a quavering tone, "Mrs. Kennedy states unequivocally that she is innocent of all charges and has no idea why she's here."

"Well, maybe she doesn't understand English." Fallon threw a nasty look directly at Morgan. "And maybe she's deaf, dumb and blind, otherwise she'd know exactly why she's here."

"Detective…" Payton quavered even more. "I must insist you speak with respect."

"Respect?" Fallon laughed. "Respect for a woman who planned to kill her husband, then tried to kill me and someone who considered her a good friend? I don't think so." He leaned over the table and stared hard into Morgan's face. "You better rethink your story, lady. I was *there*, remember? You pointed a gun at my chest and fired, or have you forgotten that little detail? You're going to jail, Mrs. Kennedy, for a long time. And this poor sucker…" He pointed at Payton who was staring at Fallon, his jaw slack with shock, "…is just never going to get you out of this!"

"You *bastard*," Morgan hissed through clenched teeth. "I'll see you ruined. My father will…"

"That's enough, Mrs. Kennedy," Perkins snapped, stepping up to the table. "Your father can't help you here. You will face a judge tomorrow morning. We will ask that bail be denied, in which case you will remain in custody until your trial, which maybe weeks, perhaps *months* away. Maybe this is the time for you and your attorney to think of asking for a deal that will lessen your sentence."

"My *sentence*? I can't go to jail!" Desperately, she turned toward Payton who had visibly blanched at the Assistant DA's words. "Ralph, *for God's sake*," she rasped. "Do something! My father pays your firm the earth in retaining fees. Oh, where is he? Daddy, Daddy, help me, please!" She buried her face in her hands and sobbed uncontrollably.

Payton, covered in confusion, did not know what to do next. He had never, in all his years of family law, had to deal with such a scene. He looked helplessly at the three law enforcement officers.

"What are you offering?" His voice was little more than a whisper.

"She turns State evidence and we ask for a reduced sentence of ten to fifteen years." Perkins said grimly. "She'll be out in about seven or eight, with good behavior."

"No, no, no!" Morgan screeched, rising to her feet. Screaming like a banshee she lunged at Fallon. "You're not sending me to jail!" Her fingernails raked his face before he could get out of the way.

"Jesus!" Fitzgerald planted his considerable size in front of the demented woman. Grabbing her wrists he pushed her back into her chair and held her there. Payton looked like he was about to pass out.

"You OK, Nick?" Perkins looked at Fallon, who nodded, wiping the blood from his face. "Better cuff her, Ed." He looked grimly at Payton. "That's it, Counselor. Your client's going back to her cell and staying there until she sees the judge. As of now, there's no deal."

As Morgan was led away, still struggling and screaming hysterically, her father arrived.

"What are you doing to my daughter?" Joseph File yelled at Perkins. "Ralph, do something," he commanded the still shaking attorney.

"There's nothing I can do for her, Joseph. I don't think anyone could do anything for her. She's beyond help…"

"What the hell are you talking about, you old fool! That's Morgan, my daughter, they're manhandling."

Payton looked at Morgan's father for along moment, then straightening his back as much as he could, he said, "Your daughter is a disgrace to your family, Joseph. I want nothing to do with her. You'd better find yourself another law firm. I wouldn't touch this if my life depended on it!" So saying, he walked away with as much dignity as his unsteady gait would allow.

File watched him leave, disbelief etched visibly on his face. Then he turned to Perkins, and with some of the arrogance gone from his tone, he asked, "What on earth did she *do*?"

Some hours later Fallon arrived at David and Andrew's apartment. He smiled sheepishly as Eric embraced him in front of the others.

"What happened to your face?" Eric asked, gently touching the gauze patch that covered Fallon's right cheek.

"Andrew's girlfriend got me," Fallon chuckled, holding onto Eric for a moment longer.

"Morgan did that?" Andrew gasped.

"Hey, she tried to shoot me earlier," Fallon laughed. "I was lucky to get away with just this scratch—thanks to you."

"I bet Nick could use a drink," Jeff said to David, who quickly made for the bar.

"What'll it be, Nick?"

"Scotch and soda—easy on the soda, Dave," Fallon replied, his arm still around Eric's waist. "Brother, am I glad to be here. What a day!"

"Sit down, sit down," Andrew coaxed. "You have to tell us everything that's happened since we last saw you at the station."

"I thought Peter could have filled you in on all that, by this time."

"Smarty," Peter chuckled. "No, I can't control my psychic sense that well—in fact, not well at all."

"Well, it certainly came in handy, earlier today," Fallon grinned at him. "If you hadn't known Andrew was in danger, he and I might be on cold slabs right now."

"Jeez, Nick," Eric murmured. "Don't even go there."

"It's true," Fallon said, seriously. "I owe my life to these guys. Thanks Dave," he said as David handed him his drink. "I want to drink to my new friends and say thanks. I just wish you weren't all about to leave," he added. "We're just getting to know one another."

"Something tells me we will be friends for a long time," Peter said.

"Is that your psychic self talking?"

"Yes, I think it is."

"Then, I'll drink to that."

"So, tell us what happened after we left," Jeff urged him, as they all settled around the fireplace.

"It was pretty ugly." Fallon related the incident with Morgan, and Andrew became dejected as he listened.

"I just can't believe she turned out to be such a bitch," he said sadly. David put his arm round his shoulder and hugged him consolingly.

Fallon continued, "Then we went back to Bob and his rookie counselor. Bob was coming unglued. I guess he knew it was all over. He started babbling about all the years he'd given to the force, blah, blah, blah. Never mind that he was one of the worst detectives there. He thought everyone owed him something. On and on he went till Perkins, the Assistant DA, told him to quit the bullshit and make a statement…so he did."

He paused and sipped his drink. He put his glass down and looked around at the others, aware that everyone was looking at him intensely.

"Guys, you're making me nervous!" he laughed.

"Get on with it!" Eric said, pinching his arm.

"Ow!" Fallon yelped. "Look, I've been smacked on the head, scratched on the face already today. A little tender loving care wouldn't come amiss right about now."

"Get on with it!" Everyone roared in unison.

"The tender loving care will come later," Eric said, amid the general laughter. "Now tell us what happened."

"It was kind of pathetic really. I actually started to feel sorry for the son of a bitch. He was cornered and he knew it. At one point he really fell to pieces, started blubbering like a kid. Anyway the story he gave us was kind of what we had suspected. He met Morgan right after her accident. She opened up to him about what a louse her husband was, how unhappy she was etc. etc. Bob sort of fell in love with her, I guess. She obviously was aware of that, and gave him just enough hope to make him believe he could get in the sack with her, one day. She knew he'd do anything for her and she began to drop hints about how much better off she'd be if hubby wasn't around anymore. So, Bob offered to take care of it for her and at first she said, oh no, that would be terrible, but after the incident with Andrew, she called Bob and told him now was the time to make good on his offer. She told him what had happened and that, at that moment, Kennedy was stretched out unconscious. She was leaving to go to her parents. Bob told her to unlock the alley door and leave a key to the apartment in the basement on top of the doorjamb." He paused to take a healthy swig of his drink.

"He must have thought this out in advance," Jeff said. "When Morgan first put the seed in his mind."

"Right," Fallon agreed. "He'd done a complete surveillance job on the apartment building and found the way in and out by which he could not be detected. One thing went wrong though. When Morgan called him he couldn't get over there right away—the Chief was having all of us in a meeting. He had to wait, by which time Kennedy had recovered, discovered Morgan was gone, and then, amazingly—he must have called Chris Swenson, his latest boyfriend, and arranged for him to come over…"

"Poor Chris," Eric said quietly.

"Yeah. If Bob had been able to get over to the apartment right away, Chris Swenson would have been spared. As it was, when Bob did get over there a couple of hours later, he found Kennedy and Chris lying naked on the rug at the foot of the bed. They were both asleep. Chris was lying slightly on top of

Kennedy. Bob put a bullet in the kid's head. Kennedy woke at that moment and started to get up. Bob picked up the horse's head and threw it down on top of him. It caved his head in and probably killed him immediately, but Bob hit him a couple of more times to make sure. Then he had to decide what to do with Chris's body.

"Bob's plan was to make it look like you had done it, Andrew. That's why Morgan kept pushing you as the perpetrator. According to her you could have gone back to the apartment after she left, had a confrontation with Jeremy, killed him and ran. But how to explain the bullet? Bob had reacted too quickly when he shot Chris. If he had bludgeoned both of them it could have looked more like a spontaneous fight, but there was the chance that Kennedy could have fought him off after he had killed Chris, so he took the easy way out. Then he had to get rid of Chris's body and we know what happened there. He didn't notice that blood from Chris's head wound had ended up on Kennedy's skin. He was in too much of a hurry to get rid of the body, and like all things Bob did, it was sloppy and under-planned. The other thing he didn't reckon on was you being the one to find Kennedy, Andrew. It threw him as he'd hoped to convince me ahead of time, after we talked to Morgan and she implicated you, that you had to be the killer.

"Instead, I got your statement first and my gut told me you didn't do it. Bob kept trying to persuade me it had to be 'the fag', and I kept telling him I didn't think so. But the big break came when Eric called me about Chris. Without that bit of information, I would never have linked him to the crime scene and Jeff probably wouldn't have gone looking for clues in the alley. When I presented Bob with Chris's watch and shoes, he knew he had to get rid of me. Of course, at that time he didn't know Jeff was the one who had discovered those effects.

"When he saw I was getting too close to the truth, the two of them put together the little charade of having Morgan pretend to make it up with Andrew and have me over at the same time. That way they could get rid of us both, two for the price of one, as it were. And, of course, they could pin Chris Swenson's murder on Andrew too. You'd left them a nice set of prints on the gun Bob used to murder him."

The friends were silent for a little while at the end of Fallon's story. Then finally, Andrew asked, "What will happen to them now?"

"Well, Bob's going to be gone forever. No hope of parole, ever. Morgan? She'll probably end up with a sentence of about fifteen to twenty. Even though she's denying ever wanting her husband murdered, there's enough there to prove she was an accessory. Her father is going to try and pull strings, and the fact that hubby was cheating on her may just help. However, the family attorney washed his hands of it, so that means Dad has to hire a new defense for her."

Andrew shook his head. "It's still so hard to believe this is the same Morgan I thought to be such a good friend. Where did all this hatred come from?"

Peter looked at his friend. "You know," he said slowly. "It isn't so hard to understand, really. Here was a woman, attractive, wealthy, with everything to live for, tormented by a duplicitous husband who had no respect for her, and who flaunted his infidelities in front of her, without any concern for what it might do to her mentally and emotionally. What I can't ever understand, is why anyone will put up with that kind of treatment for so long. Okay. You might forgive one or two indiscretions, but to have it go on and on for years…that's just pathetic."

"You're right, Peter," Jeff agreed. "We're all human, with human failings, but to allow yourself to be humiliated over and over shows some terrible weakness that borders on sickness. I know there are people everywhere trapped in unhappy relationships, but this one just seems to have been too bizarre. I'm amazed that Jeremy, at some point, couldn't have seen that he was maybe pushing it too far, and that one day she'd just snap."

"Well, we'll never know for sure, now, what made Jeremy tick," David said.

Andrew sighed. "He was too caught up in his own pleasure to ever consider what consequences it all might have had on Morgan."

"There's no doubt that his trying to seduce you, was the last straw as far as she was concerned," Fallon commented. "I think the way she saw it, there wasn't one gay guy she could trust, ever!"

"And all you ever wanted was to be her friend." Peter smiled sadly at Andrew. "If only she could have seen that, perhaps none of this would have happened."

"I'm just glad that all of you came out unscathed," Eric said. "As far as I'm concerned, and I didn't know Morgan so it makes it easier to say this…that cop and her, got what they deserved. Even if Jeremy was scum, which from the sounds of it, he was, that's not an excuse to have murdered him and an innocent bystander into the bargain. She could have just dumped him, for God's sake!"

"I think, in the end she just hated him too much," Peter remarked.

"It makes you wonder…" Jeff mused, "If her insistence that the earlier incident with the car, you know when that other guy Kevin, was killed, was in fact an accident after all."

"We'll probably never know the answer to that," Fallon said. "She's never going to confess to it, though it wouldn't surprise me if she did stage the whole thing to get rid of him."

"Oh my God." Andrew shuddered at the thought. "How could I have been so wrong about someone?"

"Hey, we all make mistakes, sometimes, when it comes to friendships," David said. "Don't let this one episode make you less trusting of your friends—your real friends, that is."

"Right!" Peter exclaimed. "And that means us. Friends to the end!"

Andrew smiled. "You guys are the best. Thank God, for true friends."

Fallon smiled contentedly as he sat at the kitchen counter and watched Eric preparing sandwiches for the two of them. They had returned to Eric's apartment and Eric had declared himself famished. Fallon had to admit he was pretty hungry too. In all the excitement and the subsequent rehashing of the day's events, no one had mentioned food.

"I wonder if the guys have suddenly realized they didn't eat tonight?" Fallon chuckled as Eric set a giant ham sandwich in front of him.

"They're probably getting their own midnight snack even as we speak." Eric grinned at him, sitting beside him and biting into his sandwich. "Mmm, that's good. I was starved."

Fallon gazed at him fondly and enjoyed watching him relishing his food. There was something innately boyish about Eric, something still unspoiled that appealed to Fallon immensely. Despite his line of work, where he could see desperate and ugly things on a daily basis, Eric remained buoyantly unjaded and not at all cynical.

"Like something to drink?" Eric was asking him between mouthfuls. "I got some fresh milk today."

"That would be great, thanks."

Eric smiled at him as he poured the milk into two glasses. "You look like you want to ask me something," he said.

"I do, but I don't want you to think I'm coming on too strong, here."

"Oh, oh. Sounds serious." Eric sat down again and gently stroked Fallon's thigh. His touch sent a shiver of desire through Fallon's body, and he frowned as he tried to concentrate on what he wanted to say.

"Don't look so worried," Eric said quietly.

"I am worried!" Fallon blurted. "I don't want to blow this…"

Eric leaned over and kissed him gently on the lips. "My big and brave and handsome cop," he chuckled softly. "You would run into a room full of crooks and thieves without a thought, but you get all jittery about asking me a little question. You can ask me anything. You're not going to blow it, Nick. Go ahead, tell me what it is you want."

"I want…you, Eric." Fallon said quietly. He took a deep breath, and then continued. "I love you. I want us to have a life together. To live together. I know this must sound nuts. We've only known each other such a short time, and I'm not one to make big changes in my life without a lot of thought. But Eric, you've touched me somehow, in a way I never thought was possible again, and suddenly I can't imagine anything else but a future with you. That's what I want, Eric…you in my life, forever."

Eric's eyes glistened as he listened to Fallon's words. "You know, when I met you at Jim and Donna's party, I knew without a doubt that you were the one for me. If you hadn't asked me out, I was going to ask you. That night when we had dinner, I was already falling in love with you. I'm a big believer in love at first sight and people being soul mates destined to meet. I know a lot of people who'd laugh at me for that, but here we are, the perfect example of it." He gripped Fallon's hand as he continued. "There is nothing I want more than to share your life, Nick. Nothing would make me happier."

They stood and embraced, their lips meeting in a scorching kiss that neither one of them wanted to end. They clung together, feeling the heat and strength of each other's bodies.

"Stay with me tonight," Eric said, breathlessly. "And promise me you'll never leave."

Fallon buried his face in the warmth of Eric's neck, and whispered, "I promise."

CHAPTER 20

Peter sighed with contentment as he stepped out onto the balcony of his home in Laguna Beach. "It's so good to be back," he said, turning to look at Jeff who was still in bed.

"You've said that just about every morning for the last month," Jeff laughed, sitting up.

"And I've meant it every morning for the last month. Look at that sky, so blue, and those little fluffy clouds…"

"Okay, Mr. California," Jeff chuckled, sliding out of bed and padding to the bathroom.

Peter sighed happily again, looking out at the tall palm trees that bordered the street below, then at the blue ocean beyond. "Paradise," he murmured to himself. He waved, as Eve, his mother, appeared heading for her car in the driveway.

"Morning darling." She smiled up at him. "I'm off to the store. Is there anything you need?"

"Don't think so. Come over and have lunch with Jeff and me when you get back." He watched admiringly as the youthful and attractive woman waved and climbed into her car. She never seems to age, he thought. Always so vibrant and beautiful.

"Who're you waving to?" Jeff asked behind him.

"Mom. She's coming for lunch later."

"Good," Jeff grunted, pulling on a pair of jeans. "Where's my coffee?"

"In the pot, O Master. Shall I bring it to you, or will you manage to come down stairs and at least watch me pour it for you?"

"Impudent varlet," Jeff snarled, advancing on him. "Come here and be punished."

"You'll have to catch me first," Peter laughed, running for the door. He bounded down the stairs with Jeff in hot pursuit. Laughing like lunatics they ran around the house till Jeff caught Peter up in a bear hug and together they fell onto the living room couch.

"Whoa!" Jeff panted. "I'm getting way too old for these high jinks."

"Right. You have to keep up your strength for more important things," Peter said teasingly.

"Brat," Jeff murmured fondly, holding Peter tightly and kissing his chin.

"I'm glad you've taken the day off," Peter whispered.

"What time do we have to be at the airport?"

"Around three. I told them we'd pick them up at the baggage claim."

Peter slipped from Jeff's arms and stood up. "C'mon. Let's have that coffee."

Jeff ambled after him into the kitchen. "I bet Andrew is beside himself with excitement about coming home today."

"You know he is," Peter chuckled. "He was delirious on the phone last night."

"He can finally put all this mess with Morgan behind him."

"Yeah. He did mention her. He says he still gets upset sometimes when he let's himself dwell on it. The fact that she's in prison is hard for him to take."

"It's where she belongs," Jeff said firmly. "She's lucky the DA cut her a deal in the end. Bransky's confession was pretty damning. She could have got life, like him. It still amazes me though, that she chose to waive her right to a trial."

"Maybe she just didn't have any fight left in her," Peter suggested. "After all, the evidence was just too damning, when you think about it."

"True. All our statements, along with Nick's, and our eyewitness accounts kind of made it impossible for her to deny her involvement. Still, I had expected her to drag it all out to the bitter end."

"I think when she was denied bail and she knew she was going to be doing jail time, she just kind of gave in to the inevitable. Anyway, being back in California will be just what Andrew needs." Peter handed Jeff a steaming mug of coffee and the two walked out onto the rear patio and sat at the table.

"This is the life," Jeff murmured contentedly, enjoying the warmth of the sun on his face and bare chest. "Oh, by the way. Nick Fallon called me at the office yesterday. I forgot to tell you."

"Oh yeah? How're he and Eric doing?"

"Eric moved in with him a couple of weeks ago. He sounded really happy."

"Good," Peter said. "That guy really needed to find someone to share his life. He was too…alone."

"I know what you mean. I just hope it hasn't all happened too quickly."

"Hey, that's a chance we all take. Some people wait forever to make that decision, and two months later, it's all over." Peter smiled slyly at him. "Look how long you waffled around."

"I did not waffle!"

"You did. Kept me waiting and waiting, just to see how long you could."

"Well, I wanted to make sure what you were feeling wasn't just lust for my body."

Peter grinned at him. "Oh, there was some of that, too."

"Don't I know it." Jeff laughed, stretching out his long legs and rubbing Peter's feet with his own. "Anyway, I just hope it works for them."

"I'm sure it will. I think Eric's just the right match for Nick and I could see they were very much in love."

"If you say so, my love, it must be so," Jeff said, smiling and getting to his feet. "I need to shower. Want to come scrub my back?"

"Your wish is my command, O Master." Peter grinned up at him.

"That's more like it." Jeff pulled Peter to his feet. For a moment, he stood still, gazing into Peter's eyes, an air of tenderness now replacing the one of banter they had just shared. "Thank you for being in my life," he whispered huskily.

"There's no where else I would rather be," Peter replied, moving into Jeff's arms. "And this is where I'll most definitely stay."

Morgan sat despondently in her cell, looking at the bulky envelope she had just received. It bore her mother's handwriting and she was loath to open it. Her mother had not been to see her since her incarceration in this women's facility in upstate New York. Morgan knew her mother was deeply humiliated by her actions. Her father had told her that his wife had not been out of the house since Morgan's arrest.

"Too embarrassed to face her friends and neighbors, I'm afraid," he had said, sadly. "She just sits around, reading and watching TV, nowadays."

"Poor Mother," Morgan had remarked, without much sympathy. After all, it was not her mother who now had to endure this prison sentence that loomed ahead of her interminably. Her father had been able to pull one or two strings.

At least she had her own cell. It was inconceivable that she might have had to share this space with someone else.

Restlessly, she stood up and walked to the window, leaving the envelope on her narrow bunk. She looked out at her grim surroundings. The concrete yard, the high perimeter wall. She longed for the comfort of her own apartment, the lush furnishings, and the expensive clothes. It would be a long time before she could indulge herself like that again…if ever. She would be old when they finally let her out. Too old to really enjoy those kind of luxuries.

I'll be decrepit and wrinkled and unattractive, she thought bitterly. No man will ever want me again. Better I just die here. But she knew she would never have the courage to attempt to take her own life. No matter how terrible all this was, she knew she would have to survive the years ahead—somehow.

Picking up the envelope, she raised the flap. It had already been opened and inspected by the prison censors. There was a short note from her mother.

Dearest Morgan,

Words cannot express how I feel right now. That you have brought shame to our family goes without saying. Nothing will ever erase this humiliation. I am sorry you are in that dreadful institution. Your father has told me how awful it is, but Morgan, what you did was even more terrible. I cannot bring myself to mention it here. Suffice to say, I pray for your soul every day.

Only God's forgiveness means anything, in the end. Pray to him, Morgan—and find salvation in his love.

Your Mother.

Angrily, Morgan tore the note to shreds. "Damn her!" she cried aloud, furiously. "That sanctimonious old witch…how dare she?" She flung the envelope against the wall and watched as its contents scattered across the cell floor. There appeared to be some photographs among the papers that now littered the floor. Curiosity now getting the better of her, Morgan stooped to pick up the photographs and peered at the first one intently.

"God!" she muttered derisively as she recognized the first picture. It was of a Christmas, years ago when Jeremy and she had visited her parents in Connecticut. Not a happy occasion, she recalled, though they were all pretending to smile in the picture.

"Bastard..." Morgan breathed as she studied Jeremy's handsome image. "It's because of you that I'm here." She threw the photo down on the bed and looked at the next one. What on earth was her Mother thinking about when she decided to send these photographs? Morgan wondered. Here was a group of her friends from high school. Next, a photo taken on deck of a cruise ship her parents had taken her on when she was only fifteen years old. As she turned the last photograph over, her breath caught in her throat and her hand trembled with shock. It was a picture of her standing with Andrew in his apartment in front of his portrait. Slowly, she sank down onto the bed, still gazing at the photo.

"Oh Andrew," she sighed slowly, tears springing into her eyes. "How happy we were, that day."

David had taken the photograph the first time she had ever visited them. She had admired Andrew's portrait, and they had proudly told them of their friend Peter, who had painted it. She had been so relaxed and carefree in the company of these two friendly and charming gay men. If only she could have been honest with them, perhaps they could have helped her through the trauma of her bad marriage and Jeremy's incessant need for male lovers.

But she could never have admitted it to anyone. It would have been all too humiliating. And now, look where it had all led her. The tears slid unchecked from her eyes as she gently touched the image of Andrew's smiling face with her fingers. How could she ever have been persuaded to use him like that? Why had she ever listened to that fat fool, Bransky? She lay back on the bed, gazing through eyes blurred with her tears at the gray ceiling above her.

A sob racked her body as gave herself up to her misery. There would be many more days, months, *years* to endure the memory of all that this had cost her. Her sobbing became louder, and outside her cell a passing guard shook her head as she paused to listen.

"Get used to it, honey," she muttered to herself as she walked on. "You're here for quite a spell."

*****THE END*****

Look out for J.P. Bowie's next

Peter Brandon novel—

SELF PORTRAIT

Due out soon!

0-595-30223-8

Printed in the United States
63429LVS00006BB/33

9 780595 302239